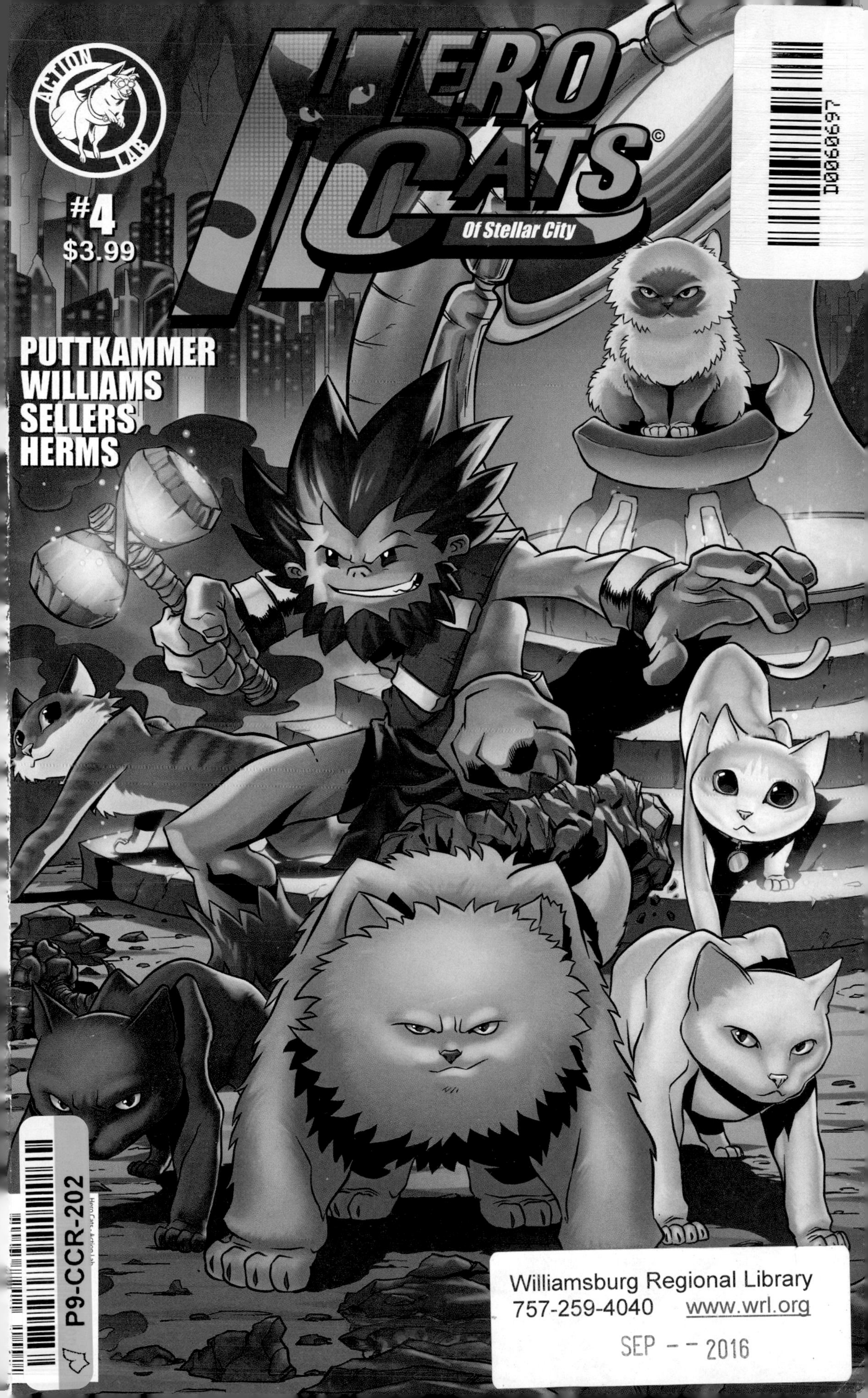
ACTION LAB
HERO CATS©
Of Stellar City
#4
$3.99
PUTTKAMMER
WILLIAMS
SELLERS
HERMS

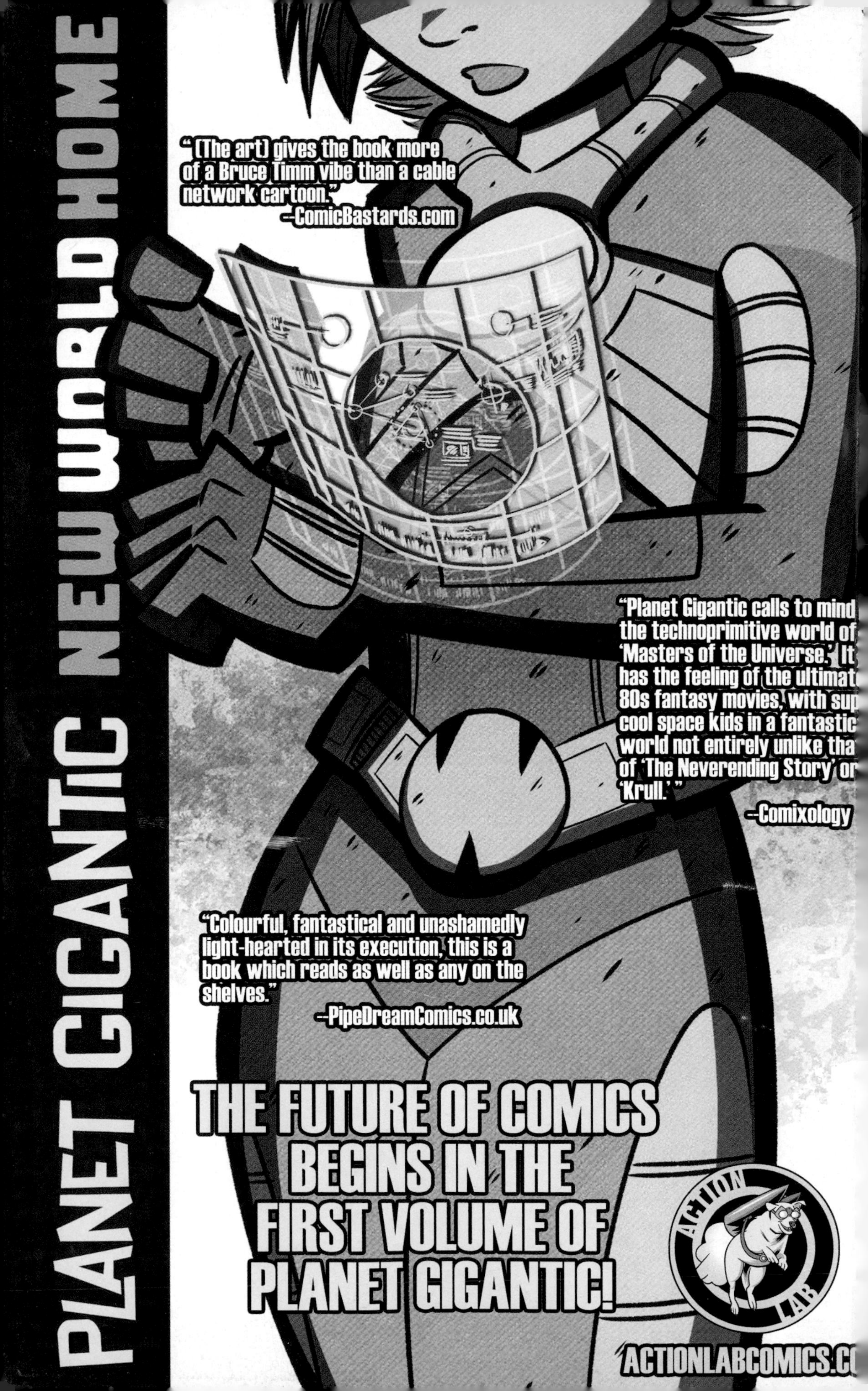
PLANET GIGANTIC NEW WORLD HOME
" [The art] gives the book more of a Bruce Timm vibe than a cable network cartoon."
--ComicBastards.com
"Planet Gigantic calls to mind the technoprimitive world of 'Masters of the Universe.' It has the feeling of the ultimat 80s fantasy movies, with sup cool space kids in a fantastic world not entirely unlike tha of 'The Neverending Story' or 'Krull.' "
--Comixology
"Colourful, fantastical and unashamedly light-hearted in its execution, this is a book which reads as well as any on the shelves."
--PipeDreamComics.co.uk
THE FUTURE OF COMICS BEGINS IN THE FIRST VOLUME OF PLANET GIGANTIC!
ACTION LAB
ACTIONLABCOMICS.C

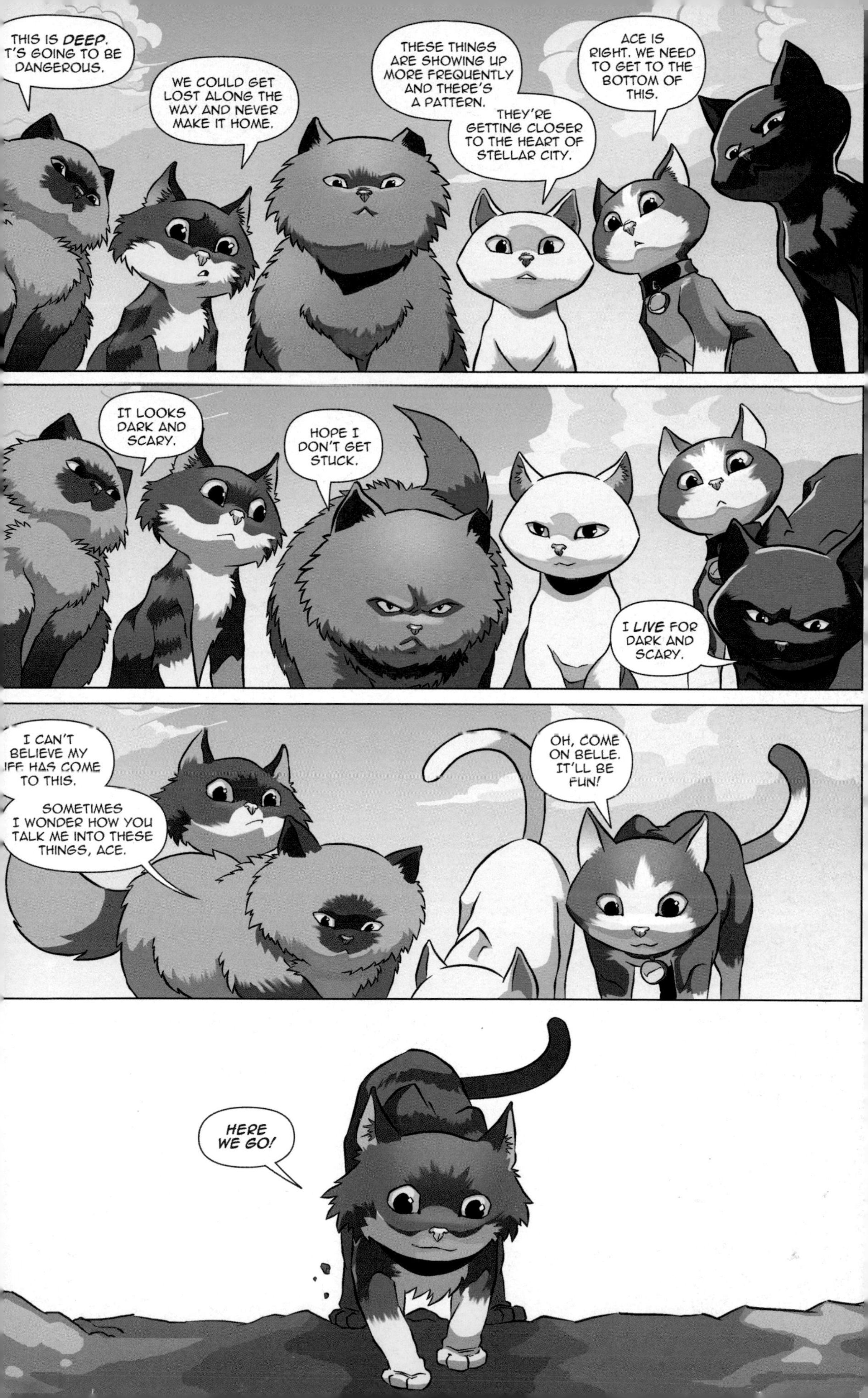
THIS IS DEEP. T'S GOING TO BE DANGEROUS.
WE COULD GET LOST ALONG THE WAY AND NEVER MAKE IT HOME.
THESE THINGS ARE SHOWING UP MORE FREQUENTLY AND THERE'S A PATTERN.
THEY'RE GETTING CLOSER TO THE HEART OF STELLAR CITY.
ACE IS RIGHT. WE NEED TO GET TO THE BOTTOM OF THIS.
IT LOOKS DARK AND SCARY.
HOPE I DON'T GET STUCK.
I LIVE FOR DARK AND SCARY.
I CAN'T BELIEVE MY IFE HAS COME TO THIS.
SOMETIMES I WONDER HOW YOU TALK ME INTO THESE THINGS, ACE.
OH, COME ON BELLE. IT'LL BE FUN!
HERE WE GO!

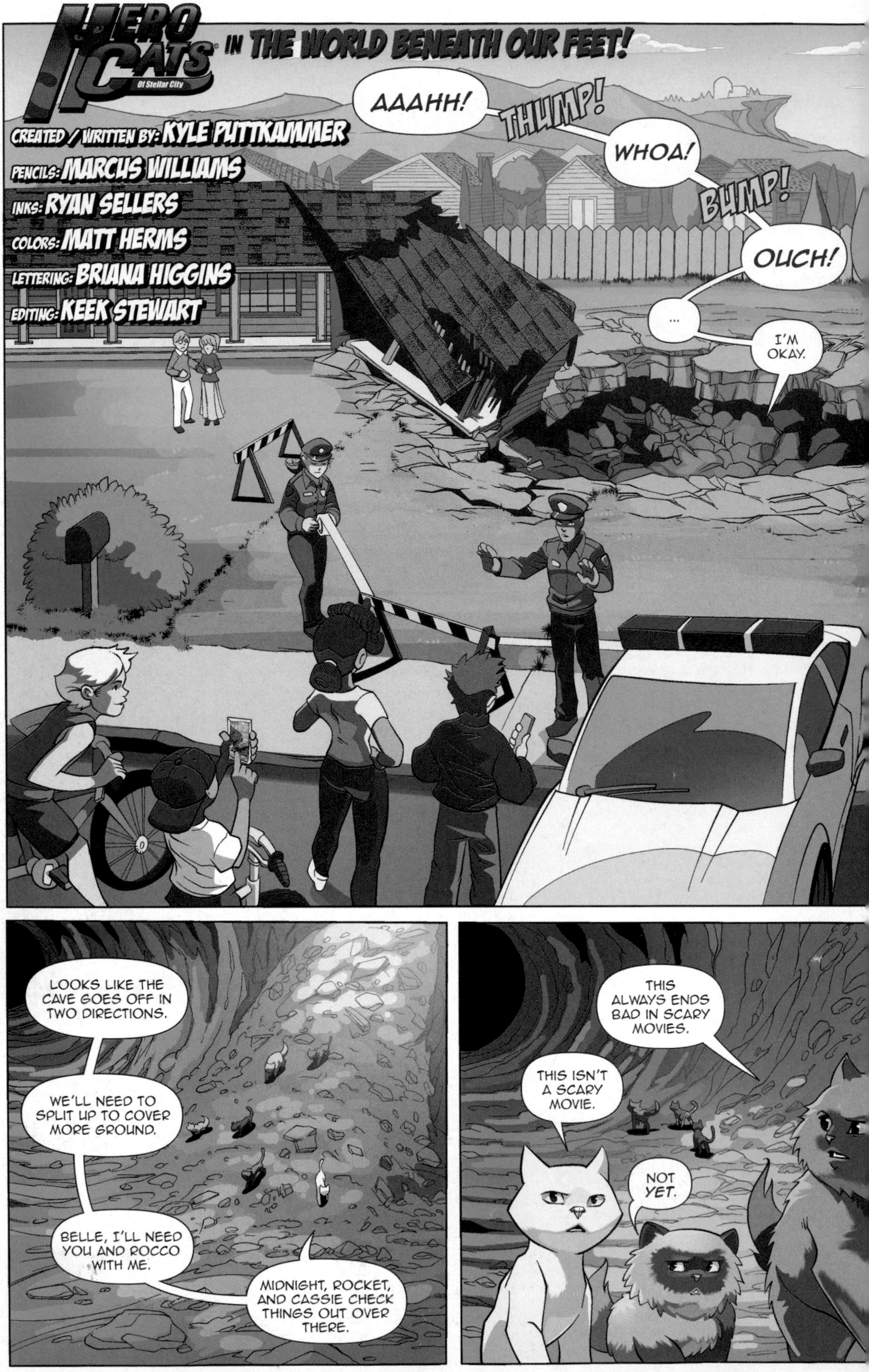
HERO CATS Of Stellar City
IN THE WORLD BENEATH OUR FEET!
CREATED / WRITTEN BY: KYLE PUTTKAMMER
PENCILS: MARCUS WILLIAMS
INKS: RYAN SELLERS
COLORS: MATT HERMS
LETTERING: BRIANA HIGGINS
EDITING: KEEK STEWART
AAAHH!
THUMP!
WHOA!
BUMP!
OUCH!
...
I'M OKAY.
LOOKS LIKE THE CAVE GOES OFF IN TWO DIRECTIONS.
WE'LL NEED TO SPLIT UP TO COVER MORE GROUND.
BELLE, I'LL NEED YOU AND ROCCO WITH ME.
MIDNIGHT, ROCKET, AND CASSIE CHECK THINGS OUT OVER THERE.
THIS ALWAYS ENDS BAD IN SCARY MOVIES.
THIS ISN'T A SCARY MOVIE.
NOT YET.

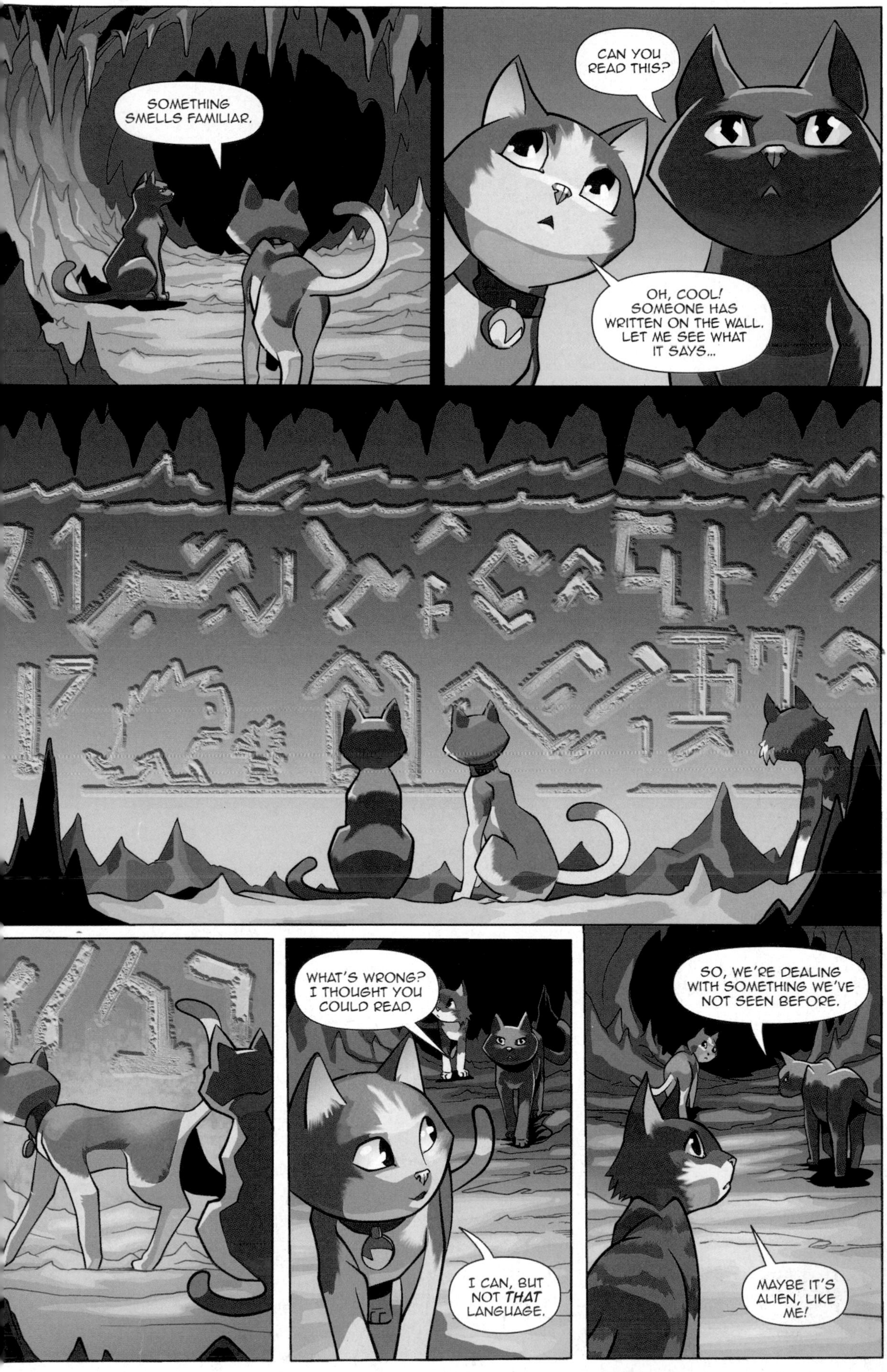
SOMETHING SMELLS FAMILIAR.
CAN YOU READ THIS?
OH, COOL! SOMEONE HAS WRITTEN ON THE WALL. LET ME SEE WHAT IT SAYS...
WHAT'S WRONG? I THOUGHT YOU COULD READ.
I CAN, BUT NOT *THAT* LANGUAGE.
SO, WE'RE DEALING WITH SOMETHING WE'VE NOT SEEN BEFORE.
MAYBE IT'S ALIEN, LIKE ME!

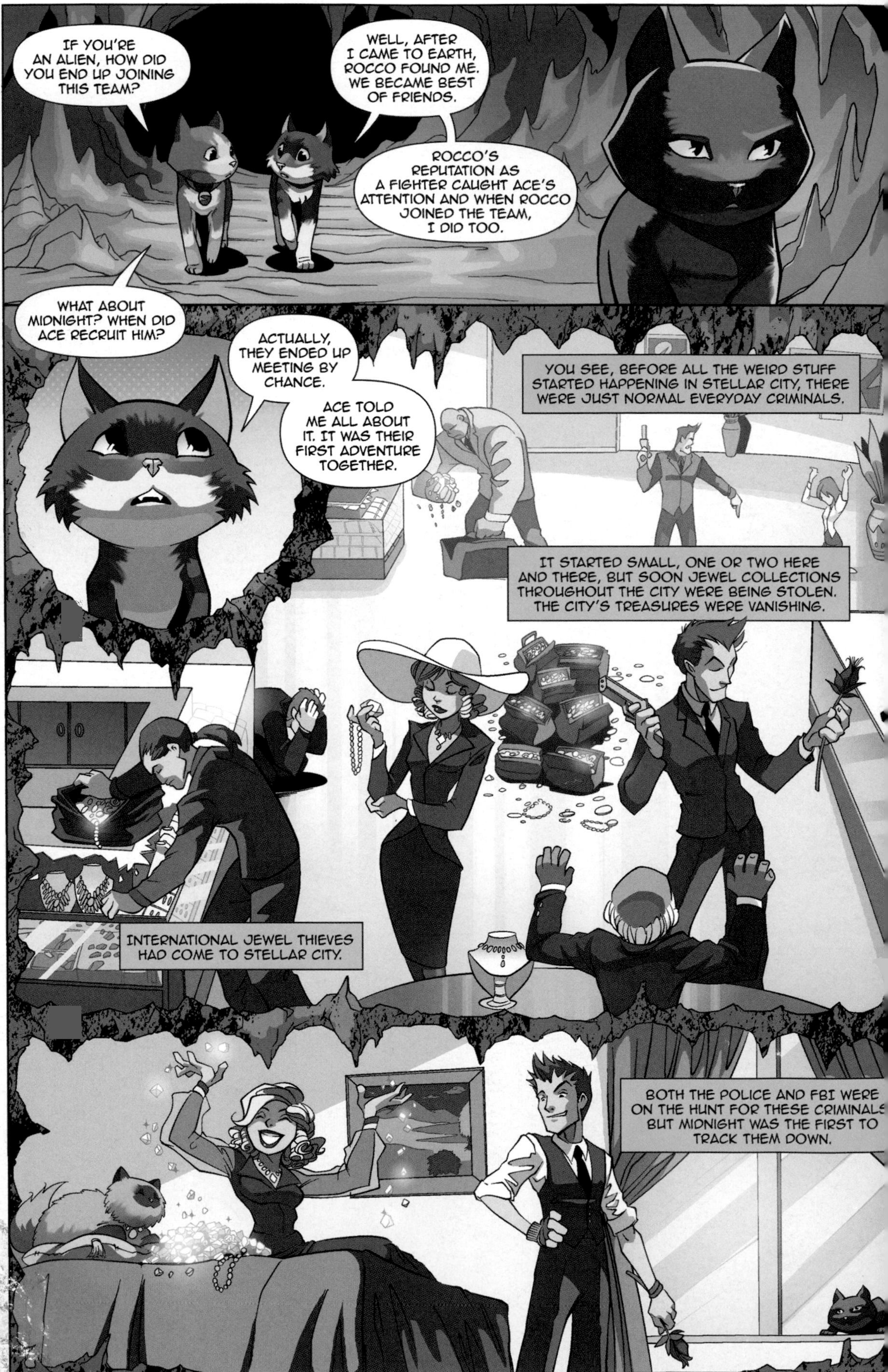
IF YOU'RE AN ALIEN, HOW DID YOU END UP JOINING THIS TEAM?
WELL, AFTER I CAME TO EARTH, ROCCO FOUND ME. WE BECAME BEST OF FRIENDS.
ROCCO'S REPUTATION AS A FIGHTER CAUGHT ACE'S ATTENTION AND WHEN ROCCO JOINED THE TEAM, I DID TOO.
WHAT ABOUT MIDNIGHT? WHEN DID ACE RECRUIT HIM?
ACTUALLY, THEY ENDED UP MEETING BY CHANCE.
ACE TOLD ME ALL ABOUT IT. IT WAS THEIR FIRST ADVENTURE TOGETHER.
YOU SEE, BEFORE ALL THE WEIRD STUFF STARTED HAPPENING IN STELLAR CITY, THERE WERE JUST NORMAL EVERYDAY CRIMINALS.
IT STARTED SMALL, ONE OR TWO HERE AND THERE, BUT SOON JEWEL COLLECTIONS THROUGHOUT THE CITY WERE BEING STOLEN. THE CITY'S TREASURES WERE VANISHING.
INTERNATIONAL JEWEL THIEVES HAD COME TO STELLAR CITY.
BOTH THE POLICE AND FBI WERE ON THE HUNT FOR THESE CRIMINALS BUT MIDNIGHT WAS THE FIRST TO TRACK THEM DOWN.

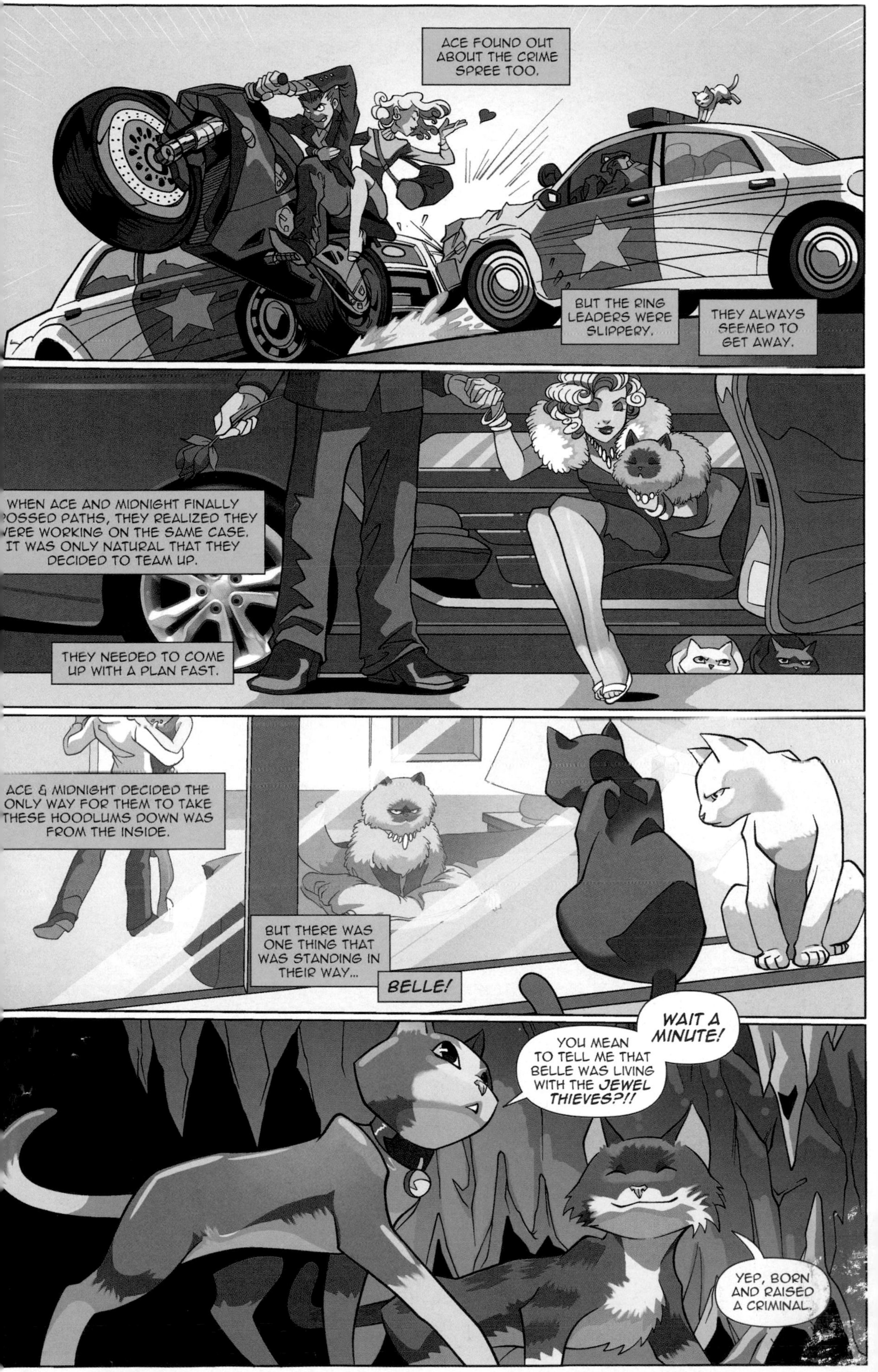
ACE FOUND OUT ABOUT THE CRIME SPREE TOO.
BUT THE RING LEADERS WERE SLIPPERY.
THEY ALWAYS SEEMED TO GET AWAY.
WHEN ACE AND MIDNIGHT FINALLY CROSSED PATHS, THEY REALIZED THEY WERE WORKING ON THE SAME CASE. IT WAS ONLY NATURAL THAT THEY DECIDED TO TEAM UP.
THEY NEEDED TO COME UP WITH A PLAN FAST.
ACE & MIDNIGHT DECIDED THE ONLY WAY FOR THEM TO TAKE THESE HOODLUMS DOWN WAS FROM THE INSIDE.
BUT THERE WAS ONE THING THAT WAS STANDING IN THEIR WAY...
BELLE!
WAIT A MINUTE!
YOU MEAN TO TELL ME THAT BELLE WAS LIVING WITH THE JEWEL THIEVES?!!
YEP, BORN AND RAISED A CRIMINAL.

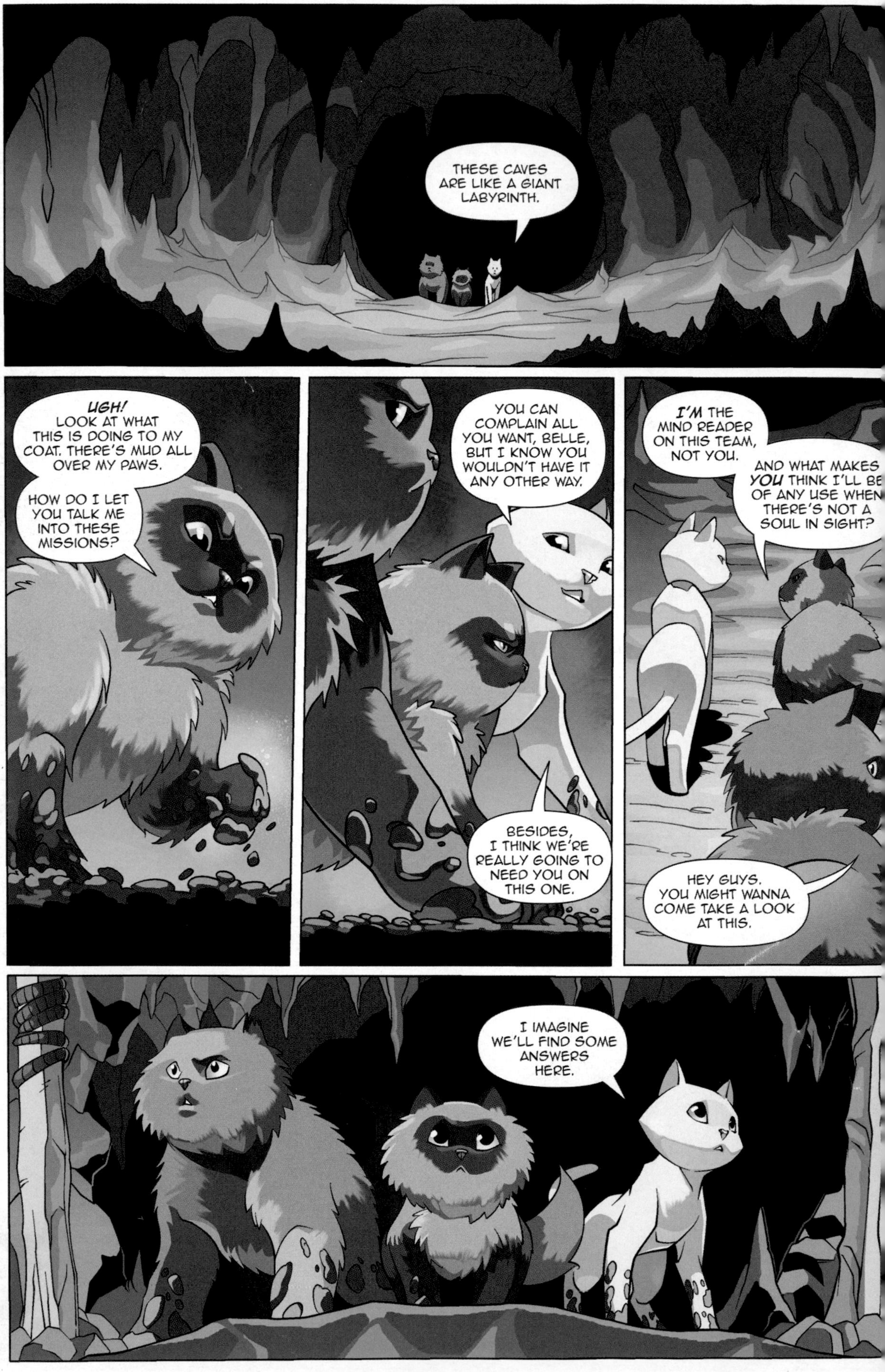
THESE CAVES ARE LIKE A GIANT LABYRINTH.
UGH! LOOK AT WHAT THIS IS DOING TO MY COAT. THERE'S MUD ALL OVER MY PAWS.
HOW DO I LET YOU TALK ME INTO THESE MISSIONS?
YOU CAN COMPLAIN ALL YOU WANT, BELLE, BUT I KNOW YOU WOULDN'T HAVE IT ANY OTHER WAY.
BESIDES, I THINK WE'RE REALLY GOING TO NEED YOU ON THIS ONE.
I'M THE MIND READER ON THIS TEAM, NOT YOU.
AND WHAT MAKES YOU THINK I'LL BE OF ANY USE WHEN THERE'S NOT A SOUL IN SIGHT?
HEY GUYS. YOU MIGHT WANNA COME TAKE A LOOK AT THIS.
I IMAGINE WE'LL FIND SOME ANSWERS HERE.

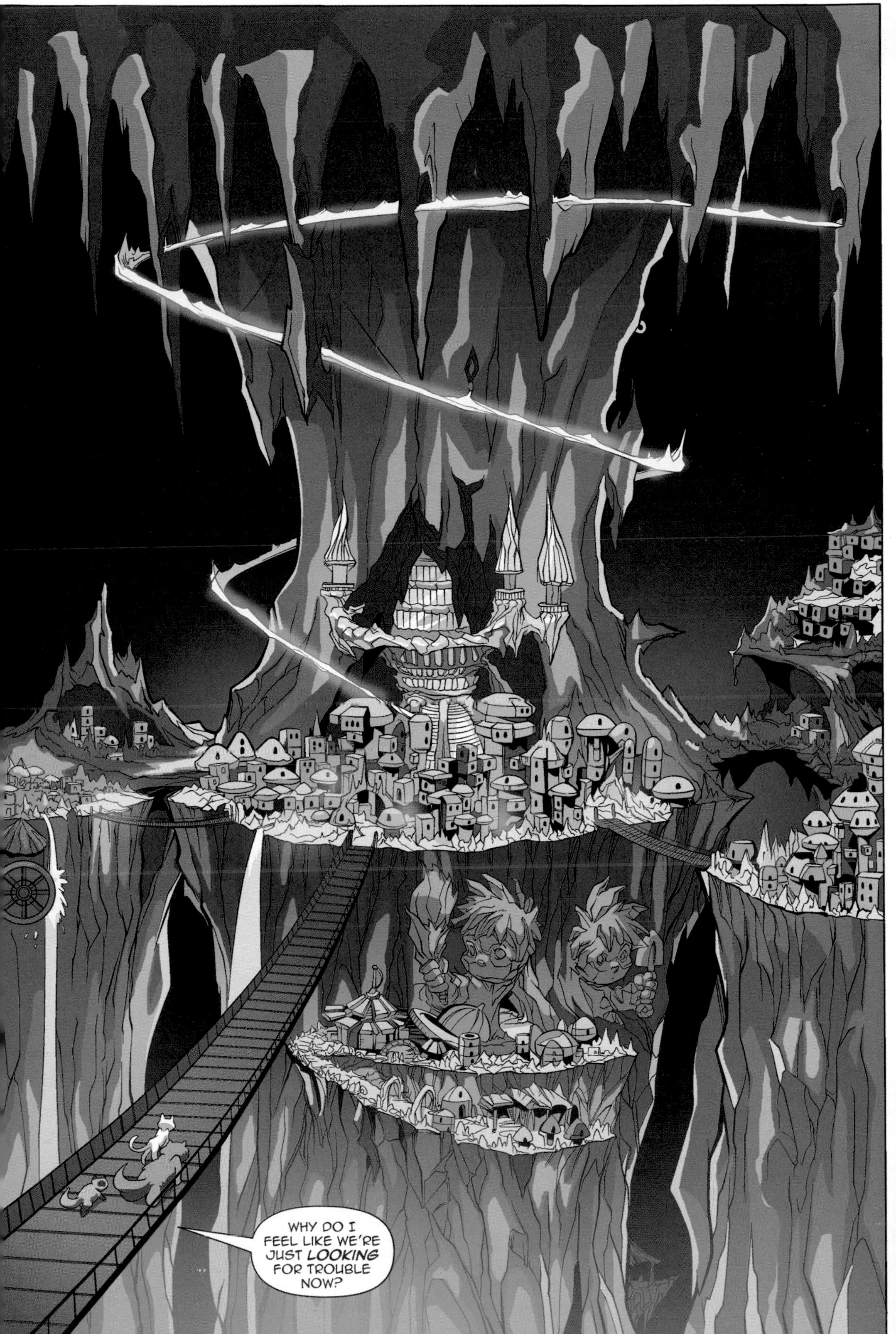
WHY DO I FEEL LIKE WE'RE JUST LOOKING FOR TROUBLE NOW?

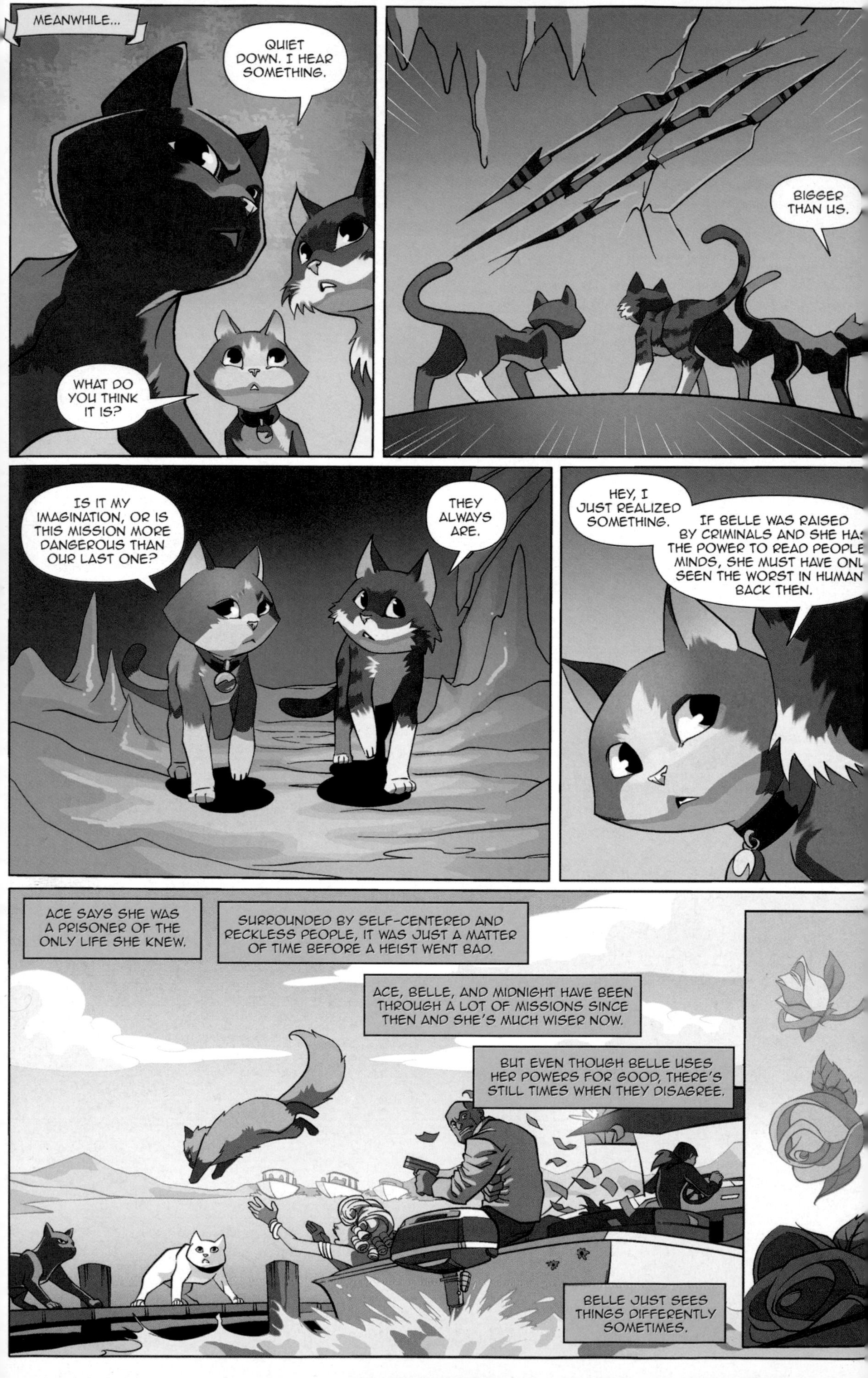
MEANWHILE...
QUIET DOWN. I HEAR SOMETHING.
WHAT DO YOU THINK IT IS?
BIGGER THAN US.
IS IT MY IMAGINATION, OR IS THIS MISSION MORE DANGEROUS THAN OUR LAST ONE?
THEY ALWAYS ARE.
HEY, I JUST REALIZED SOMETHING.
IF BELLE WAS RAISED BY CRIMINALS AND SHE HAS THE POWER TO READ PEOPLE'S MINDS, SHE MUST HAVE ONLY SEEN THE WORST IN HUMANS BACK THEN.
ACE SAYS SHE WAS A PRISONER OF THE ONLY LIFE SHE KNEW.
SURROUNDED BY SELF-CENTERED AND RECKLESS PEOPLE, IT WAS JUST A MATTER OF TIME BEFORE A HEIST WENT BAD.
ACE, BELLE, AND MIDNIGHT HAVE BEEN THROUGH A LOT OF MISSIONS SINCE THEN AND SHE'S MUCH WISER NOW.
BUT EVEN THOUGH BELLE USES HER POWERS FOR GOOD, THERE'S STILL TIMES WHEN THEY DISAGREE.
BELLE JUST SEES THINGS DIFFERENTLY SOMETIMES.

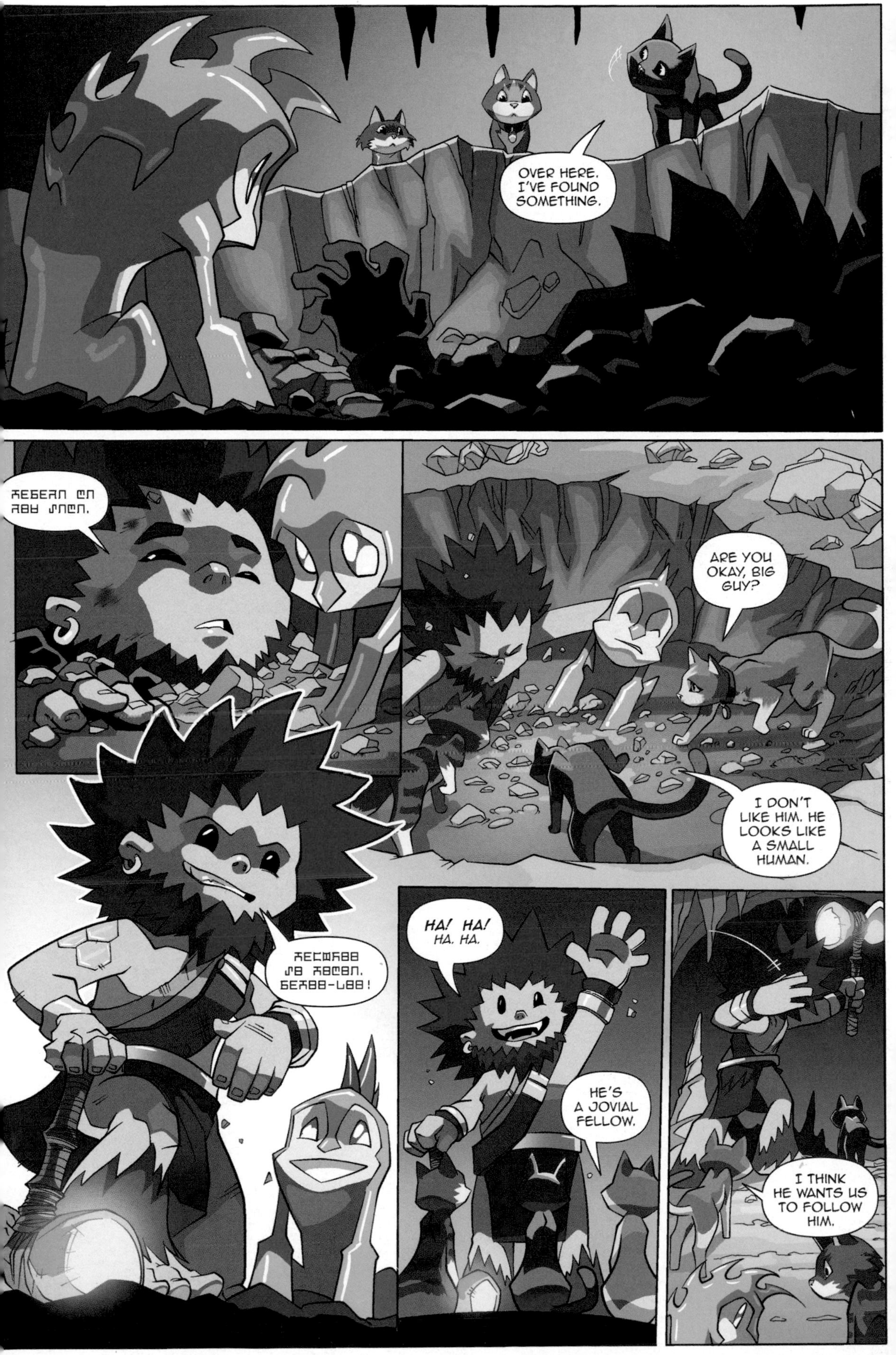
OVER HERE. I'VE FOUND SOMETHING.
ARE YOU OKAY, BIG GUY?
I DON'T LIKE HIM. HE LOOKS LIKE A SMALL HUMAN.
HA! HA! HA. HA.
HE'S A JOVIAL FELLOW.
I THINK HE WANTS US TO FOLLOW HIM.

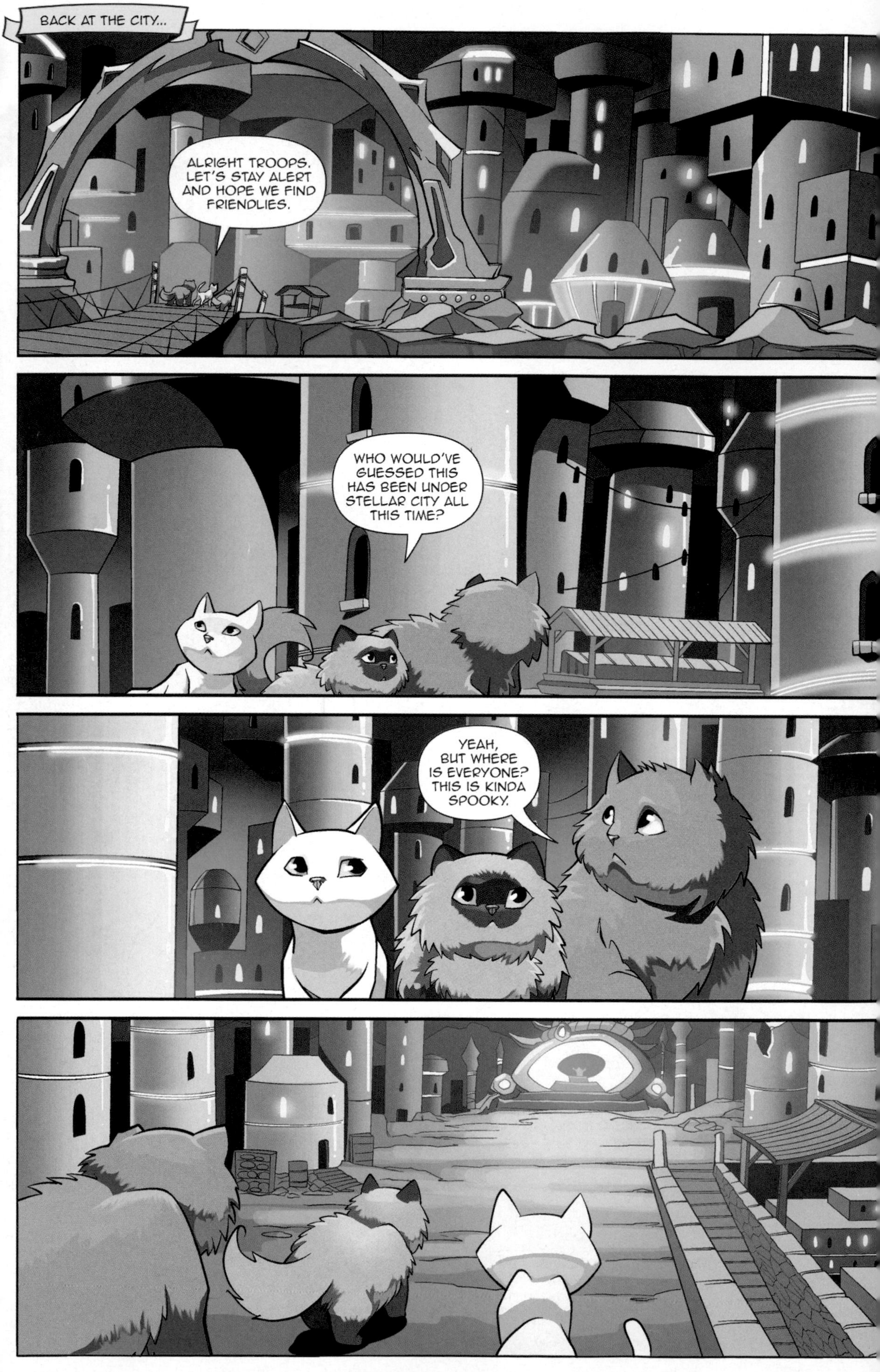
BACK AT THE CITY...
ALRIGHT TROOPS. LET'S STAY ALERT AND HOPE WE FIND FRIENDLIES.
WHO WOULD'VE GUESSED THIS HAS BEEN UNDER STELLAR CITY ALL THIS TIME?
YEAH, BUT WHERE IS EVERYONE? THIS IS KINDA SPOOKY.

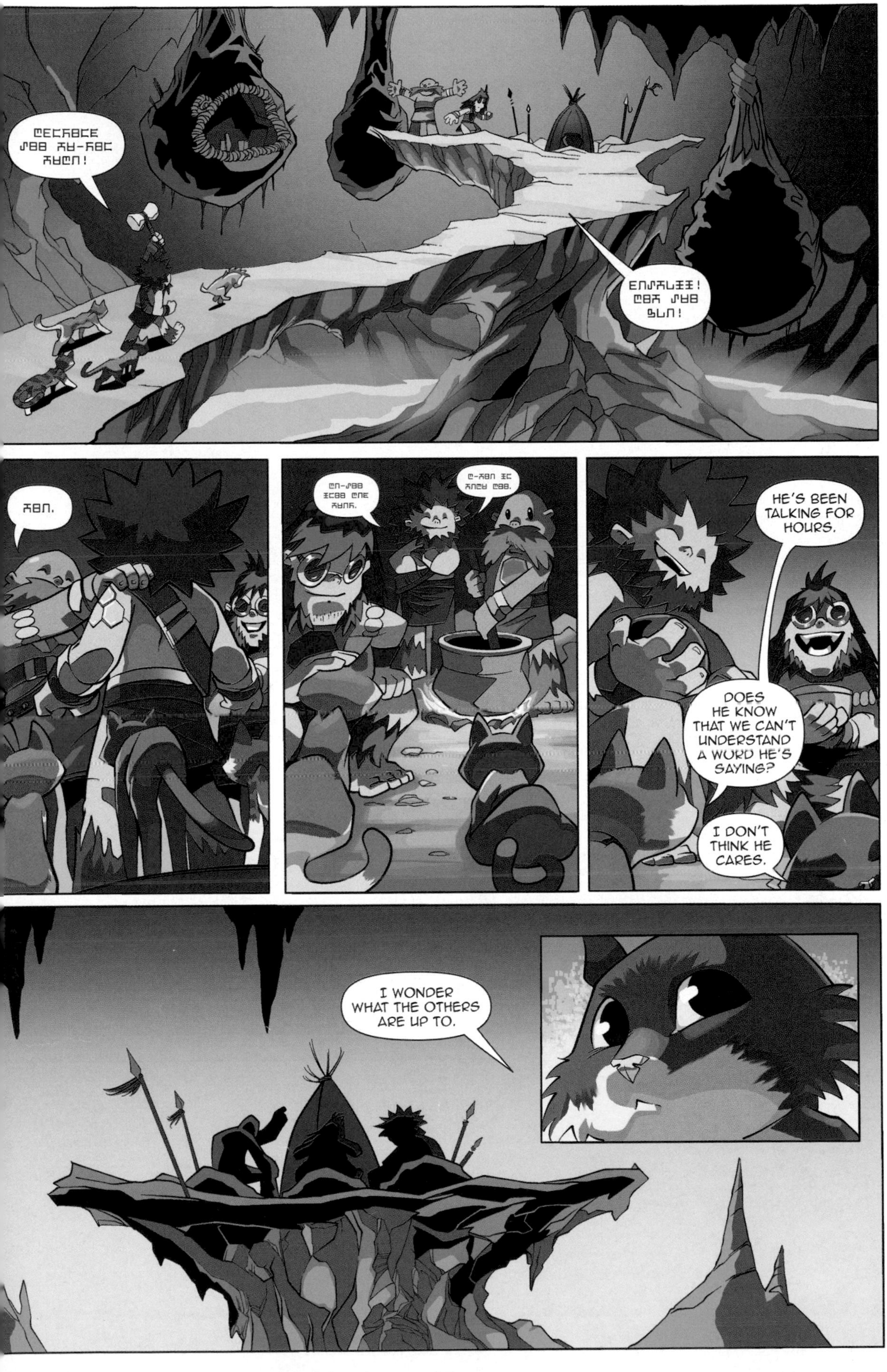
HE'S BEEN TALKING FOR HOURS.
DOES HE KNOW THAT WE CAN'T UNDERSTAND A WORD HE'S SAYING?
I DON'T THINK HE CARES.
I WONDER WHAT THE OTHERS ARE UP TO.

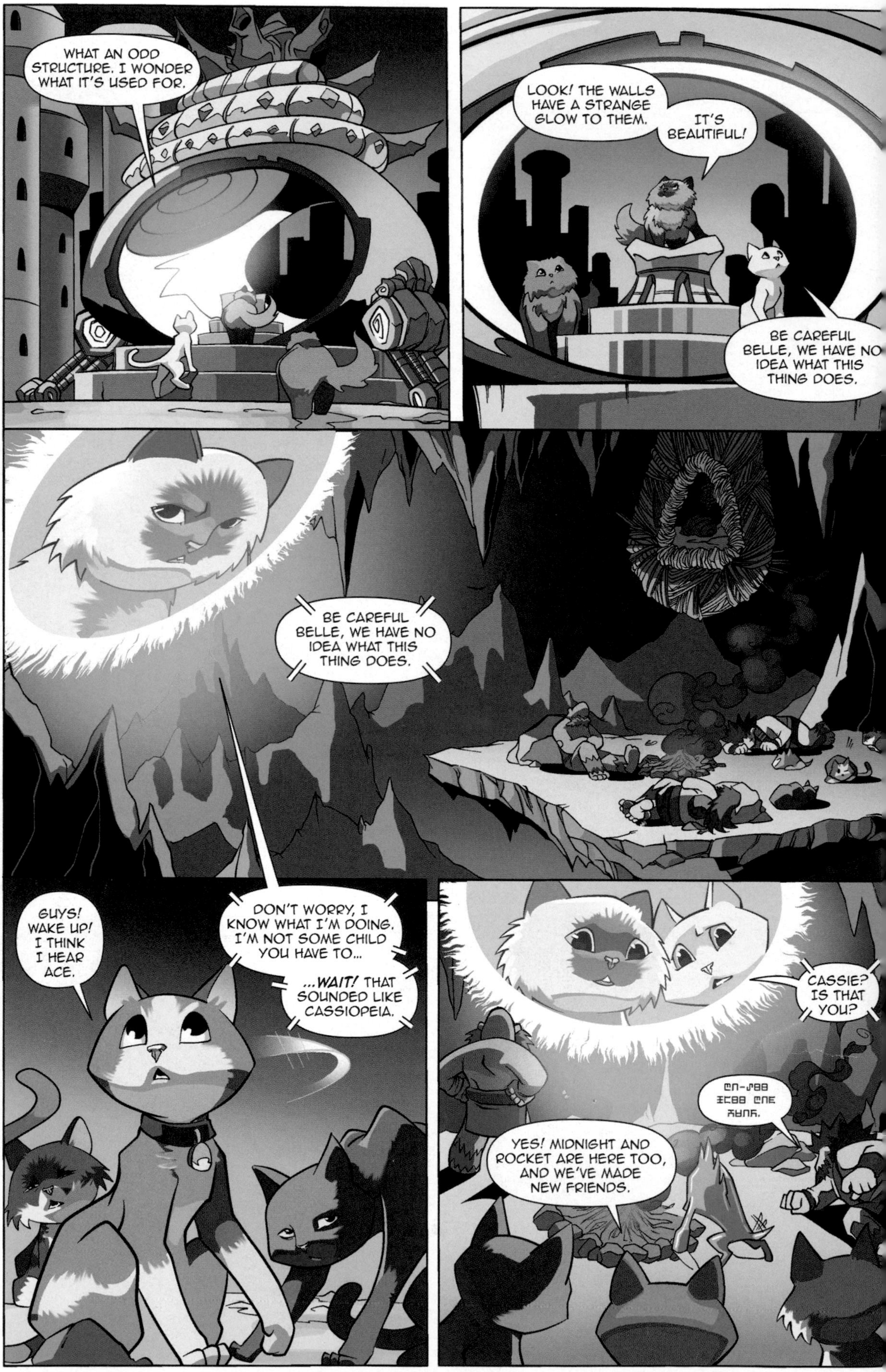
WHAT AN ODD STRUCTURE. I WONDER WHAT IT'S USED FOR.
LOOK! THE WALLS HAVE A STRANGE GLOW TO THEM.
IT'S BEAUTIFUL!
BE CAREFUL BELLE, WE HAVE NO IDEA WHAT THIS THING DOES.
BE CAREFUL BELLE, WE HAVE NO IDEA WHAT THIS THING DOES.
GUYS! WAKE UP! I THINK I HEAR ACE.
DON'T WORRY, I KNOW WHAT I'M DOING. I'M NOT SOME CHILD YOU HAVE TO...
...WAIT! THAT SOUNDED LIKE CASSIOPEIA.
CASSIE? IS THAT YOU?
YES! MIDNIGHT AND ROCKET ARE HERE TOO, AND WE'VE MADE NEW FRIENDS.

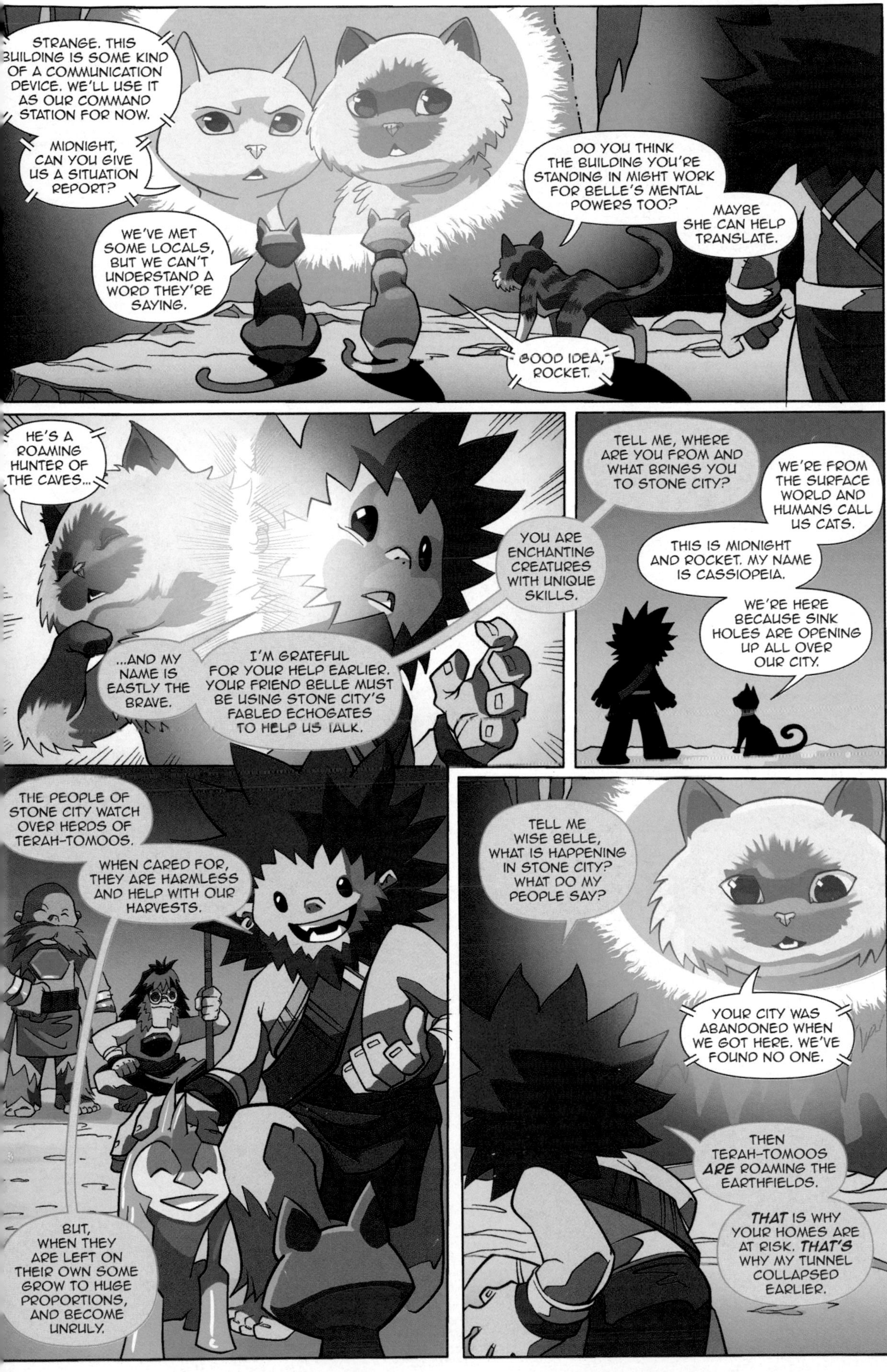

STRANGE. THIS BUILDING IS SOME KIND OF A COMMUNICATION DEVICE. WE'LL USE IT AS OUR COMMAND STATION FOR NOW.
MIDNIGHT, CAN YOU GIVE US A SITUATION REPORT?
WE'VE MET SOME LOCALS, BUT WE CAN'T UNDERSTAND A WORD THEY'RE SAYING.
DO YOU THINK THE BUILDING YOU'RE STANDING IN MIGHT WORK FOR BELLE'S MENTAL POWERS TOO?
MAYBE SHE CAN HELP TRANSLATE.
GOOD IDEA, ROCKET.
HE'S A ROAMING HUNTER OF THE CAVES...
...AND MY NAME IS EASTLY THE BRAVE.
I'M GRATEFUL FOR YOUR HELP EARLIER. YOUR FRIEND BELLE MUST BE USING STONE CITY'S FABLED ECHOGATES TO HELP US TALK.
YOU ARE ENCHANTING CREATURES WITH UNIQUE SKILLS.
TELL ME, WHERE ARE YOU FROM AND WHAT BRINGS YOU TO STONE CITY?
WE'RE FROM THE SURFACE WORLD AND HUMANS CALL US CATS.
THIS IS MIDNIGHT AND ROCKET. MY NAME IS CASSIOPEIA.
WE'RE HERE BECAUSE SINK HOLES ARE OPENING UP ALL OVER OUR CITY.
THE PEOPLE OF STONE CITY WATCH OVER HERDS OF TERAH-TOMOOS.
WHEN CARED FOR, THEY ARE HARMLESS AND HELP WITH OUR HARVESTS.
BUT, WHEN THEY ARE LEFT ON THEIR OWN SOME GROW TO HUGE PROPORTIONS, AND BECOME UNRULY.
TELL ME WISE BELLE, WHAT IS HAPPENING IN STONE CITY? WHAT DO MY PEOPLE SAY?
YOUR CITY WAS ABANDONED WHEN WE GOT HERE. WE'VE FOUND NO ONE.
THEN TERAH-TOMOOS *ARE* ROAMING THE EARTHFIELDS.
THAT IS WHY YOUR HOMES ARE AT RISK. *THAT'S* WHY MY TUNNEL COLLAPSED EARLIER.

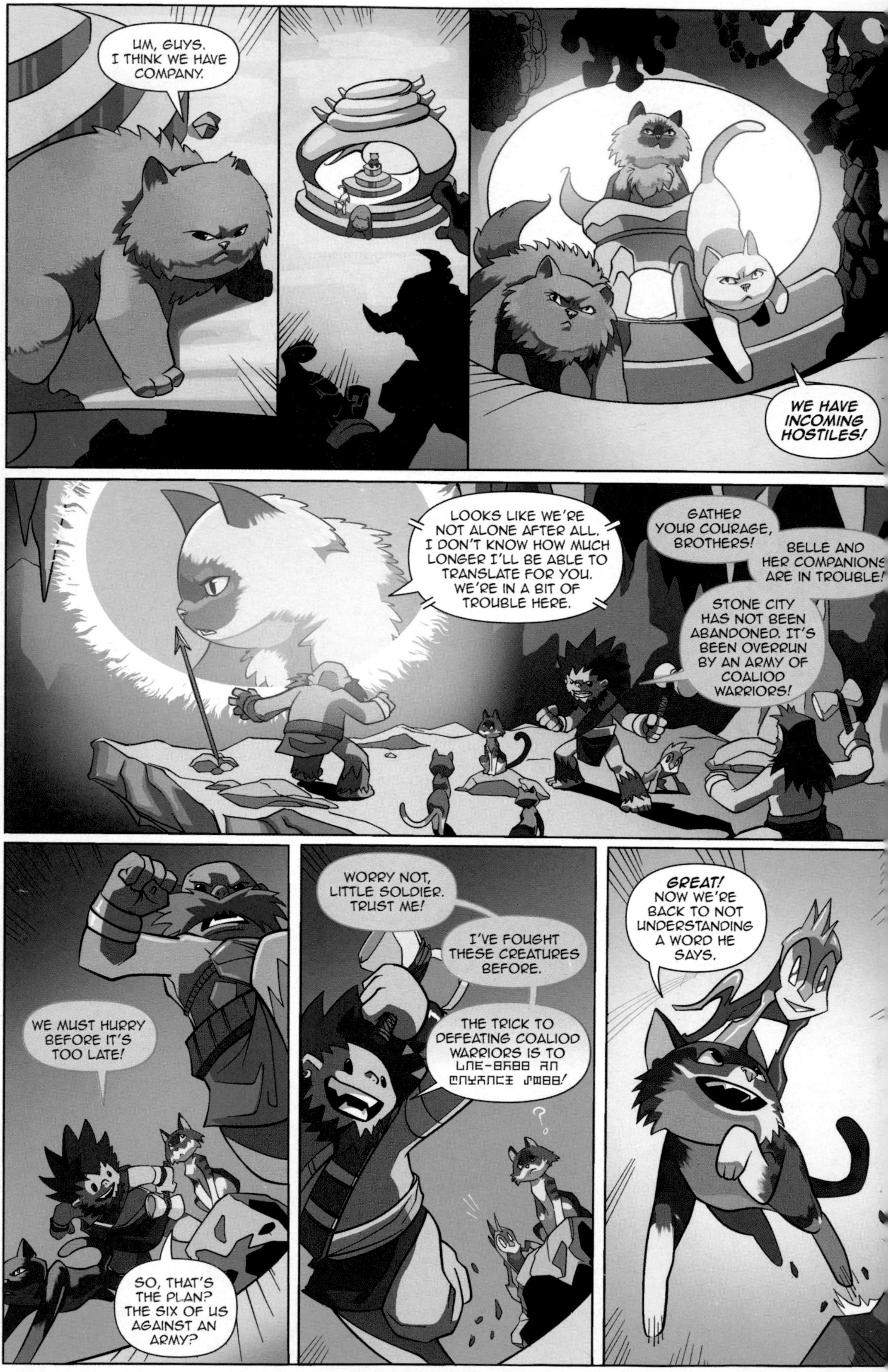
UM, GUYS. I THINK WE HAVE COMPANY.
WE HAVE INCOMING HOSTILES!
LOOKS LIKE WE'RE NOT ALONE AFTER ALL. I DON'T KNOW HOW MUCH LONGER I'LL BE ABLE TO TRANSLATE FOR YOU. WE'RE IN A BIT OF TROUBLE HERE.
GATHER YOUR COURAGE, BROTHERS!
BELLE AND HER COMPANIONS ARE IN TROUBLE!
STONE CITY HAS NOT BEEN ABANDONED. IT'S BEEN OVERRUN BY AN ARMY OF COALIOD WARRIORS!
WE MUST HURRY BEFORE IT'S TOO LATE!
SO, THAT'S THE PLAN? THE SIX OF US AGAINST AN ARMY?
WORRY NOT, LITTLE SOLDIER. TRUST ME!
I'VE FOUGHT THESE CREATURES BEFORE.
THE TRICK TO DEFEATING COALIOD WARRIORS IS TO
?
GREAT! NOW WE'RE BACK TO NOT UNDERSTANDING A WORD HE SAYS.

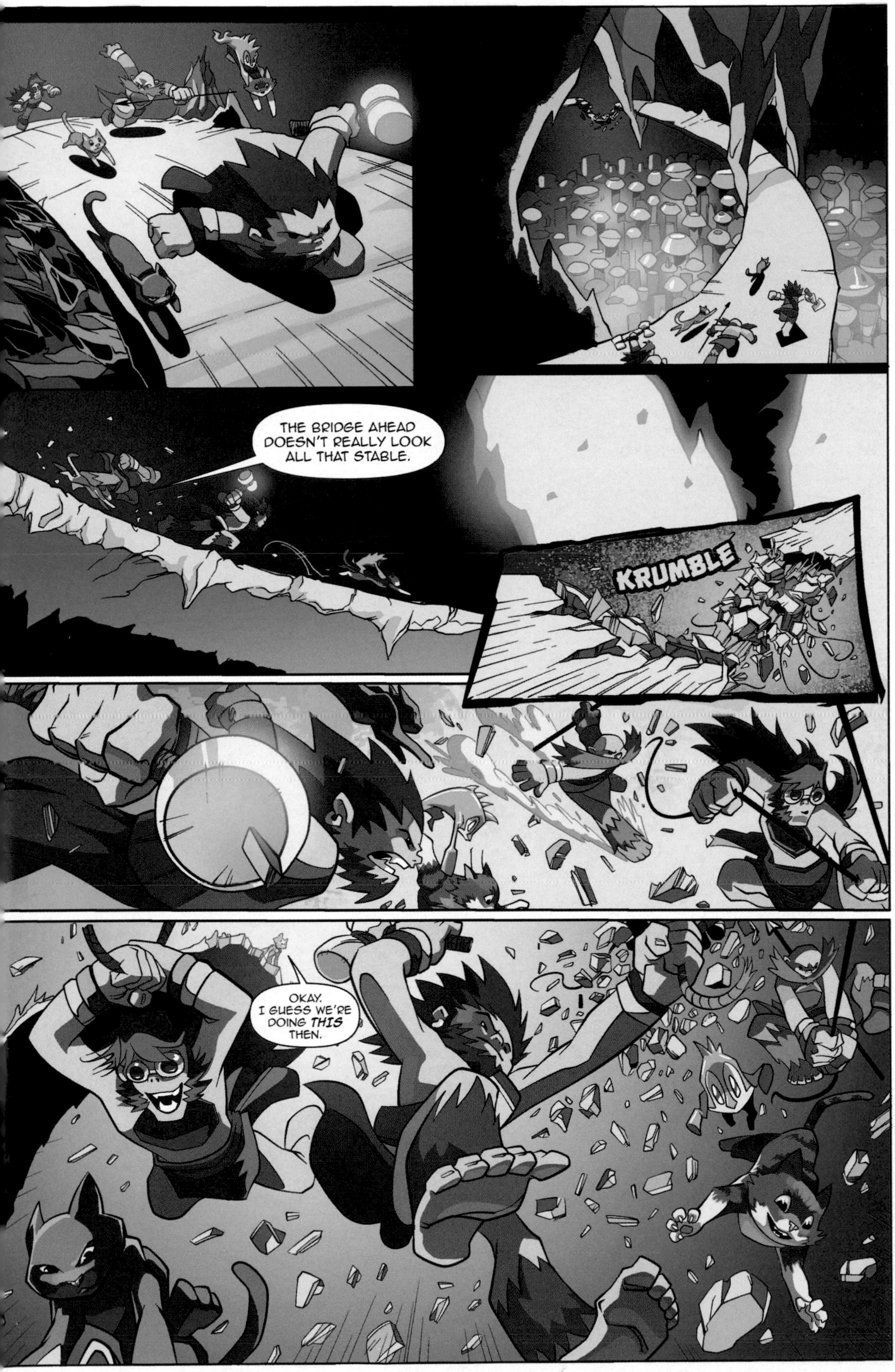
THE BRIDGE AHEAD DOESN'T REALLY LOOK ALL THAT STABLE.
KRUMBLE
OKAY. I GUESS WE'RE DOING *THIS* THEN.

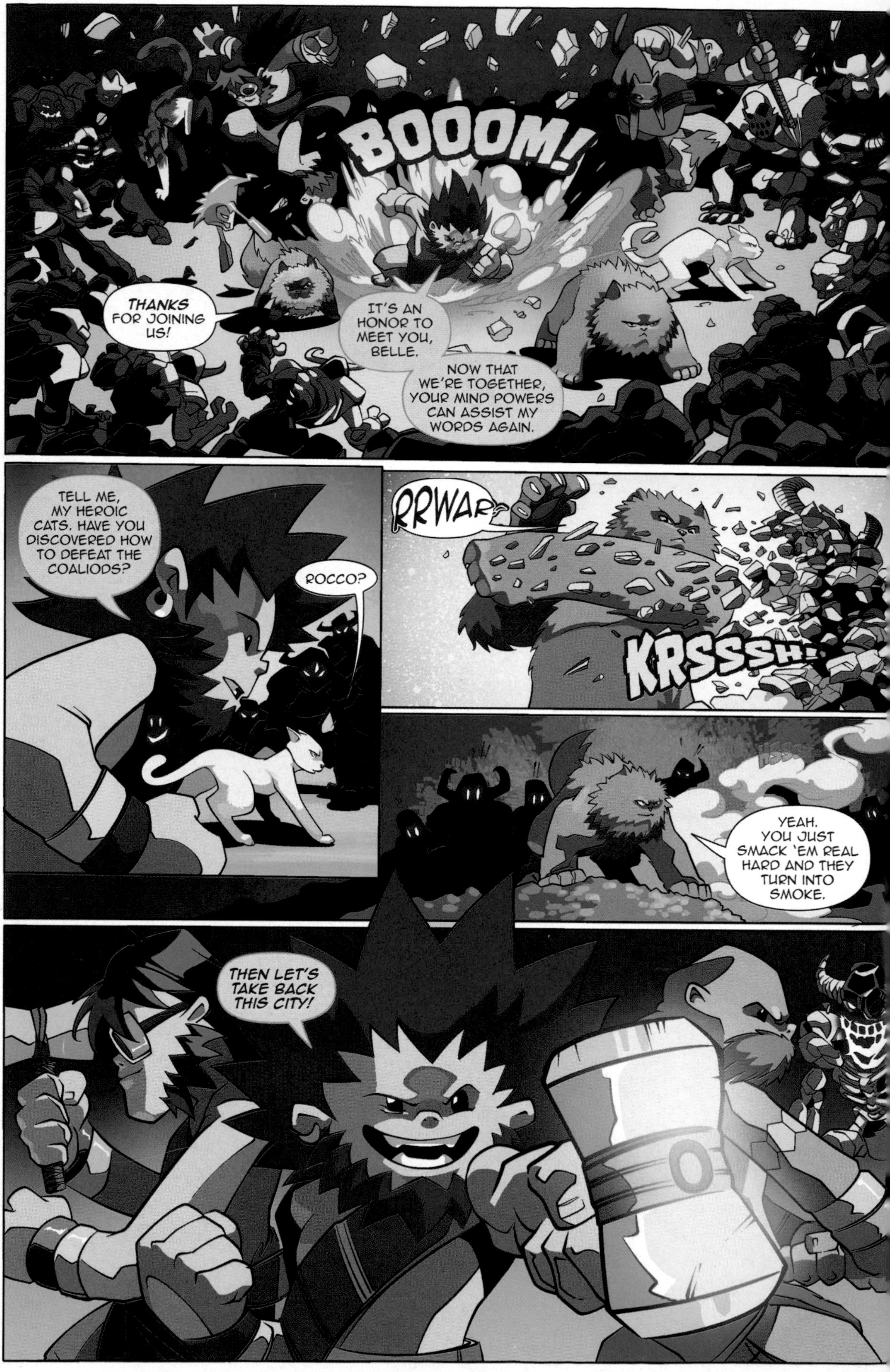
BOOOM!
THANKS FOR JOINING US!
IT'S AN HONOR TO MEET YOU, BELLE.
NOW THAT WE'RE TOGETHER, YOUR MIND POWERS CAN ASSIST MY WORDS AGAIN.
TELL ME, MY HEROIC CATS. HAVE YOU DISCOVERED HOW TO DEFEAT THE COALIODS?
ROCCO?
RRWAR
KRSSSH!
YEAH. YOU JUST SMACK 'EM REAL HARD AND THEY TURN INTO SMOKE.
THEN LET'S TAKE BACK THIS CITY!

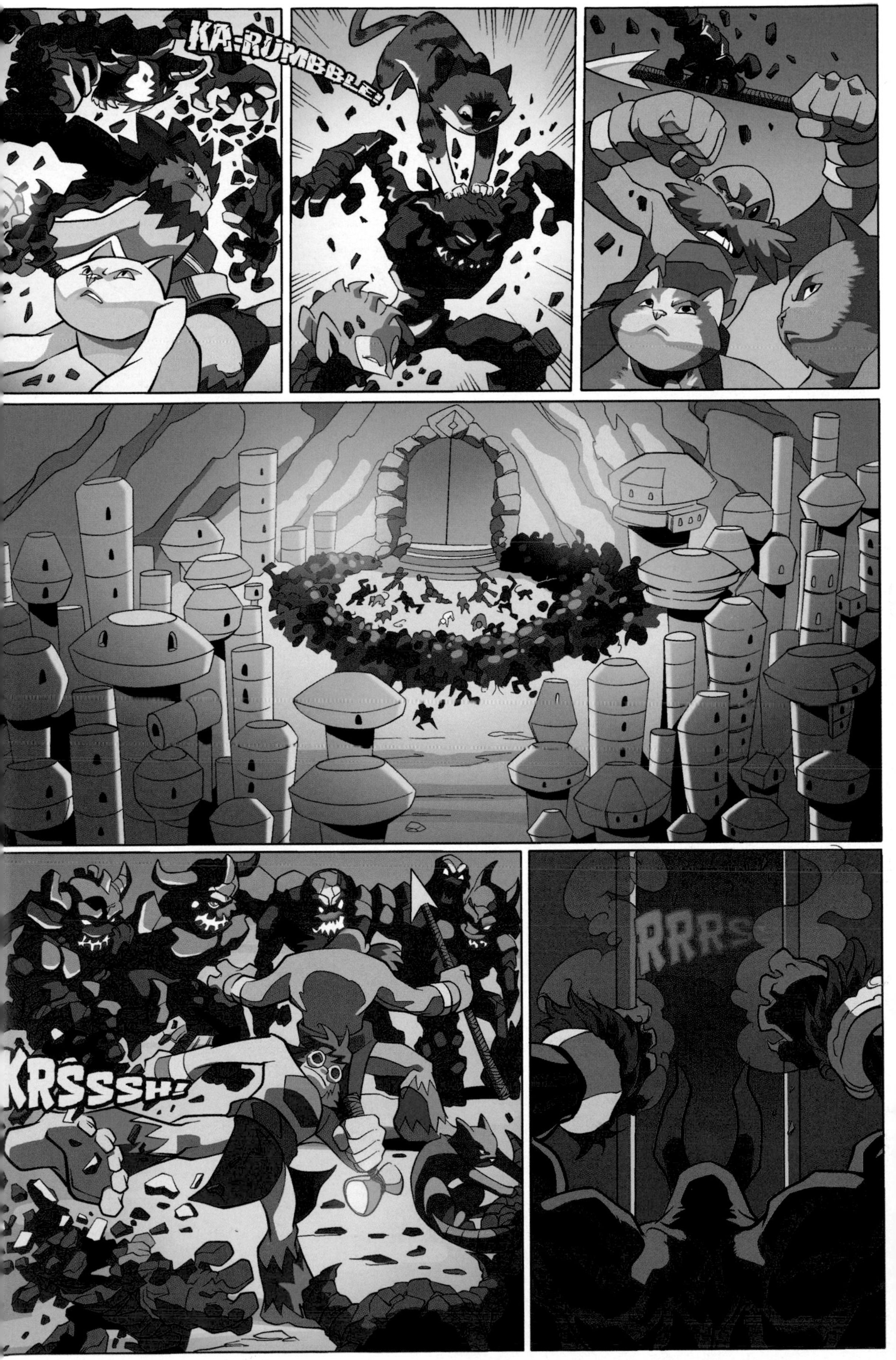
KA-RUMBBLE!
KRSSSH!
RRRS

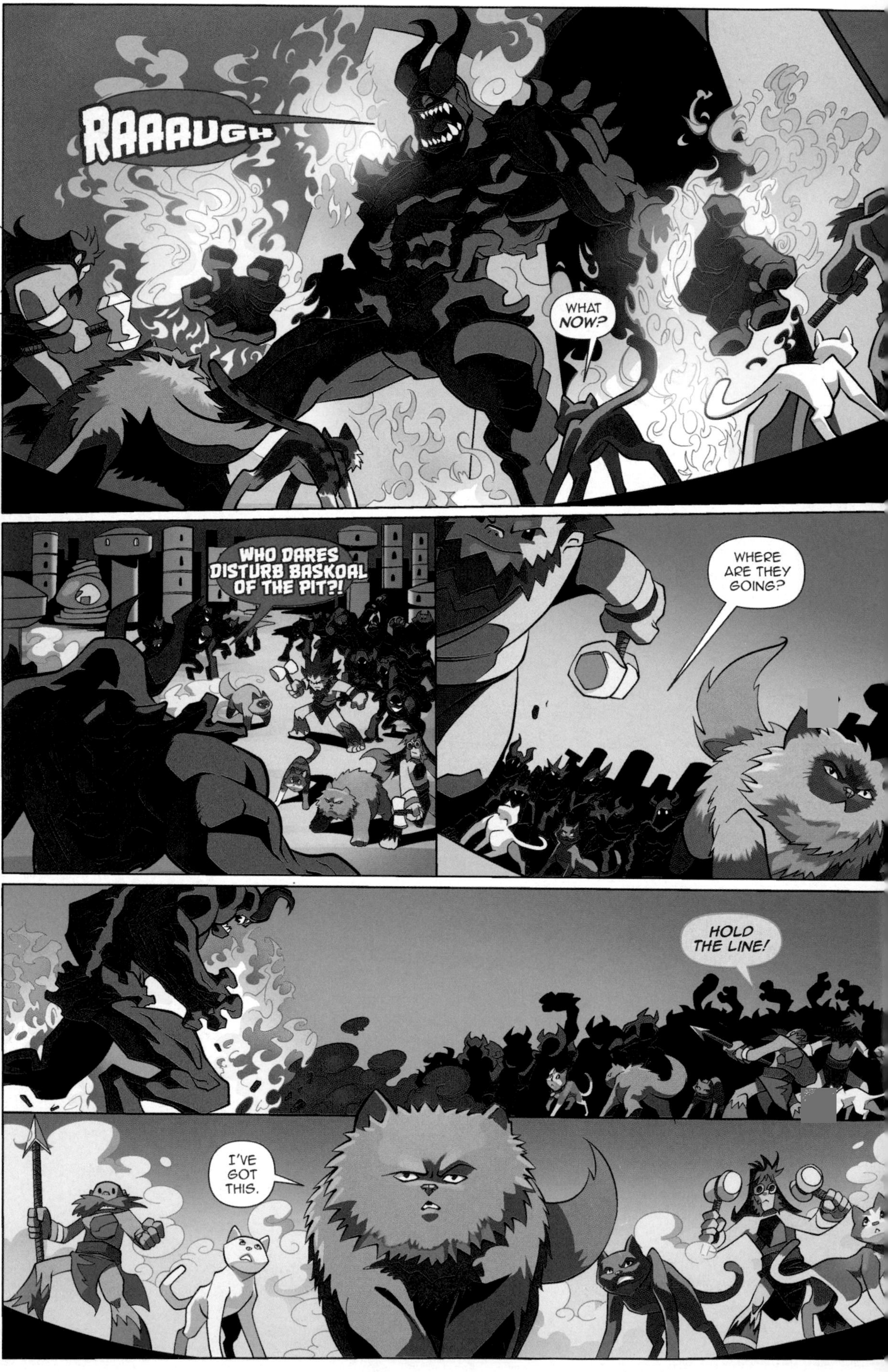
RAAAUGH
WHAT NOW?
WHO DARES DISTURB BASKOAL OF THE PIT?!
WHERE ARE THEY GOING?
HOLD THE LINE!
I'VE GOT THIS.

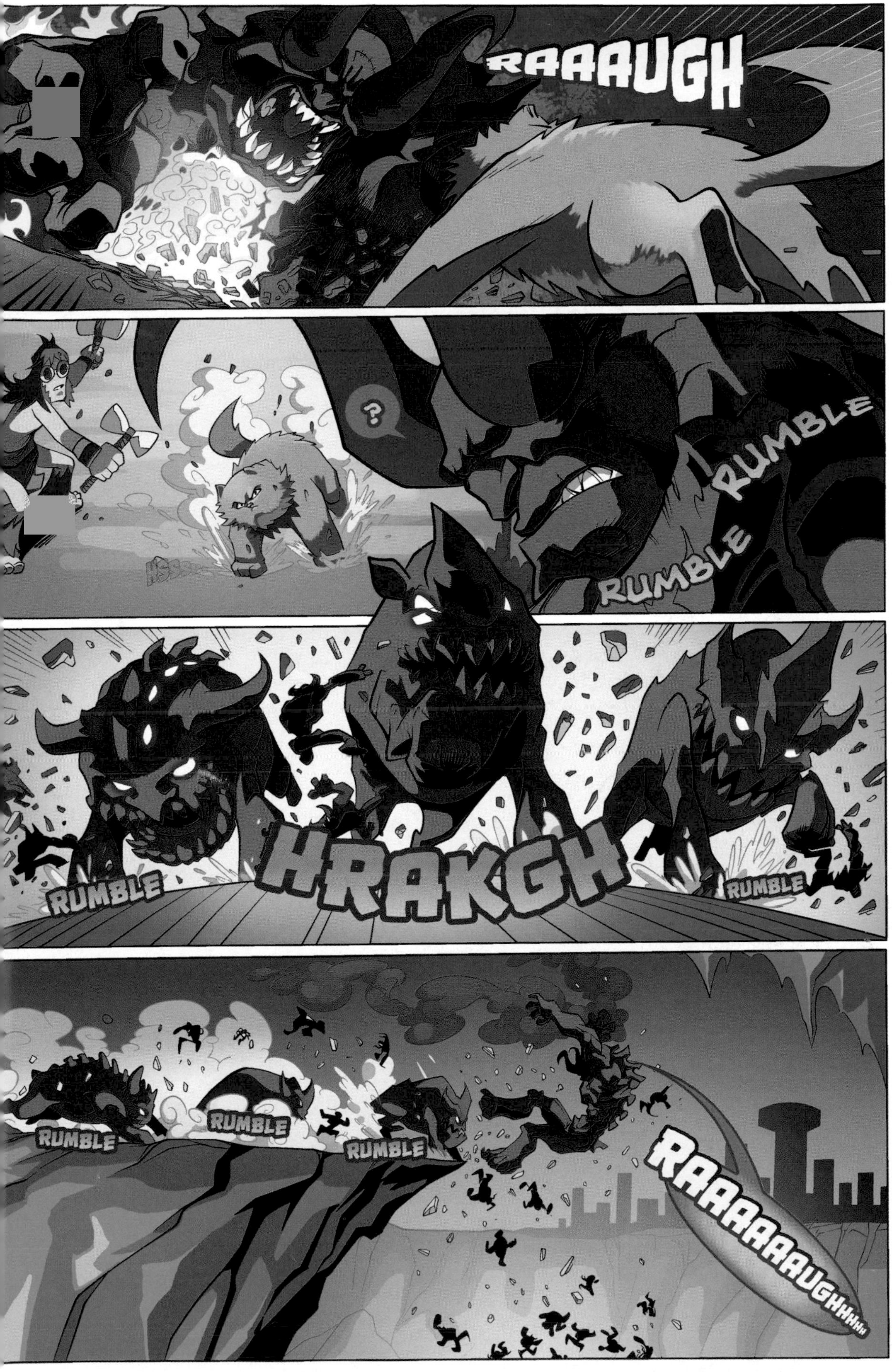
RAAAUGH
?
RUMBLE
RUMBLE
RUMBLE
HRAKGH
RUMBLE
RUMBLE
RUMBLE
RUMBLE
RUMBLE
RAAAAAAUGHHHHHH

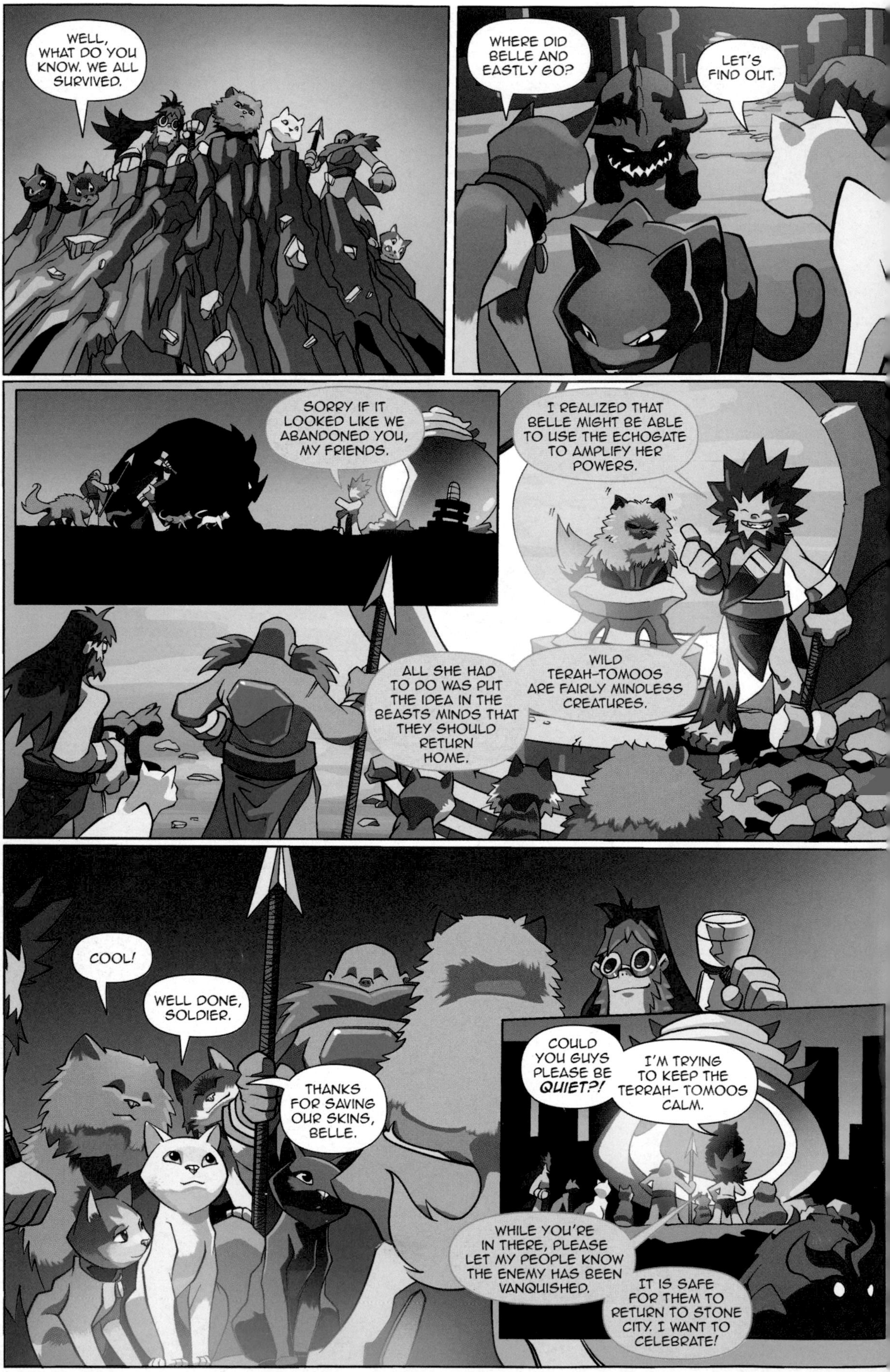
WELL, WHAT DO YOU KNOW. WE ALL SURVIVED.
WHERE DID BELLE AND EASTLY GO?
LET'S FIND OUT.
SORRY IF IT LOOKED LIKE WE ABANDONED YOU, MY FRIENDS.
I REALIZED THAT BELLE MIGHT BE ABLE TO USE THE ECHOGATE TO AMPLIFY HER POWERS.
WILD TERAH-TOMOOS ARE FAIRLY MINDLESS CREATURES.
ALL SHE HAD TO DO WAS PUT THE IDEA IN THE BEASTS MINDS THAT THEY SHOULD RETURN HOME.
COOL!
WELL DONE, SOLDIER.
THANKS FOR SAVING OUR SKINS, BELLE.
COULD YOU GUYS PLEASE BE QUIET?!
I'M TRYING TO KEEP THE TERRAH- TOMOOS CALM.
WHILE YOU'RE IN THERE, PLEASE LET MY PEOPLE KNOW THE ENEMY HAS BEEN VANQUISHED.
IT IS SAFE FOR THEM TO RETURN TO STONE CITY. I WANT TO CELEBRATE!

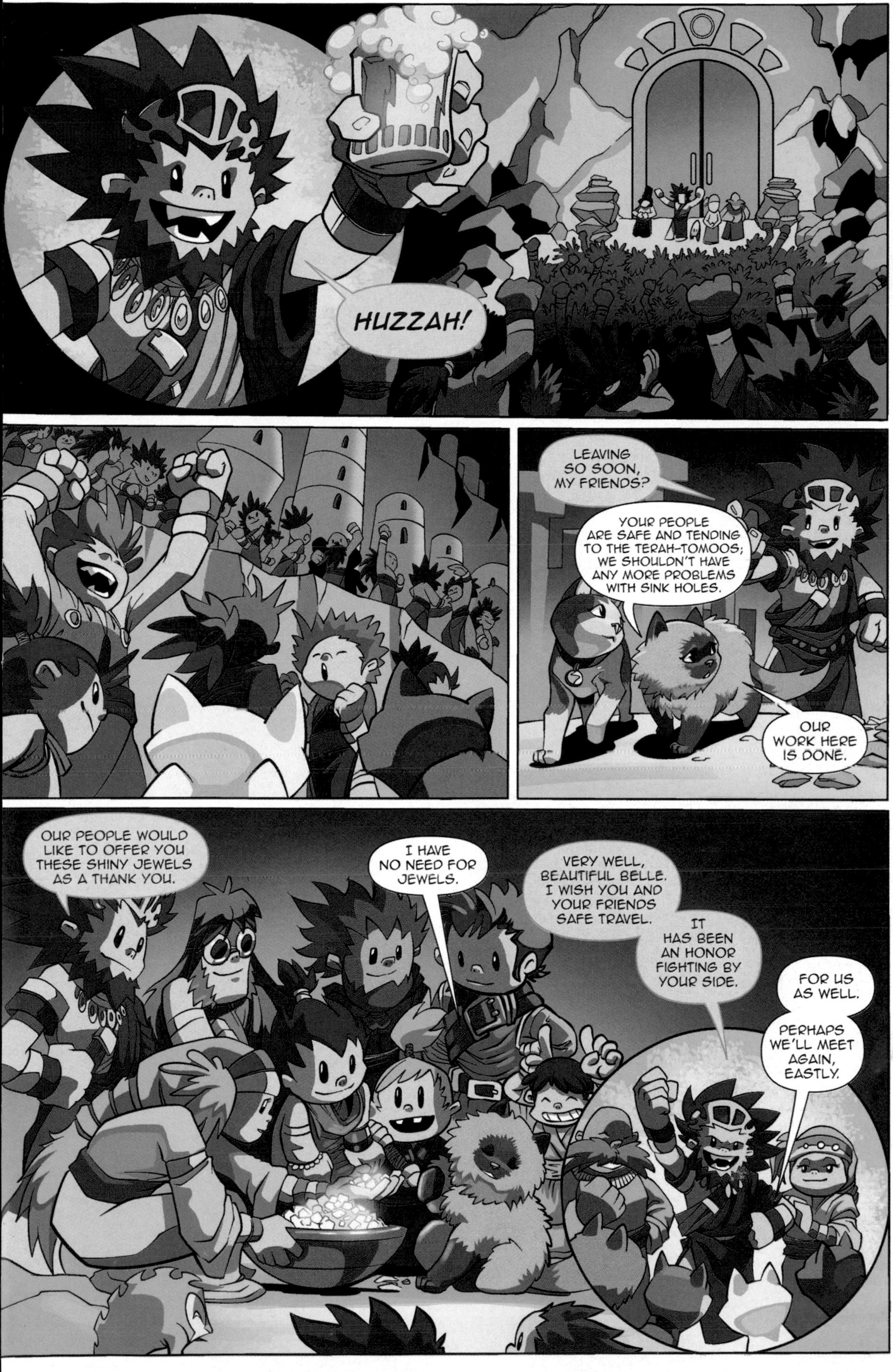
HUZZAH!
LEAVING SO SOON, MY FRIENDS?
YOUR PEOPLE ARE SAFE AND TENDING TO THE TERAH-TOMOOS; WE SHOULDN'T HAVE ANY MORE PROBLEMS WITH SINK HOLES.
OUR WORK HERE IS DONE.
OUR PEOPLE WOULD LIKE TO OFFER YOU THESE SHINY JEWELS AS A THANK YOU.
I HAVE NO NEED FOR JEWELS.
VERY WELL, BEAUTIFUL BELLE. I WISH YOU AND YOUR FRIENDS SAFE TRAVEL.
IT HAS BEEN AN HONOR FIGHTING BY YOUR SIDE.
FOR US AS WELL.
PERHAPS WE'LL MEET AGAIN, EASTLY.

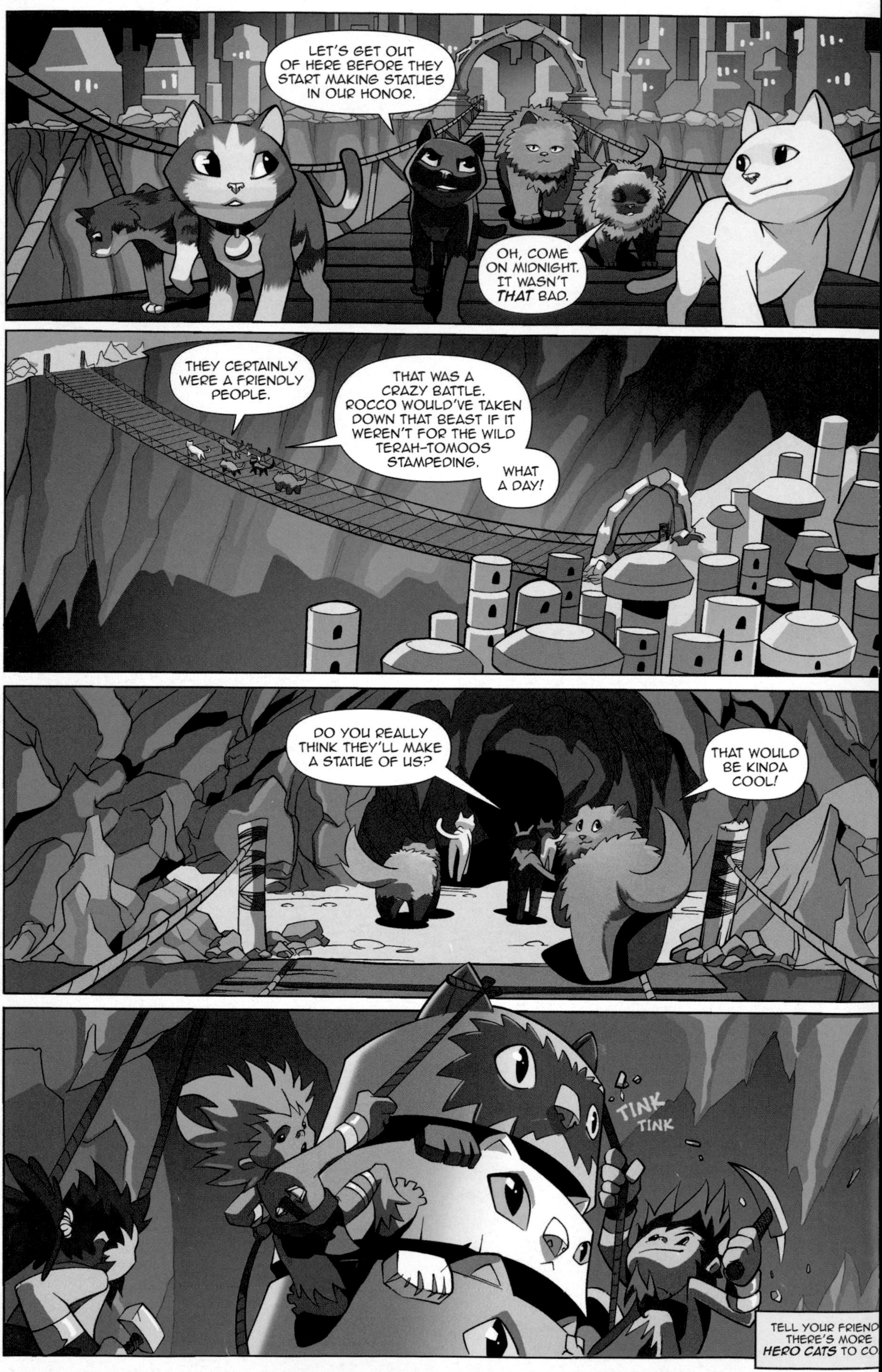
LET'S GET OUT OF HERE BEFORE THEY START MAKING STATUES IN OUR HONOR.
OH, COME ON MIDNIGHT. IT WASN'T *THAT* BAD.
THEY CERTAINLY WERE A FRIENDLY PEOPLE.
THAT WAS A CRAZY BATTLE. ROCCO WOULD'VE TAKEN DOWN THAT BEAST IF IT WEREN'T FOR THE WILD TERAH-TOMOOS STAMPEDING.
WHAT A DAY!
DO YOU REALLY THINK THEY'LL MAKE A STATUE OF US?
THAT WOULD BE KINDA COOL!
TINK
TINK
TELL YOUR FRIEND
THERE'S MORE
HERO CATS TO CO

HERO CHAT

OUR FANS ARE SO MUCH FUN TO MEET AT COVENTIONS!

THANK YOU FOR STOPPING BY ARTIST ALLEY AND SUPPORTING THE TEAM. THEY'RE JUST GETTING STARTED, SO HOPEFULLY KYLE, MARCUS, TRACY, & THE REST OF THE GANG WILL BE IN YOUR TOWN SOON.

-Bandit-

STAY STELLAR!

NEXT UP: SPACE BUGS

email Kyle Puttkammer @ kyle@galacticquest.com

BONUS COVER BY "SONIC THE HEDGHOG" ARTIST TRACY YARDLEY!

Bryan Seaton - Publisher
Kevin Freeman - President
Dave Dwonch - Creative Director
Shawn Gabborin - Editor in Chief
Jamal Igle & Kelly Dale - Co-Directors of Marketing
Jim Dietz - Social Media Director
Jeremy Whitley - Education Outreach Director
Chad Cicconi & Colleen Boyd - Associate Editors

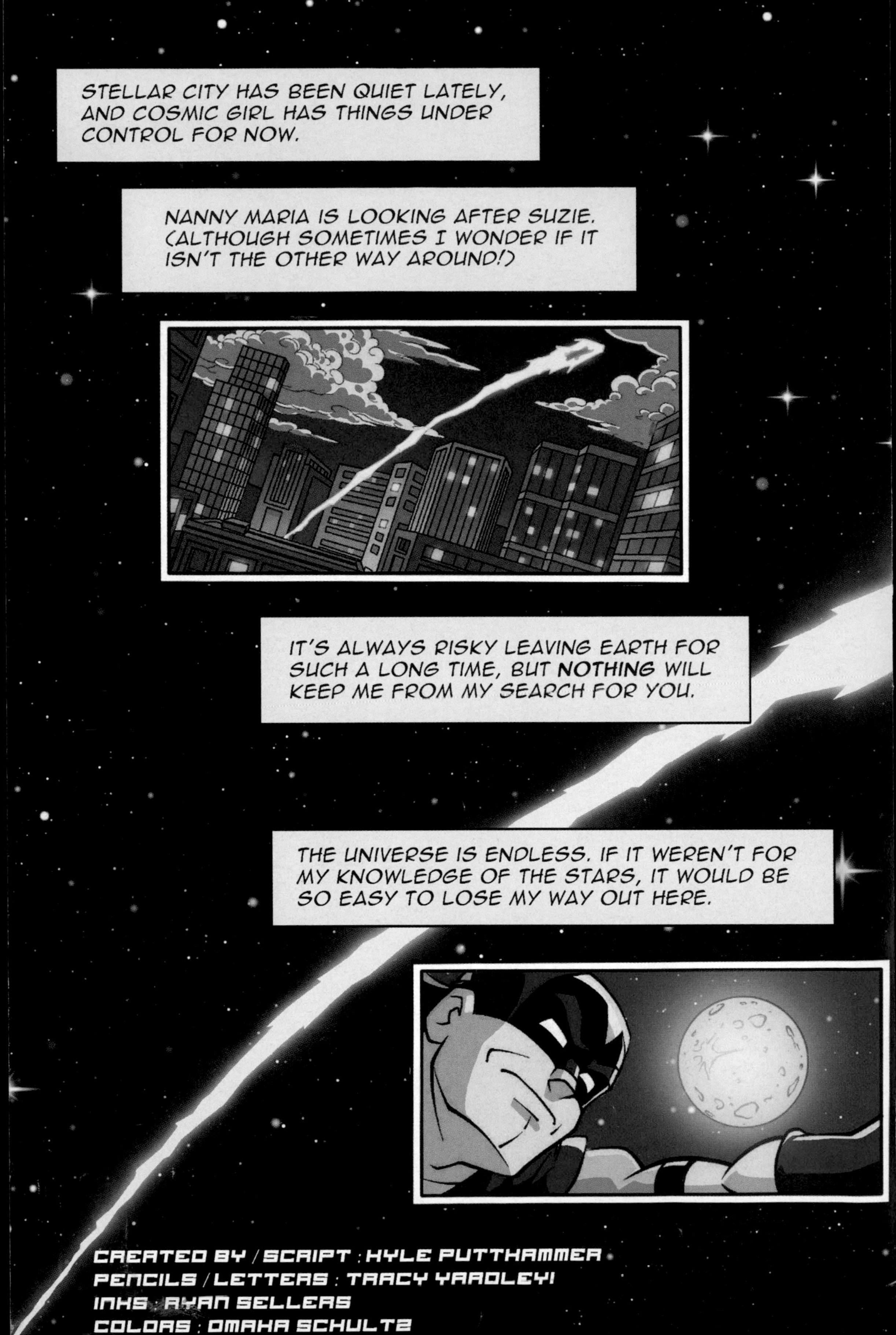
STELLAR CITY HAS BEEN QUIET LATELY, AND COSMIC GIRL HAS THINGS UNDER CONTROL FOR NOW.
NANNY MARIA IS LOOKING AFTER SUZIE. (ALTHOUGH SOMETIMES I WONDER IF IT ISN'T THE OTHER WAY AROUND!)
IT'S ALWAYS RISKY LEAVING EARTH FOR SUCH A LONG TIME, BUT **NOTHING** WILL KEEP ME FROM MY SEARCH FOR YOU.
THE UNIVERSE IS ENDLESS. IF IT WEREN'T FOR MY KNOWLEDGE OF THE STARS, IT WOULD BE SO EASY TO LOSE MY WAY OUT HERE.
CREATED BY / SCRIPT : KYLE PUTTKAMMER
PENCILS / LETTERS : TRACY YARDLEY!
INKS : RYAN SELLERS
COLORS : OMAHA SCHULTZ

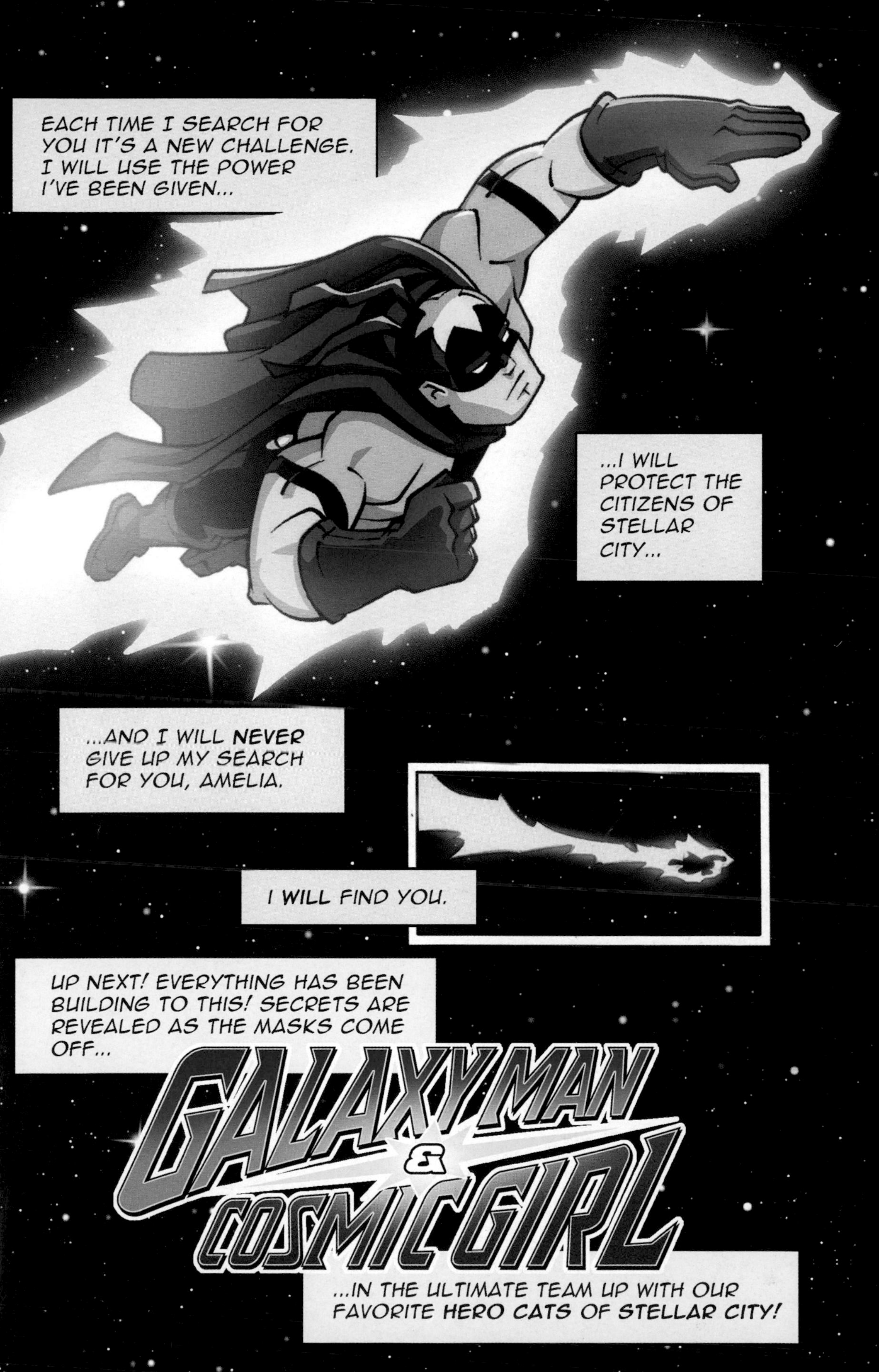
EACH TIME I SEARCH FOR YOU IT'S A NEW CHALLENGE. I WILL USE THE POWER I'VE BEEN GIVEN...
...I WILL PROTECT THE CITIZENS OF STELLAR CITY...
...AND I WILL NEVER GIVE UP MY SEARCH FOR YOU, AMELIA.
I WILL FIND YOU.
UP NEXT! EVERYTHING HAS BEEN BUILDING TO THIS! SECRETS ARE REVEALED AS THE MASKS COME OFF...
GALAXY MAN & COSMIC GIRL
...IN THE ULTIMATE TEAM UP WITH OUR FAVORITE HERO CATS OF STELLAR CITY!

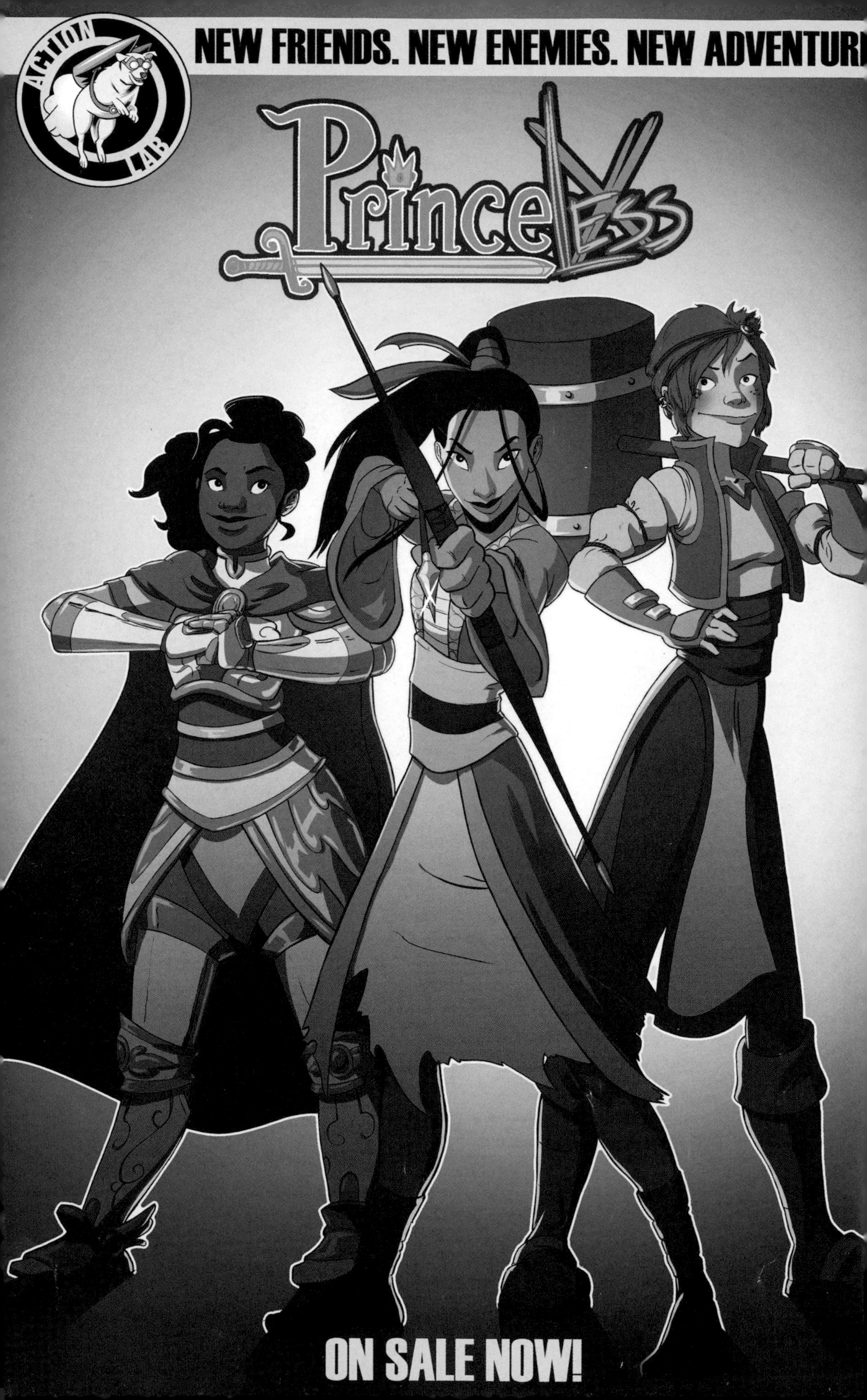
ACTION LAB
NEW FRIENDS. NEW ENEMIES. NEW ADVENTUR
Princeless
ON SALE NOW!

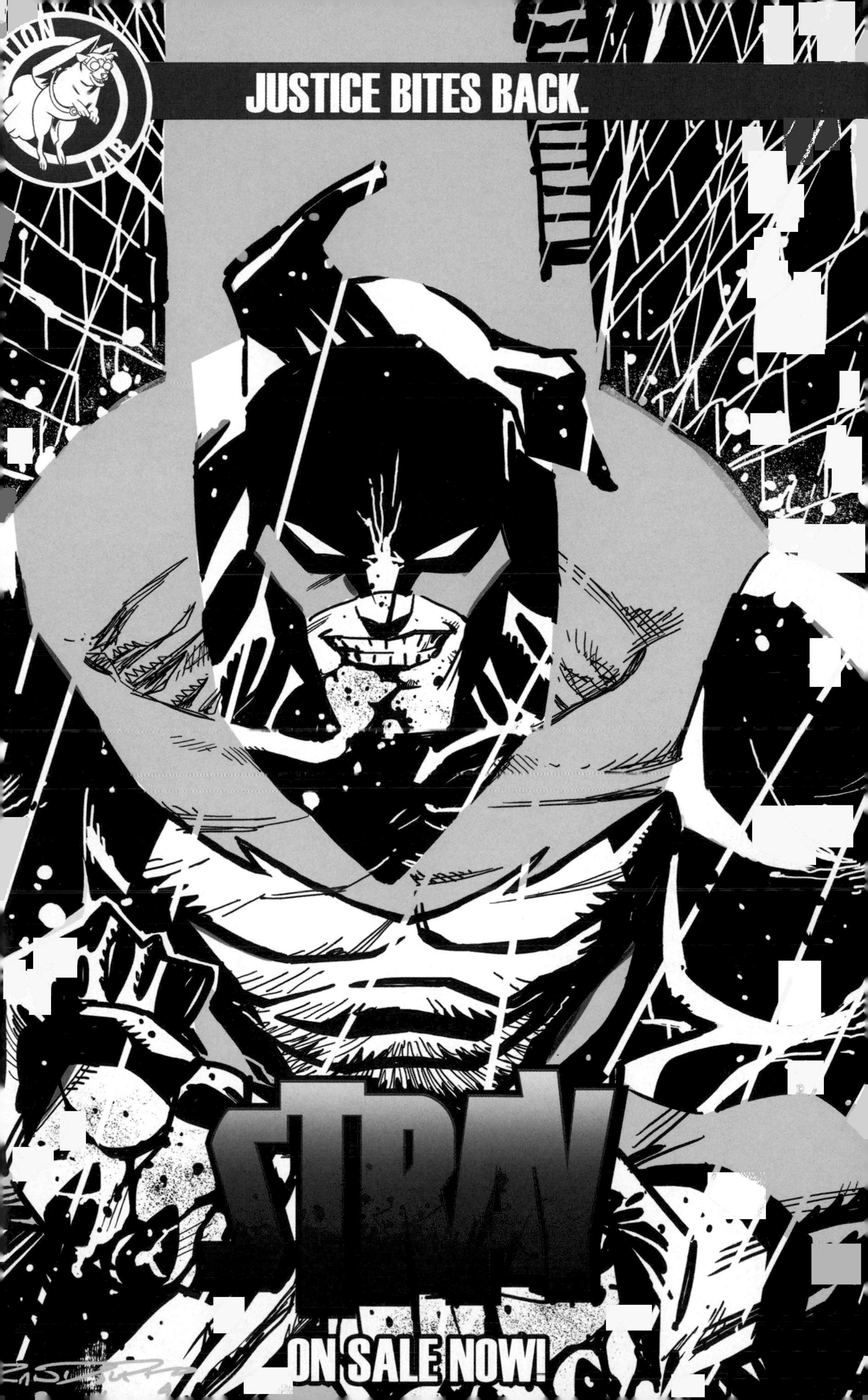
JUSTICE BITES BACK.
STRAY
ON SALE NOW!

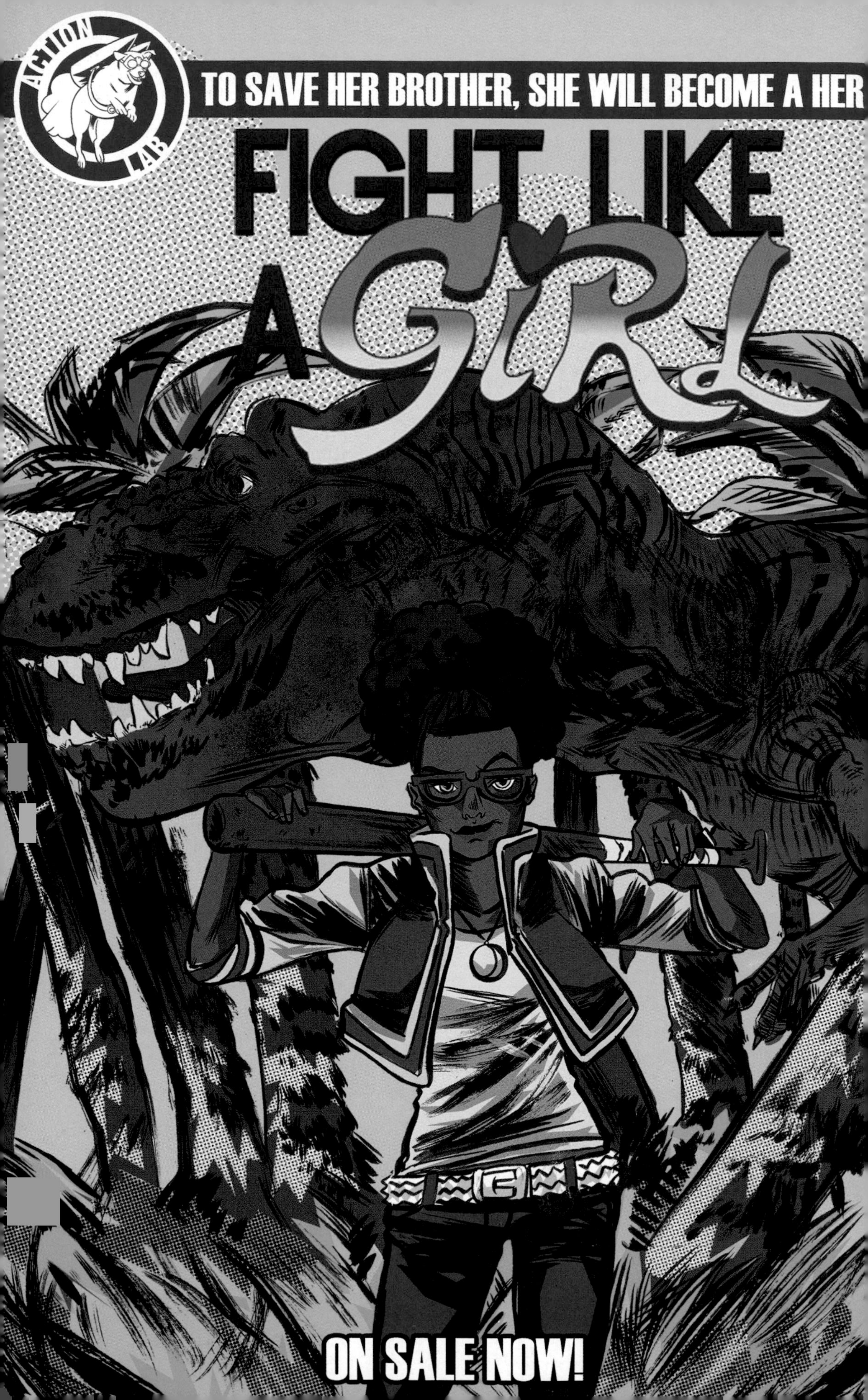
ACTION LAB
TO SAVE HER BROTHER, SHE WILL BECOME A HER
FIGHT LIKE A GIRL
ON SALE NOW!

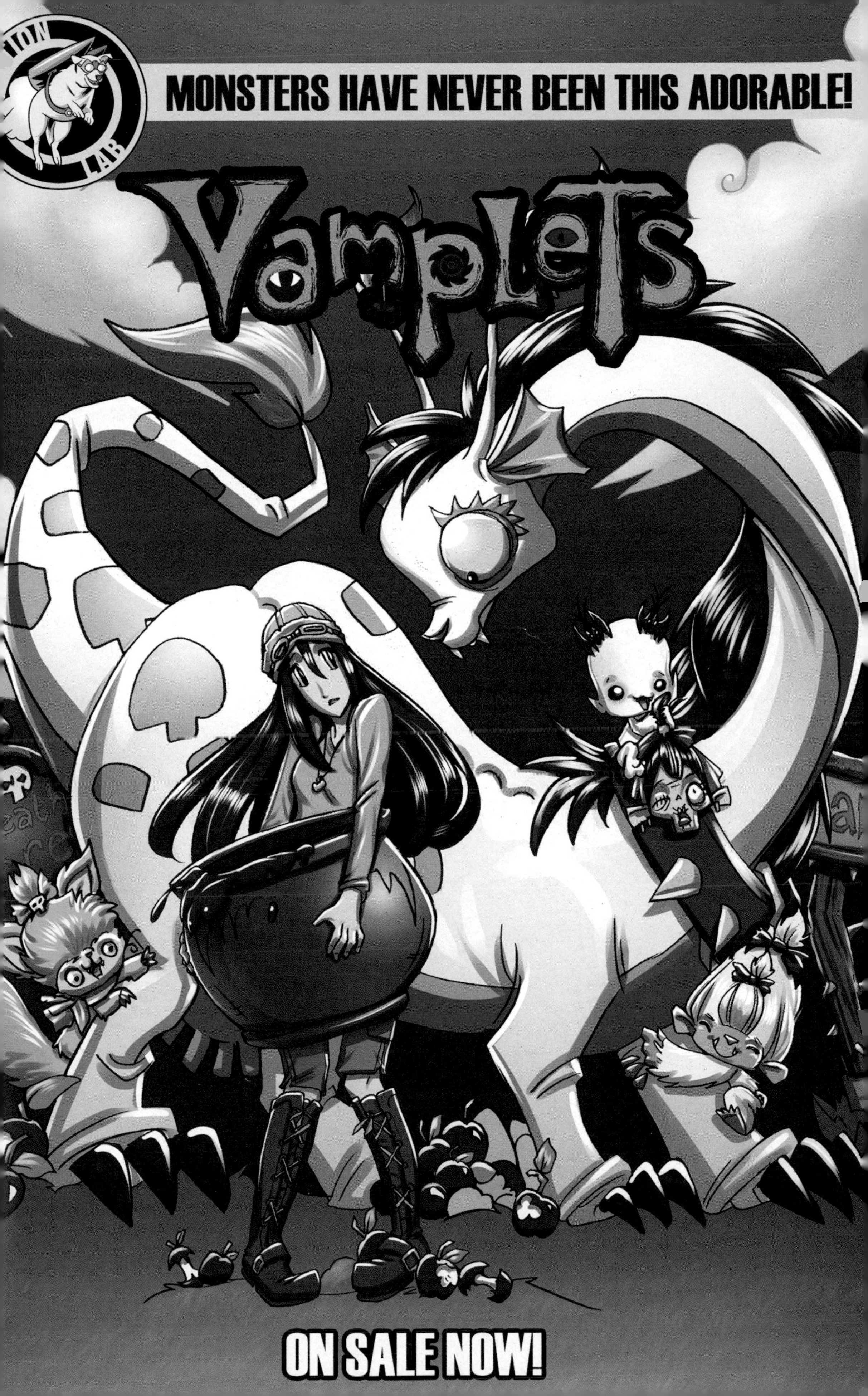
MONSTERS HAVE NEVER BEEN THIS ADORABLE!
Vamplets
ON SALE NOW!

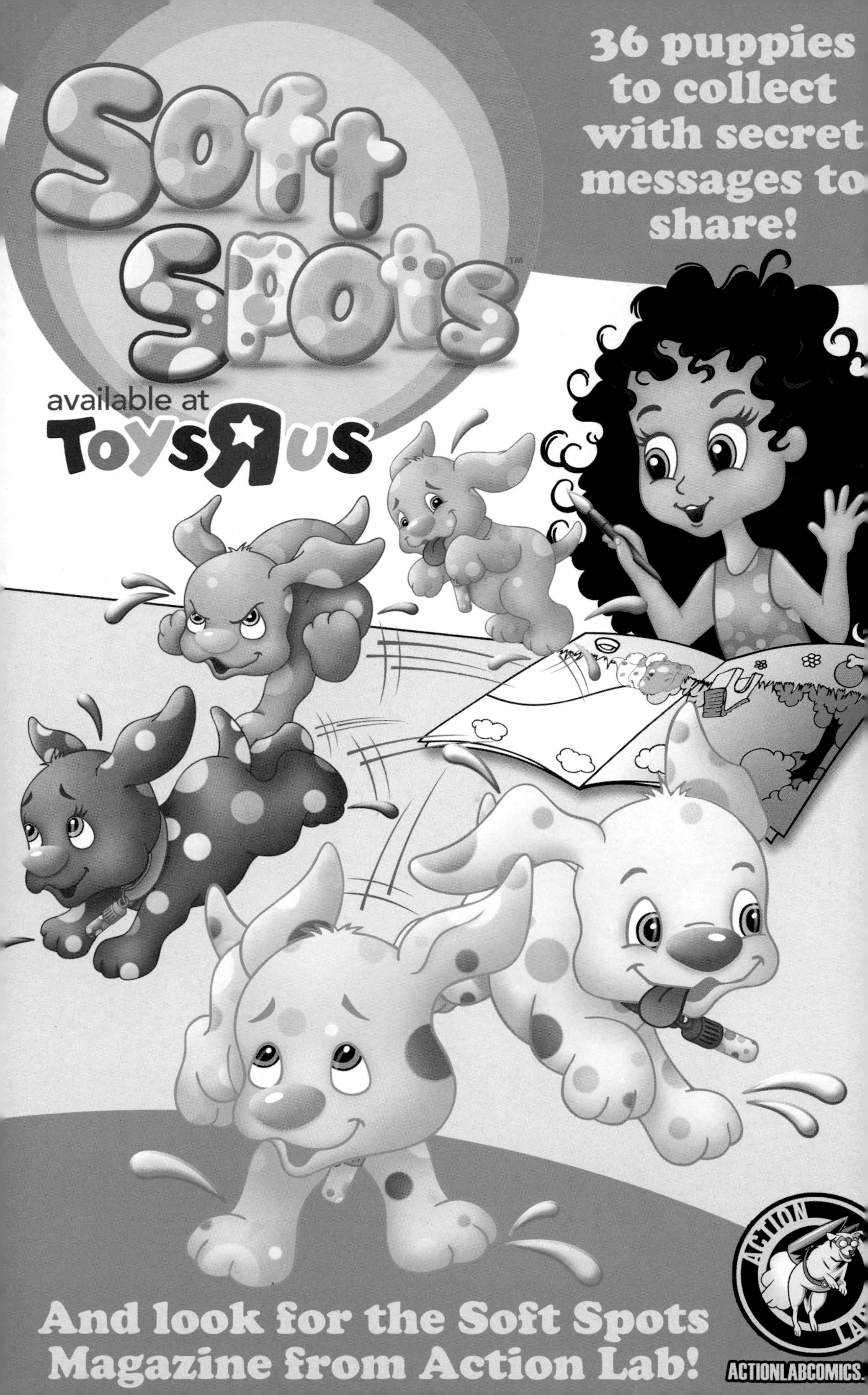

Soft Spots™
available at
ToysRUs®
36 puppies to collect with secret messages to share!
And look for the Soft Spots Magazine from Action Lab!
ACTION LAB
ACTIONLABCOMICS.

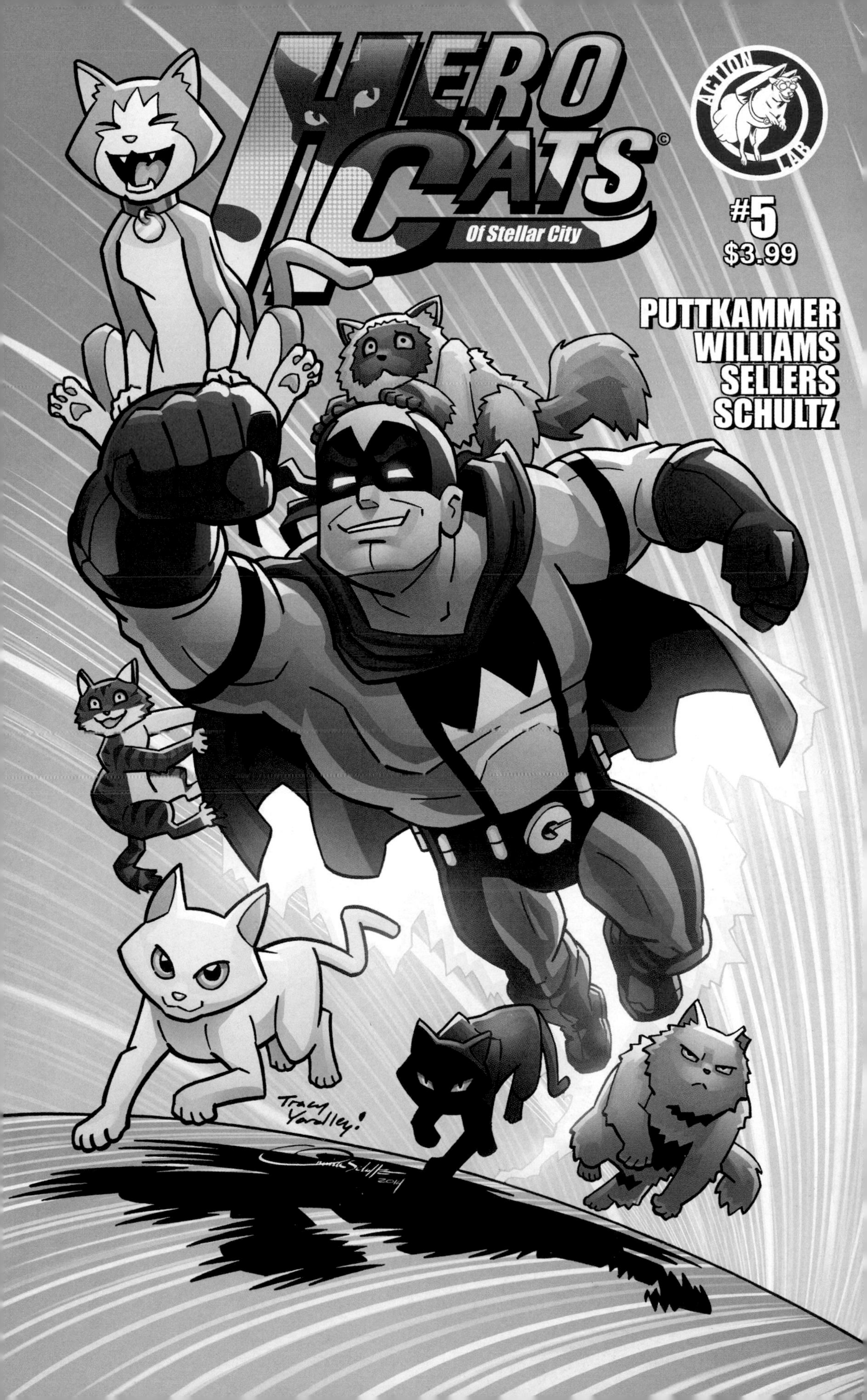
HERO CATS©
Of Stellar City
ACTION LAB
#5
$3.99
PUTTKAMMER
WILLIAMS
SELLERS
SCHULTZ
Tracy Yardley!

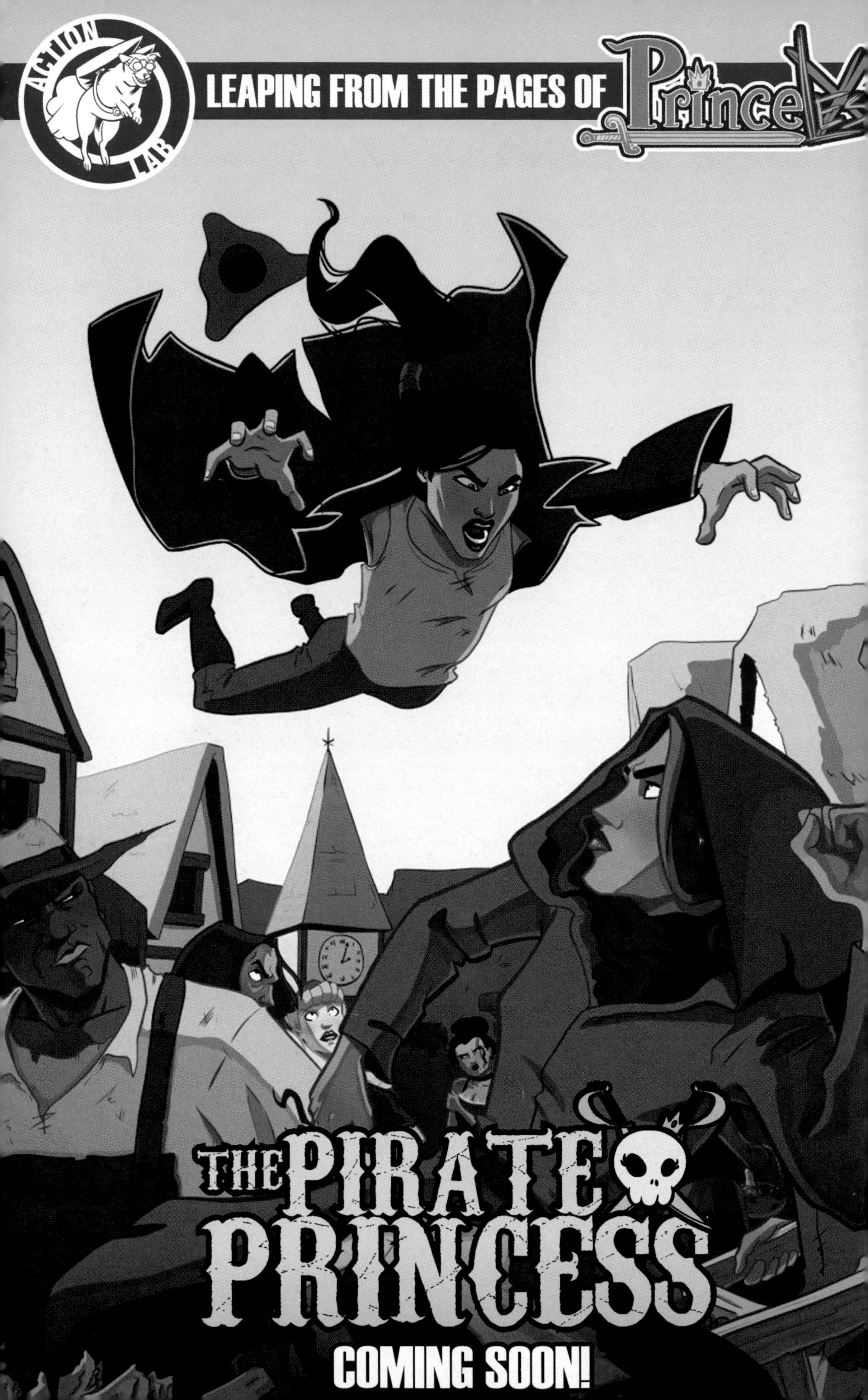

ACTION LAB
LEAPING FROM THE PAGES OF
Princeless
THE PIRATE PRINCESS
COMING SOON!

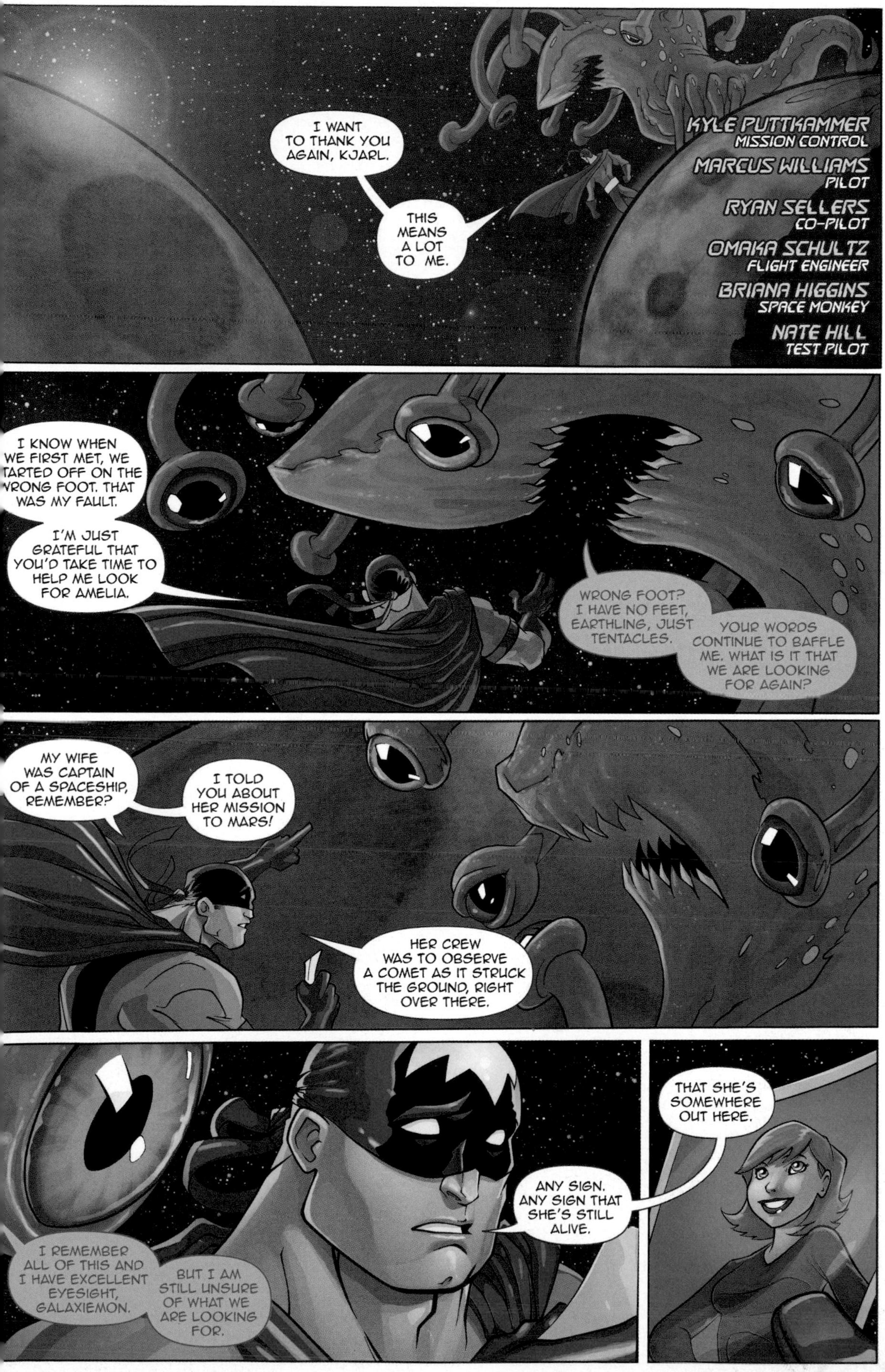

I WANT TO THANK YOU AGAIN, KJARL.
THIS MEANS A LOT TO ME.
KYLE PUTTKAMMER MISSION CONTROL
MARCUS WILLIAMS PILOT
RYAN SELLERS CO-PILOT
OMAKA SCHULTZ FLIGHT ENGINEER
BRIANA HIGGINS SPACE MONKEY
NATE HILL TEST PILOT
I KNOW WHEN WE FIRST MET, WE TARTED OFF ON THE VRONG FOOT. THAT WAS MY FAULT.
I'M JUST GRATEFUL THAT YOU'D TAKE TIME TO HELP ME LOOK FOR AMELIA.
WRONG FOOT? I HAVE NO FEET, EARTHLING, JUST TENTACLES.
YOUR WORDS CONTINUE TO BAFFLE ME. WHAT IS IT THAT WE ARE LOOKING FOR AGAIN?
MY WIFE WAS CAPTAIN OF A SPACESHIP, REMEMBER?
I TOLD YOU ABOUT HER MISSION TO MARS!
HER CREW WAS TO OBSERVE A COMET AS IT STRUCK THE GROUND, RIGHT OVER THERE.
I REMEMBER ALL OF THIS AND I HAVE EXCELLENT EYESIGHT, GALAXIEMON.
BUT I AM STILL UNSURE OF WHAT WE ARE LOOKING FOR.
ANY SIGN. ANY SIGN THAT SHE'S STILL ALIVE.
THAT SHE'S SOMEWHERE OUT HERE.

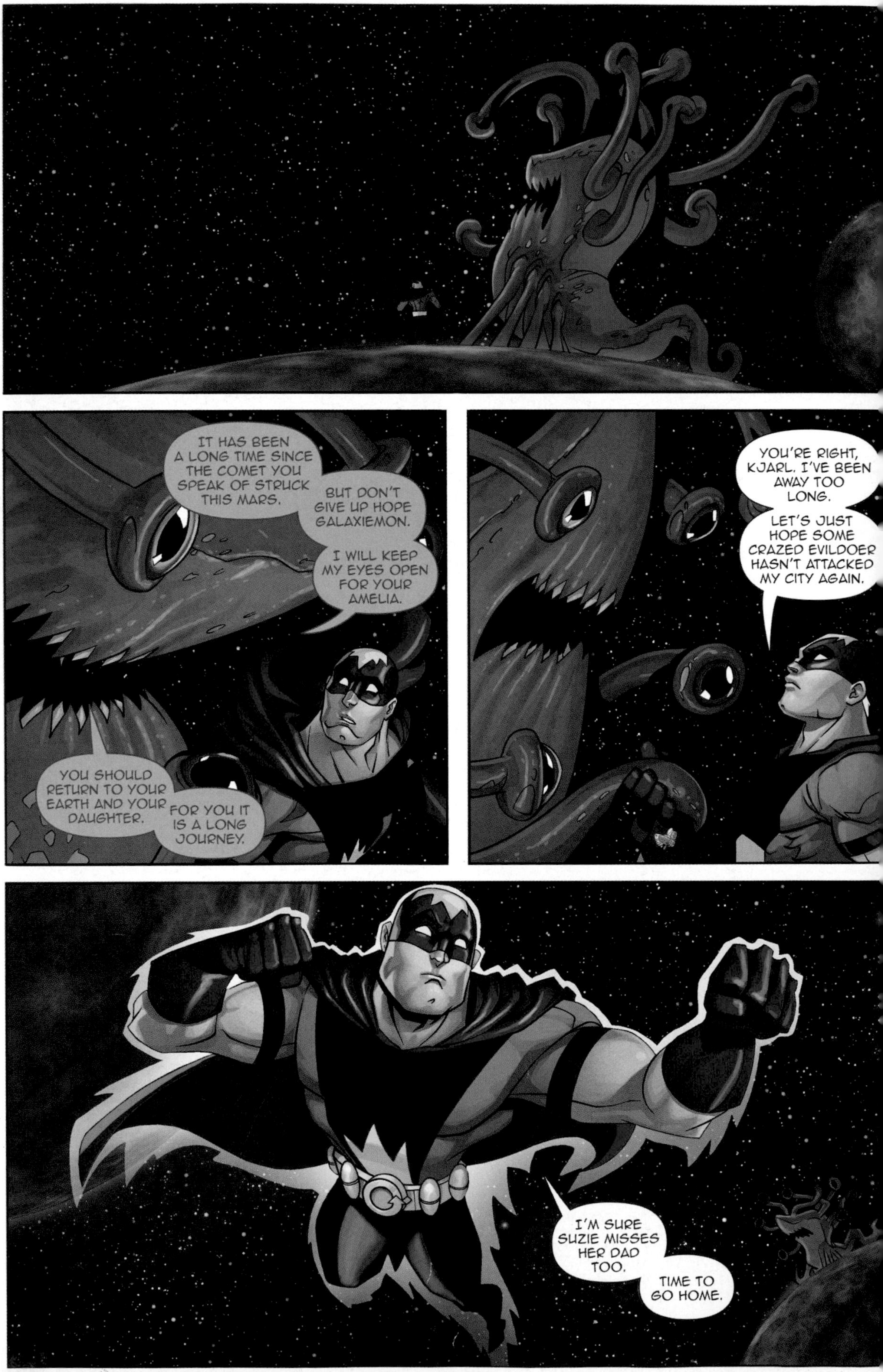
IT HAS BEEN A LONG TIME SINCE THE COMET YOU SPEAK OF STRUCK THIS MARS.
BUT DON'T GIVE UP HOPE GALAXIEMON.
I WILL KEEP MY EYES OPEN FOR YOUR AMELIA.
YOU SHOULD RETURN TO YOUR EARTH AND YOUR DAUGHTER.
FOR YOU IT IS A LONG JOURNEY.
YOU'RE RIGHT, KJARL. I'VE BEEN AWAY TOO LONG.
LET'S JUST HOPE SOME CRAZED EVILDOER HASN'T ATTACKED MY CITY AGAIN.
I'M SURE SUZIE MISSES HER DAD TOO.
TIME TO GO HOME.

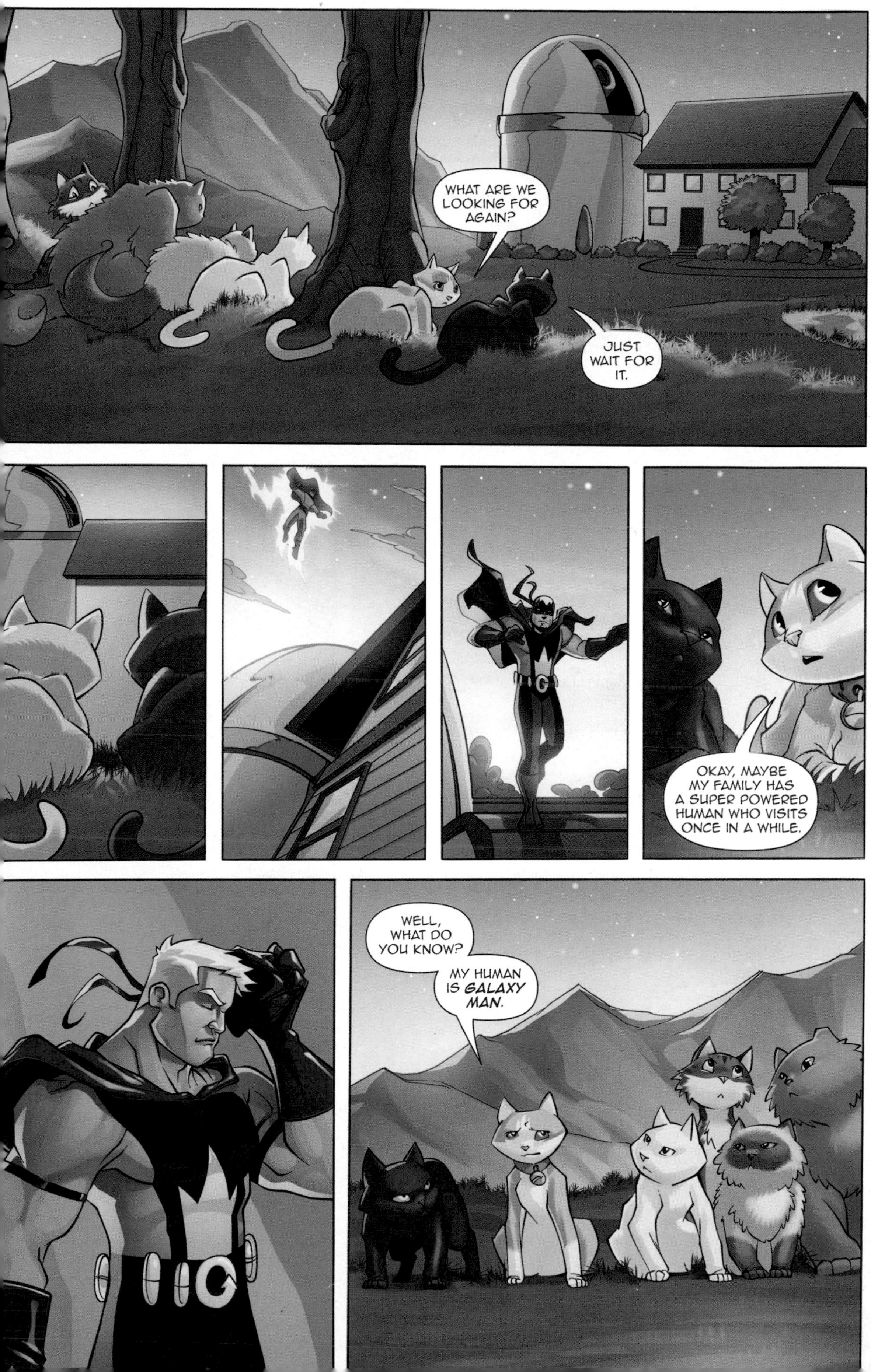
WHAT ARE WE LOOKING FOR AGAIN?
JUST WAIT FOR IT.
OKAY, MAYBE MY FAMILY HAS A SUPER POWERED HUMAN WHO VISITS ONCE IN A WHILE.
WELL, WHAT DO YOU KNOW?
MY HUMAN IS *GALAXY MAN*.

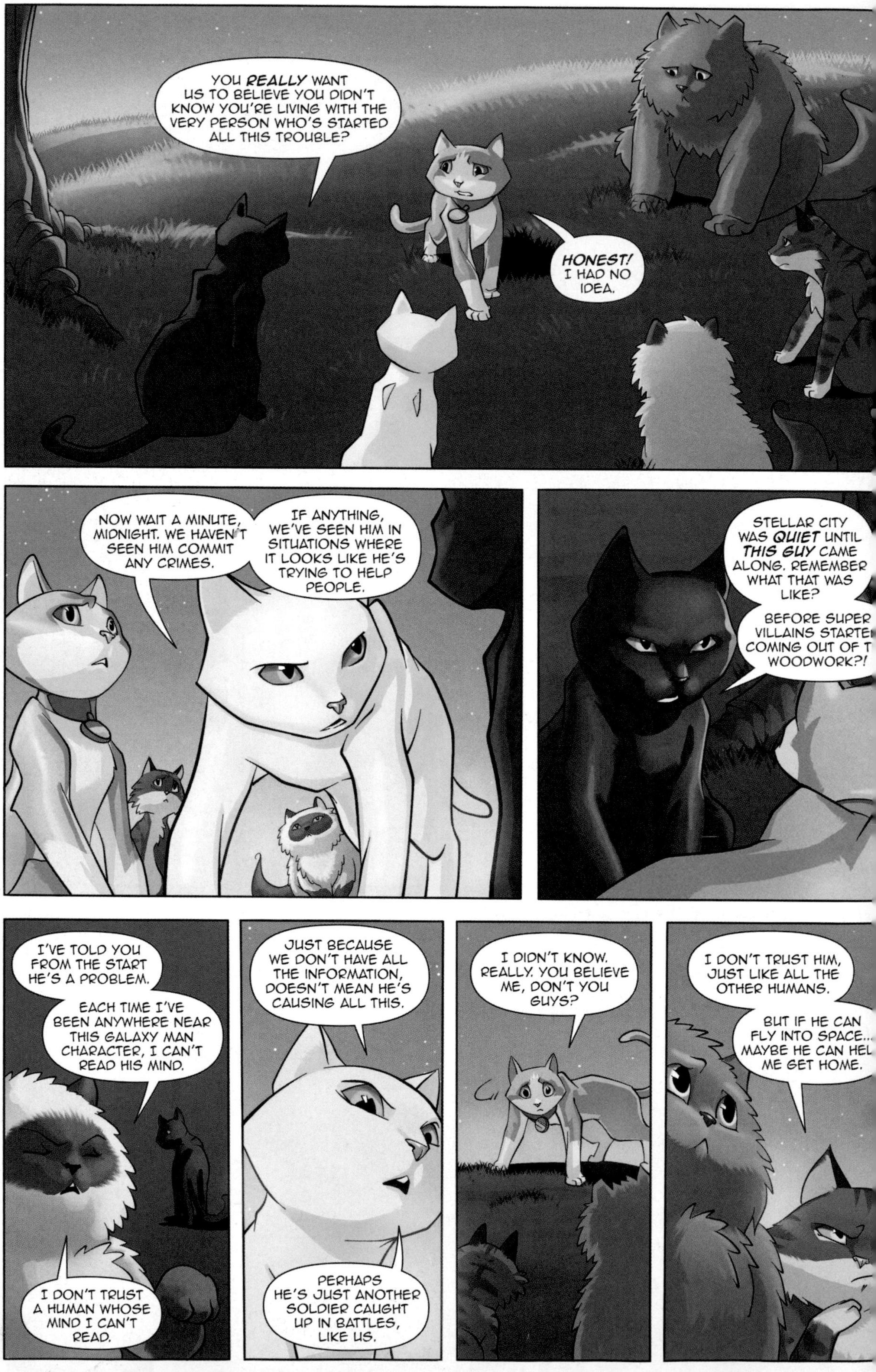

YOU *REALLY* WANT US TO BELIEVE YOU DIDN'T KNOW YOU'RE LIVING WITH THE VERY PERSON WHO'S STARTED ALL THIS TROUBLE?
HONEST! I HAD NO IDEA.
NOW WAIT A MINUTE, MIDNIGHT. WE HAVEN'T SEEN HIM COMMIT ANY CRIMES.
IF ANYTHING, WE'VE SEEN HIM IN SITUATIONS WHERE IT LOOKS LIKE HE'S TRYING TO HELP PEOPLE.
STELLAR CITY WAS *QUIET* UNTIL *THIS GUY* CAME ALONG. REMEMBER WHAT THAT WAS LIKE?
BEFORE SUPER VILLAINS STARTE COMING OUT OF T WOODWORK?!
I'VE TOLD YOU FROM THE START HE'S A PROBLEM.
EACH TIME I'VE BEEN ANYWHERE NEAR THIS GALAXY MAN CHARACTER, I CAN'T READ HIS MIND.
I DON'T TRUST A HUMAN WHOSE MIND I CAN'T READ.
JUST BECAUSE WE DON'T HAVE ALL THE INFORMATION, DOESN'T MEAN HE'S CAUSING ALL THIS.
PERHAPS HE'S JUST ANOTHER SOLDIER CAUGHT UP IN BATTLES, LIKE US.
I DIDN'T KNOW. REALLY. YOU BELIEVE ME, DON'T YOU GUYS?
I DON'T TRUST HIM, JUST LIKE ALL THE OTHER HUMANS.
BUT IF HE CAN FLY INTO SPACE... MAYBE HE CAN HEL ME GET HOME.

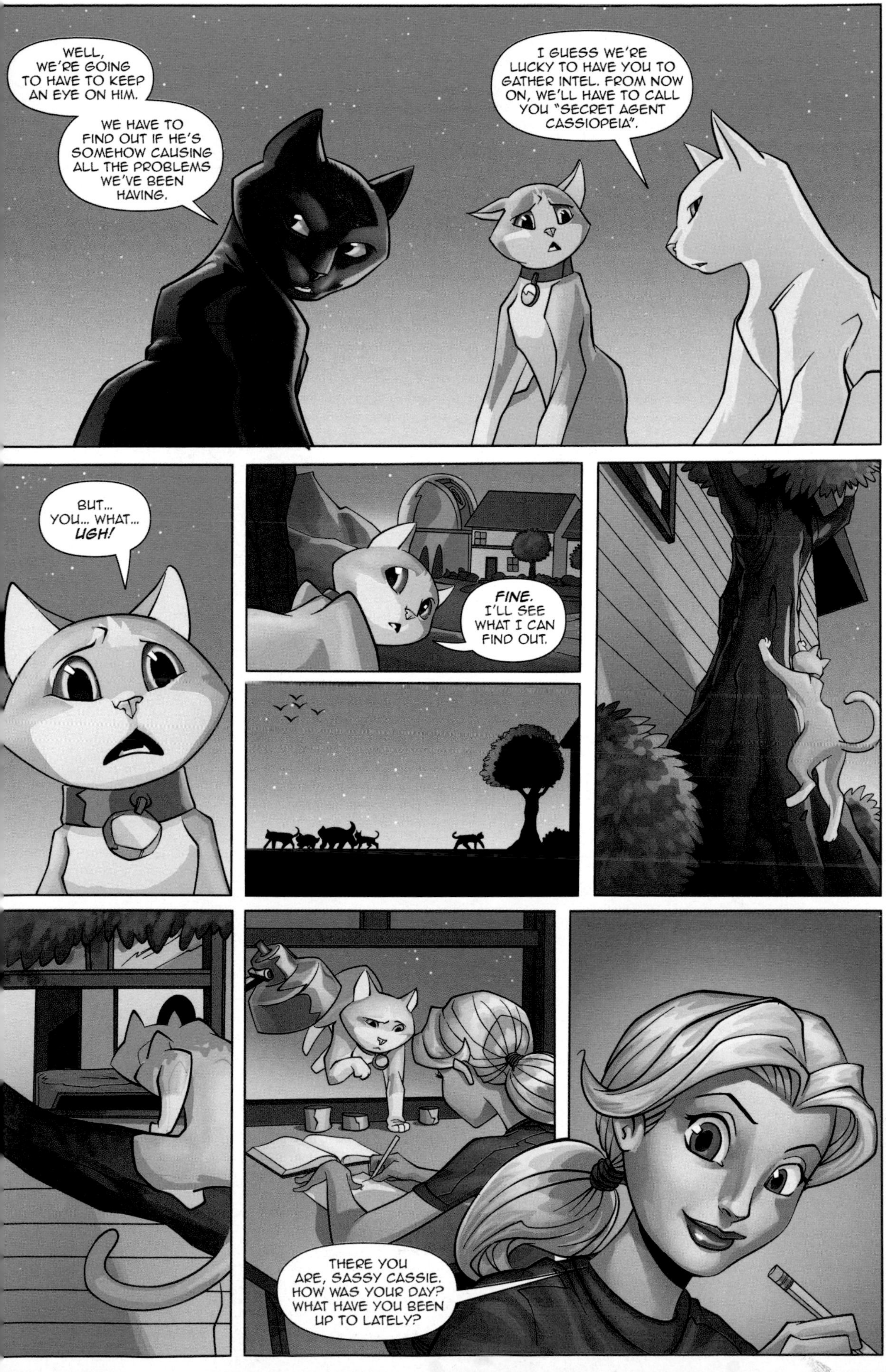
WELL, WE'RE GOING TO HAVE TO KEEP AN EYE ON HIM.
WE HAVE TO FIND OUT IF HE'S SOMEHOW CAUSING ALL THE PROBLEMS WE'VE BEEN HAVING.
I GUESS WE'RE LUCKY TO HAVE YOU TO GATHER INTEL. FROM NOW ON, WE'LL HAVE TO CALL YOU "SECRET AGENT CASSIOPEIA".
BUT... YOU... WHAT... UGH!
FINE. I'LL SEE WHAT I CAN FIND OUT.
THERE YOU ARE, SASSY CASSIE. HOW WAS YOUR DAY? WHAT HAVE YOU BEEN UP TO LATELY?

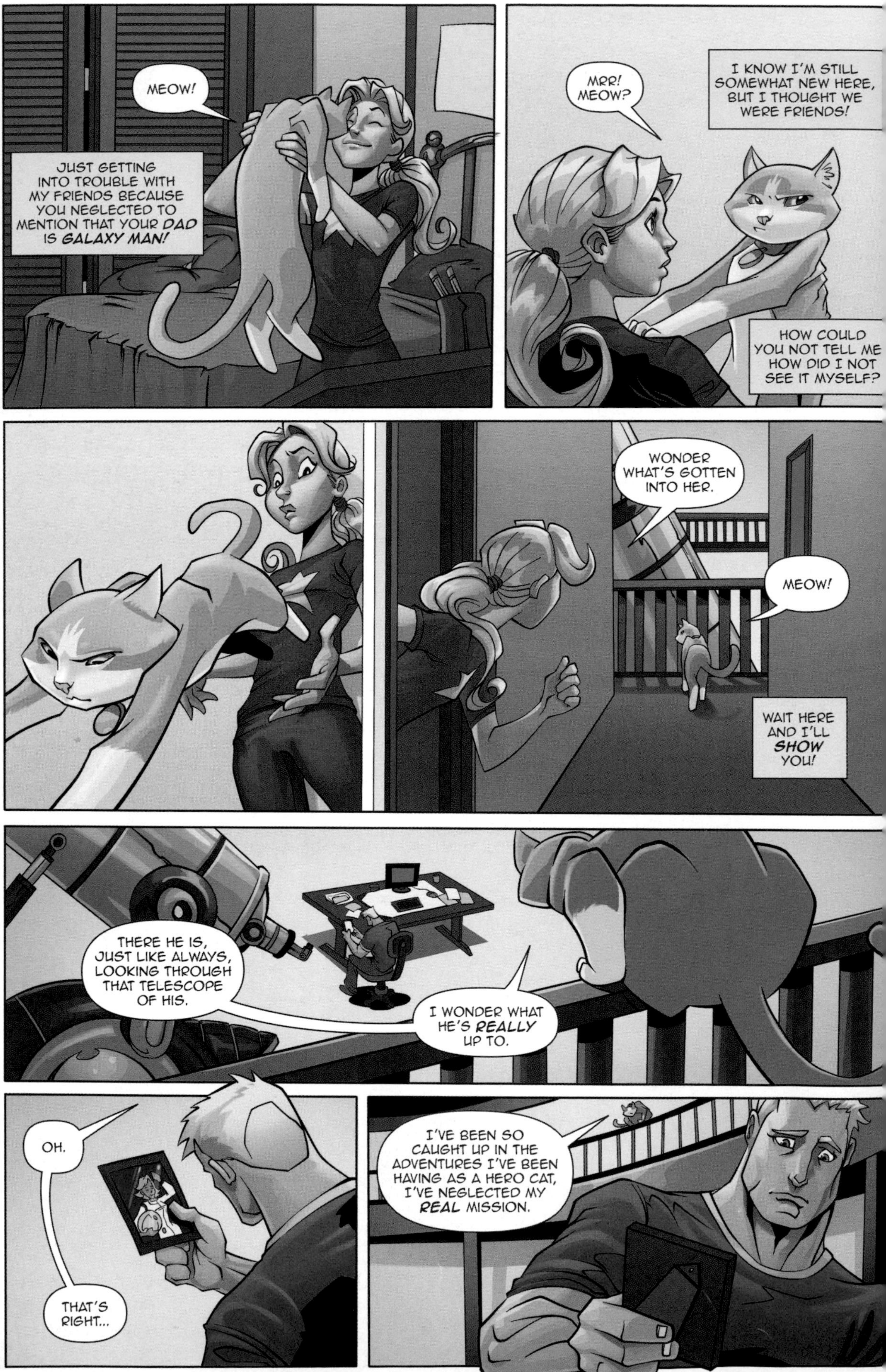
MEOW!
JUST GETTING INTO TROUBLE WITH MY FRIENDS BECAUSE YOU NEGLECTED TO MENTION THAT YOUR DAD IS GALAXY MAN!
MRR! MEOW?
I KNOW I'M STILL SOMEWHAT NEW HERE, BUT I THOUGHT WE WERE FRIENDS!
HOW COULD YOU NOT TELL ME HOW DID I NOT SEE IT MYSELF?
WONDER WHAT'S GOTTEN INTO HER.
MEOW!
WAIT HERE AND I'LL SHOW YOU!
THERE HE IS, JUST LIKE ALWAYS, LOOKING THROUGH THAT TELESCOPE OF HIS.
I WONDER WHAT HE'S REALLY UP TO.
OH.
THAT'S RIGHT...
I'VE BEEN SO CAUGHT UP IN THE ADVENTURES I'VE BEEN HAVING AS A HERO CAT, I'VE NEGLECTED MY REAL MISSION.

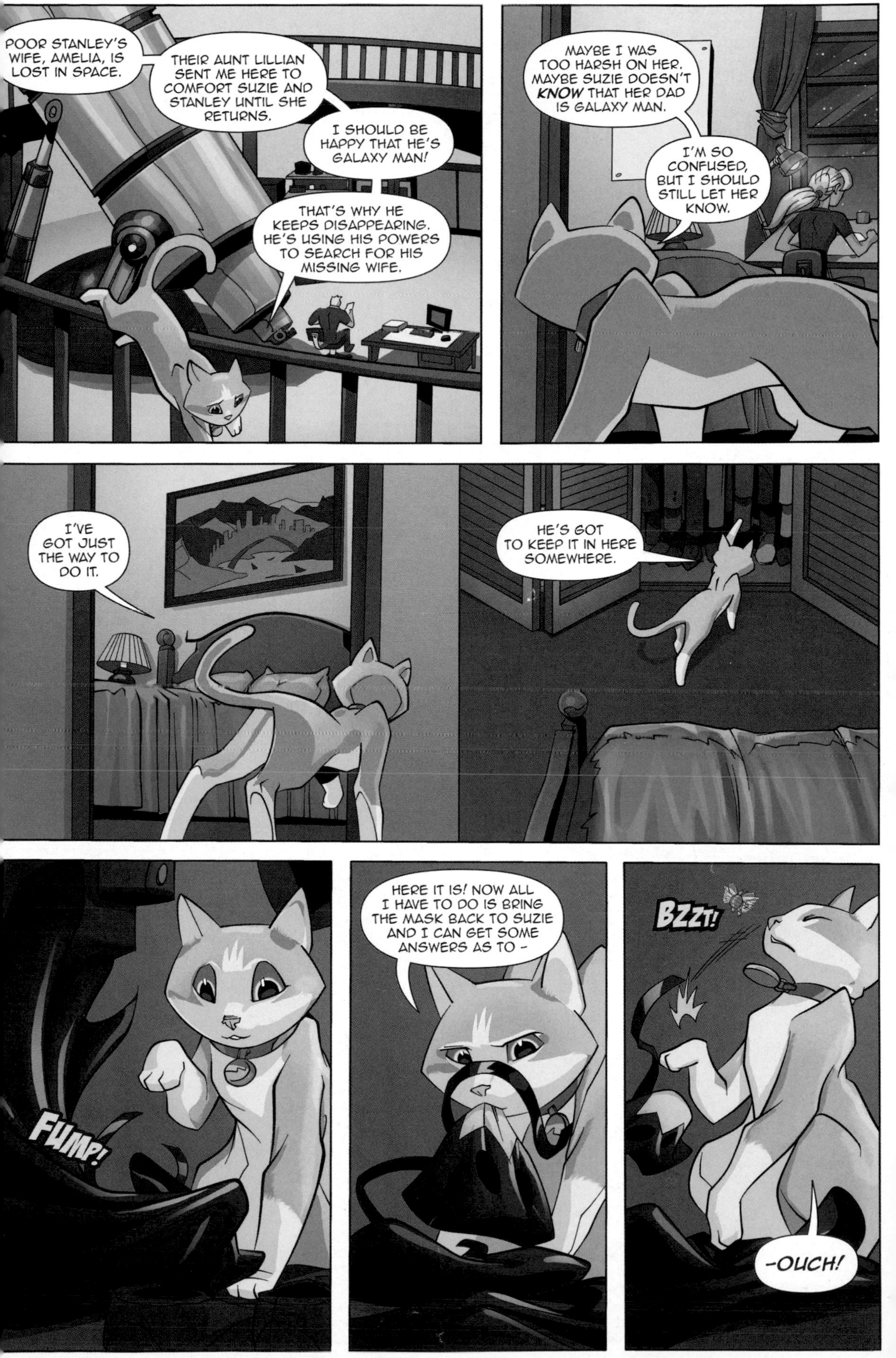
POOR STANLEY'S WIFE, AMELIA, IS LOST IN SPACE.
THEIR AUNT LILLIAN SENT ME HERE TO COMFORT SUZIE AND STANLEY UNTIL SHE RETURNS.
I SHOULD BE HAPPY THAT HE'S GALAXY MAN!
THAT'S WHY HE KEEPS DISAPPEARING. HE'S USING HIS POWERS TO SEARCH FOR HIS MISSING WIFE.
MAYBE I WAS TOO HARSH ON HER. MAYBE SUZIE DOESN'T KNOW THAT HER DAD IS GALAXY MAN.
I'M SO CONFUSED, BUT I SHOULD STILL LET HER KNOW.
I'VE GOT JUST THE WAY TO DO IT.
HE'S GOT TO KEEP IT IN HERE SOMEWHERE.
FUMP!
HERE IT IS! NOW ALL I HAVE TO DO IS BRING THE MASK BACK TO SUZIE AND I CAN GET SOME ANSWERS AS TO -
BZZT!
-OUCH!

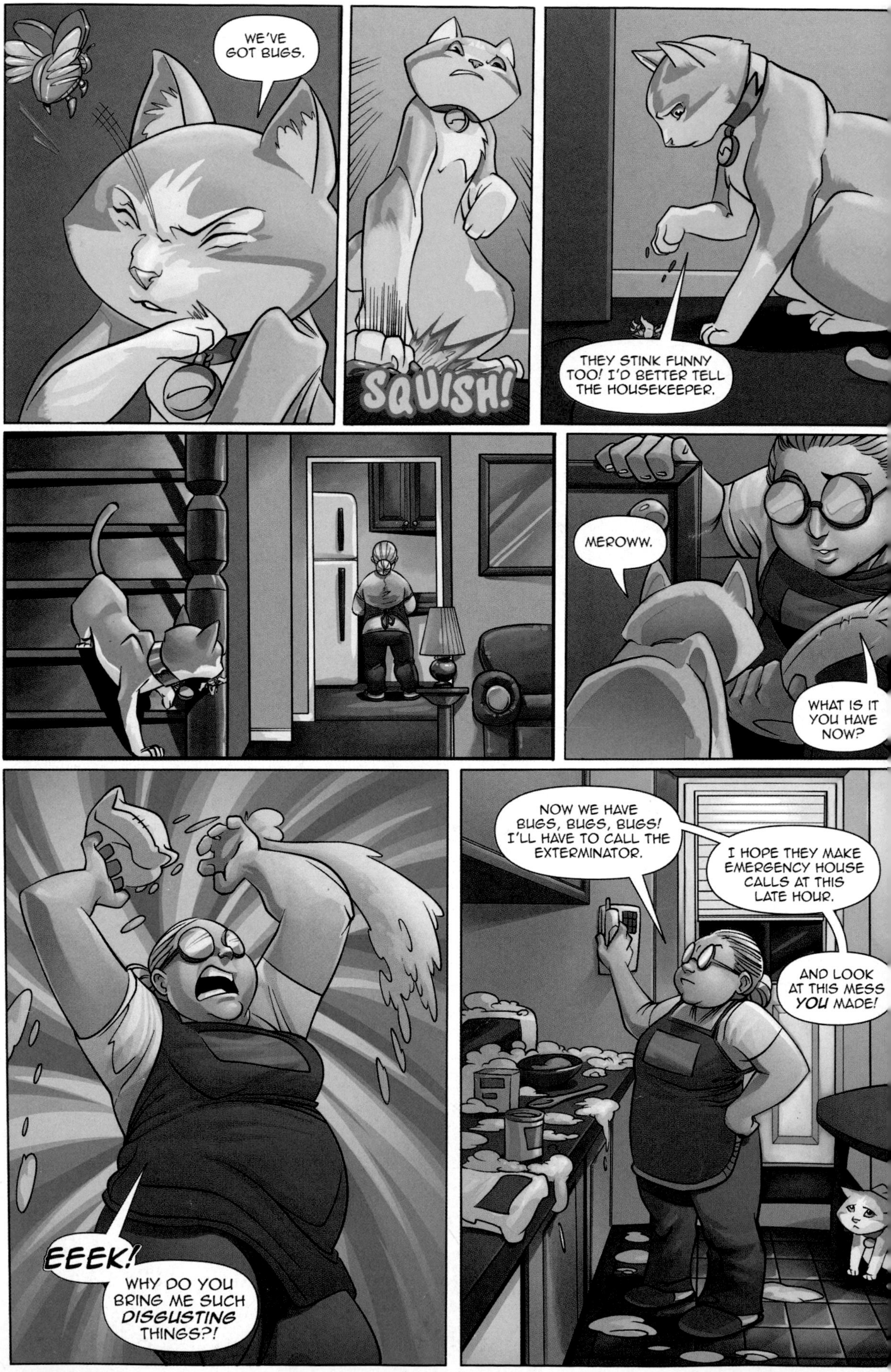
WE'VE GOT BUGS.
SQUISH!
THEY STINK FUNNY TOO! I'D BETTER TELL THE HOUSEKEEPER.
MEROWW.
WHAT IS IT YOU HAVE NOW?
EEEK!
WHY DO YOU BRING ME SUCH DISGUSTING THINGS?!
NOW WE HAVE BUGS, BUGS, BUGS! I'LL HAVE TO CALL THE EXTERMINATOR.
I HOPE THEY MAKE EMERGENCY HOUSE CALLS AT THIS LATE HOUR.
AND LOOK AT THIS MESS YOU MADE!

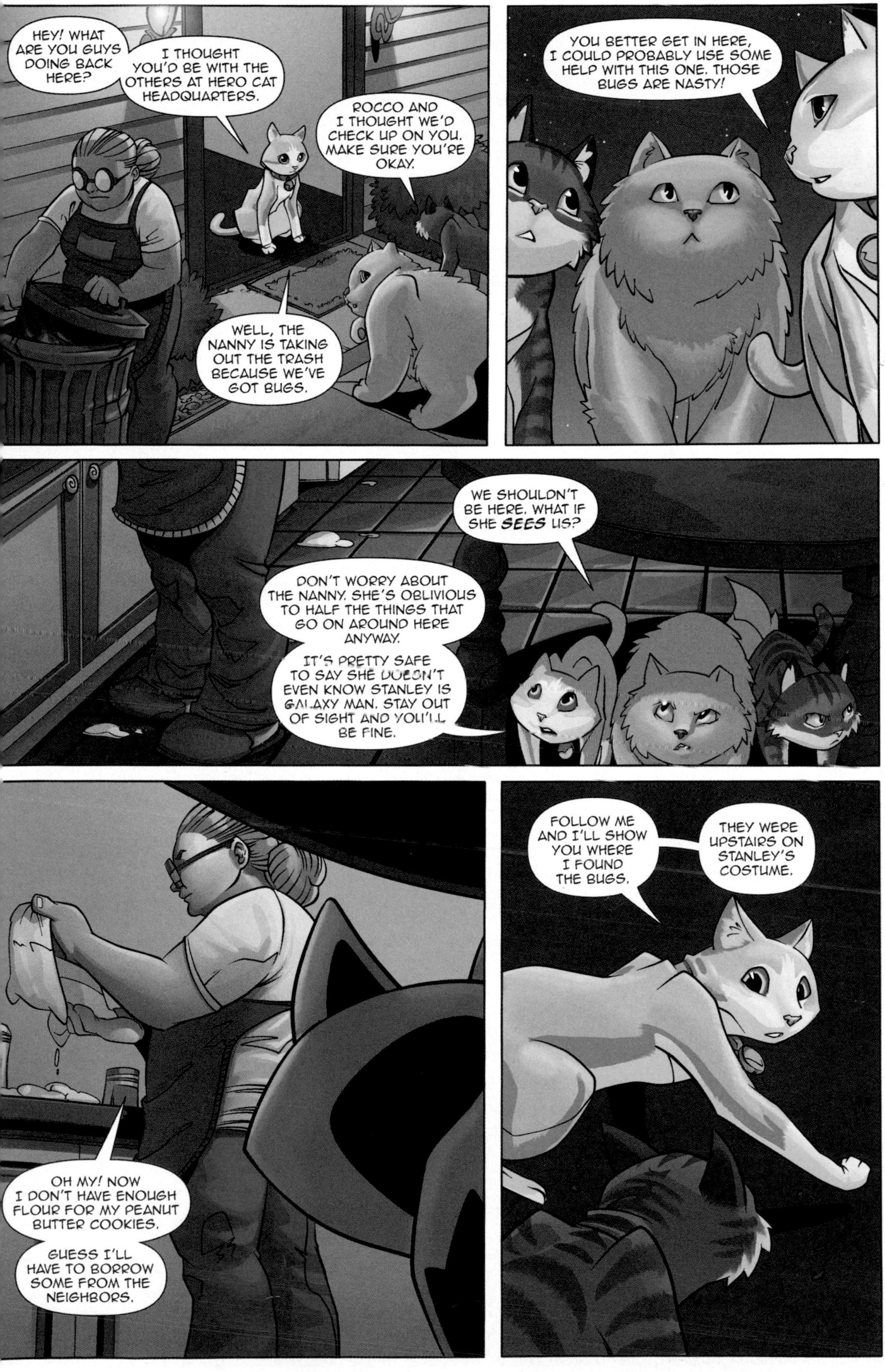
HEY! WHAT ARE YOU GUYS DOING BACK HERE?
I THOUGHT YOU'D BE WITH THE OTHERS AT HERO CAT HEADQUARTERS.
ROCCO AND I THOUGHT WE'D CHECK UP ON YOU. MAKE SURE YOU'RE OKAY.
WELL, THE NANNY IS TAKING OUT THE TRASH BECAUSE WE'VE GOT BUGS.
YOU BETTER GET IN HERE, I COULD PROBABLY USE SOME HELP WITH THIS ONE. THOSE BUGS ARE NASTY!
WE SHOULDN'T BE HERE. WHAT IF SHE SEES US?
DON'T WORRY ABOUT THE NANNY. SHE'S OBLIVIOUS TO HALF THE THINGS THAT GO ON AROUND HERE ANYWAY.
IT'S PRETTY SAFE TO SAY SHE DOESN'T EVEN KNOW STANLEY IS GALAXY MAN. STAY OUT OF SIGHT AND YOU'LL BE FINE.
OH MY! NOW I DON'T HAVE ENOUGH FLOUR FOR MY PEANUT BUTTER COOKIES.
GUESS I'LL HAVE TO BORROW SOME FROM THE NEIGHBORS.
FOLLOW ME AND I'LL SHOW YOU WHERE I FOUND THE BUGS.
THEY WERE UPSTAIRS ON STANLEY'S COSTUME.

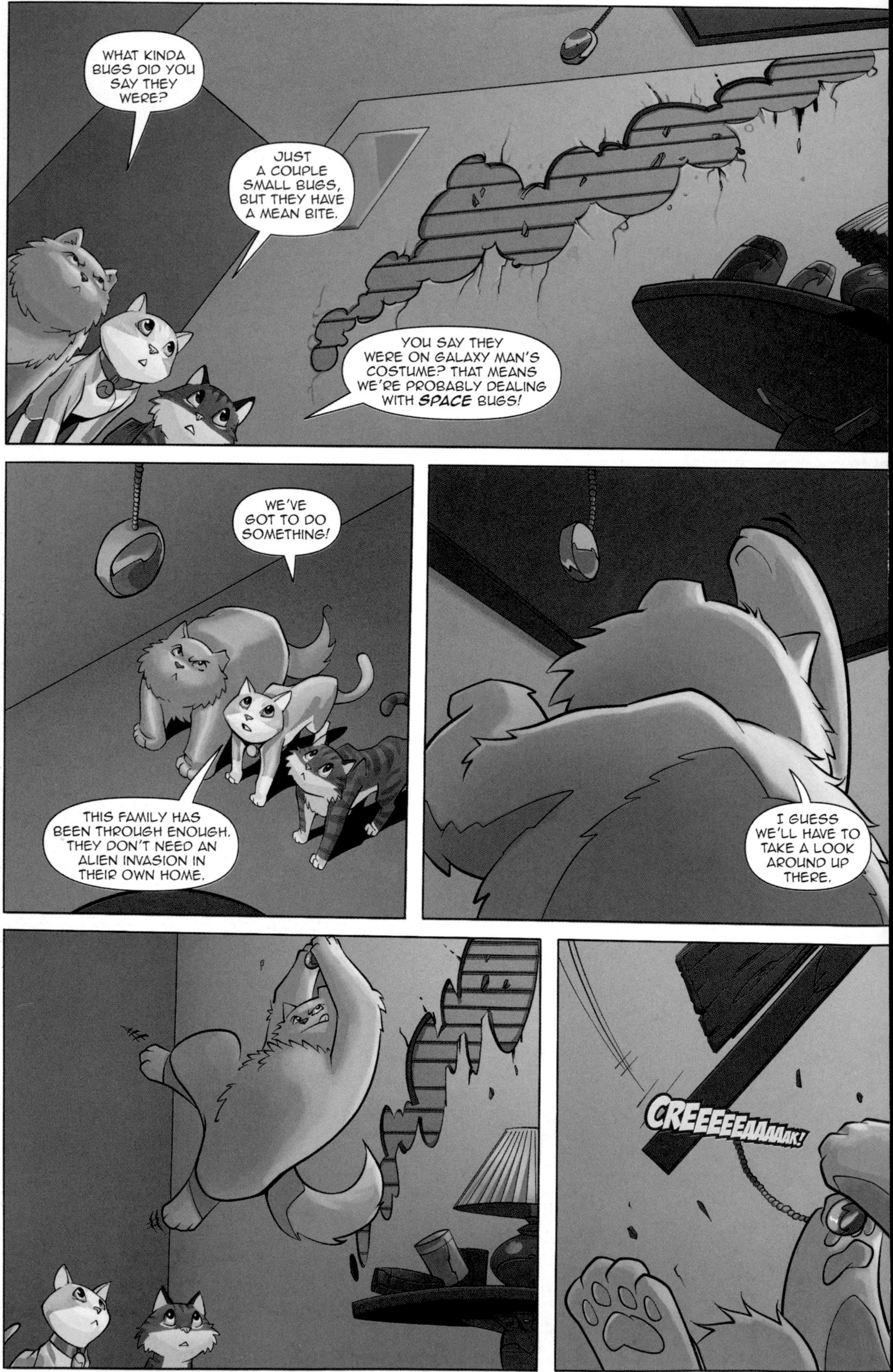
WHAT KINDA BUGS DID YOU SAY THEY WERE?
JUST A COUPLE SMALL BUGS, BUT THEY HAVE A MEAN BITE.
YOU SAY THEY WERE ON GALAXY MAN'S COSTUME? THAT MEANS WE'RE PROBABLY DEALING WITH SPACE BUGS!
WE'VE GOT TO DO SOMETHING!
THIS FAMILY HAS BEEN THROUGH ENOUGH. THEY DON'T NEED AN ALIEN INVASION IN THEIR OWN HOME.
I GUESS WE'LL HAVE TO TAKE A LOOK AROUND UP THERE.
CREEEEEAAAAAK!

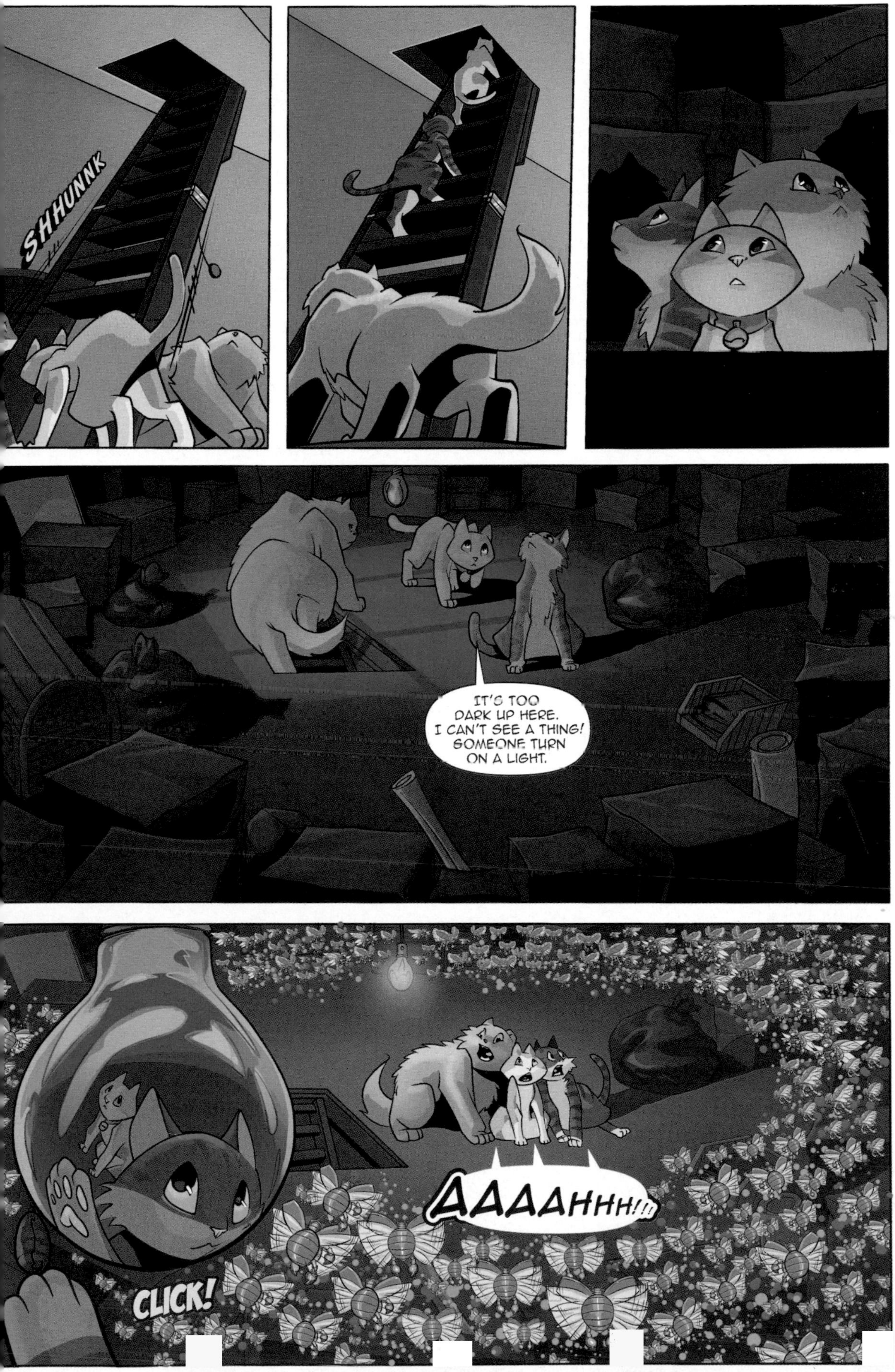
SHHUNNK
IT'S TOO DARK UP HERE. I CAN'T SEE A THING! SOMEONE TURN ON A LIGHT.
CLICK!
AAAAHHH!!!

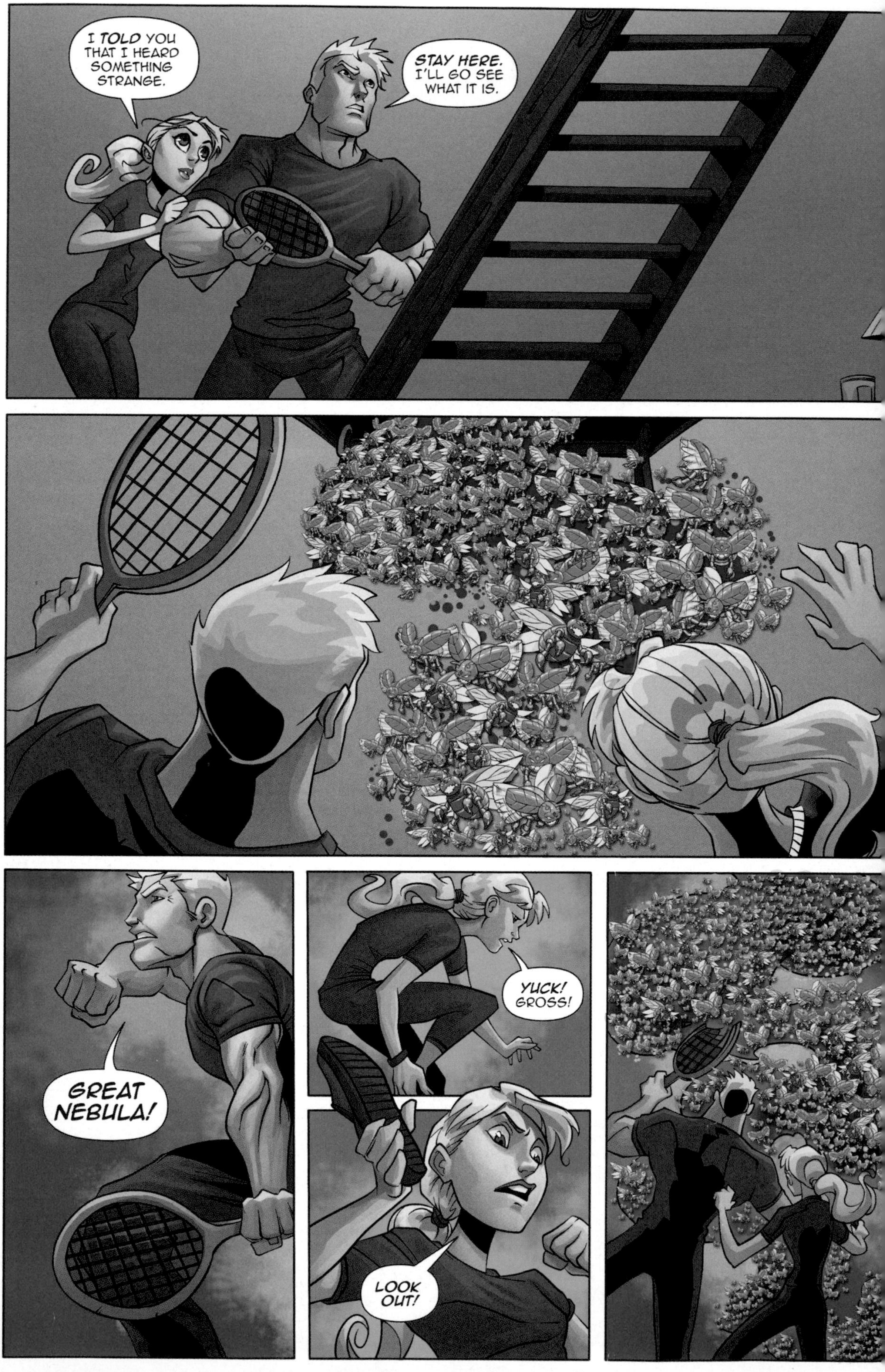
I TOLD YOU THAT I HEARD SOMETHING STRANGE.
STAY HERE. I'LL GO SEE WHAT IT IS.
GREAT NEBULA!
YUCK! GROSS!
LOOK OUT!

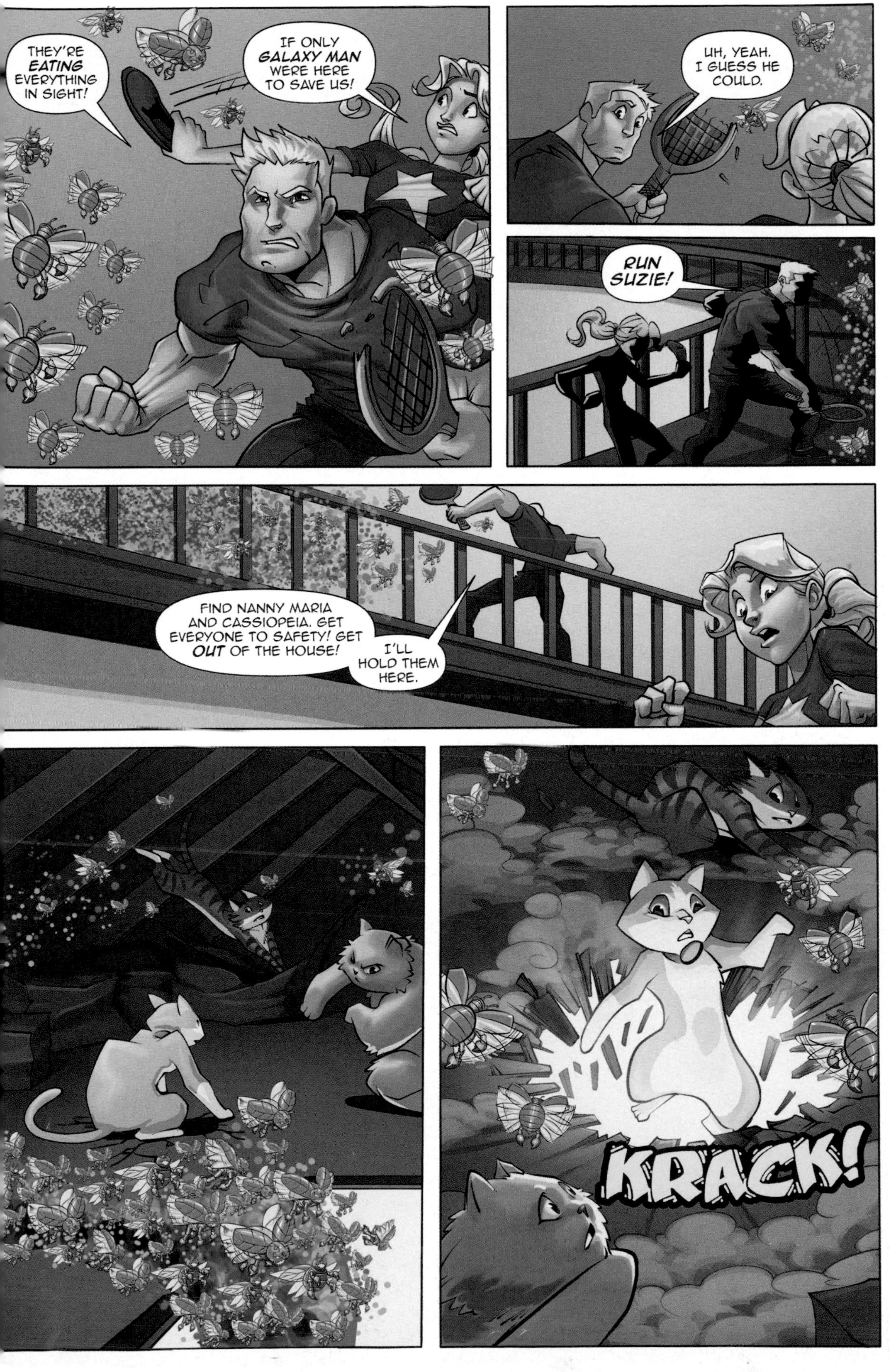
THEY'RE EATING EVERYTHING IN SIGHT!
IF ONLY GALAXY MAN WERE HERE TO SAVE US!
UH, YEAH. I GUESS HE COULD.
RUN SUZIE!
FIND NANNY MARIA AND CASSIOPEIA. GET EVERYONE TO SAFETY! GET OUT OF THE HOUSE!
I'LL HOLD THEM HERE.
KRACK!

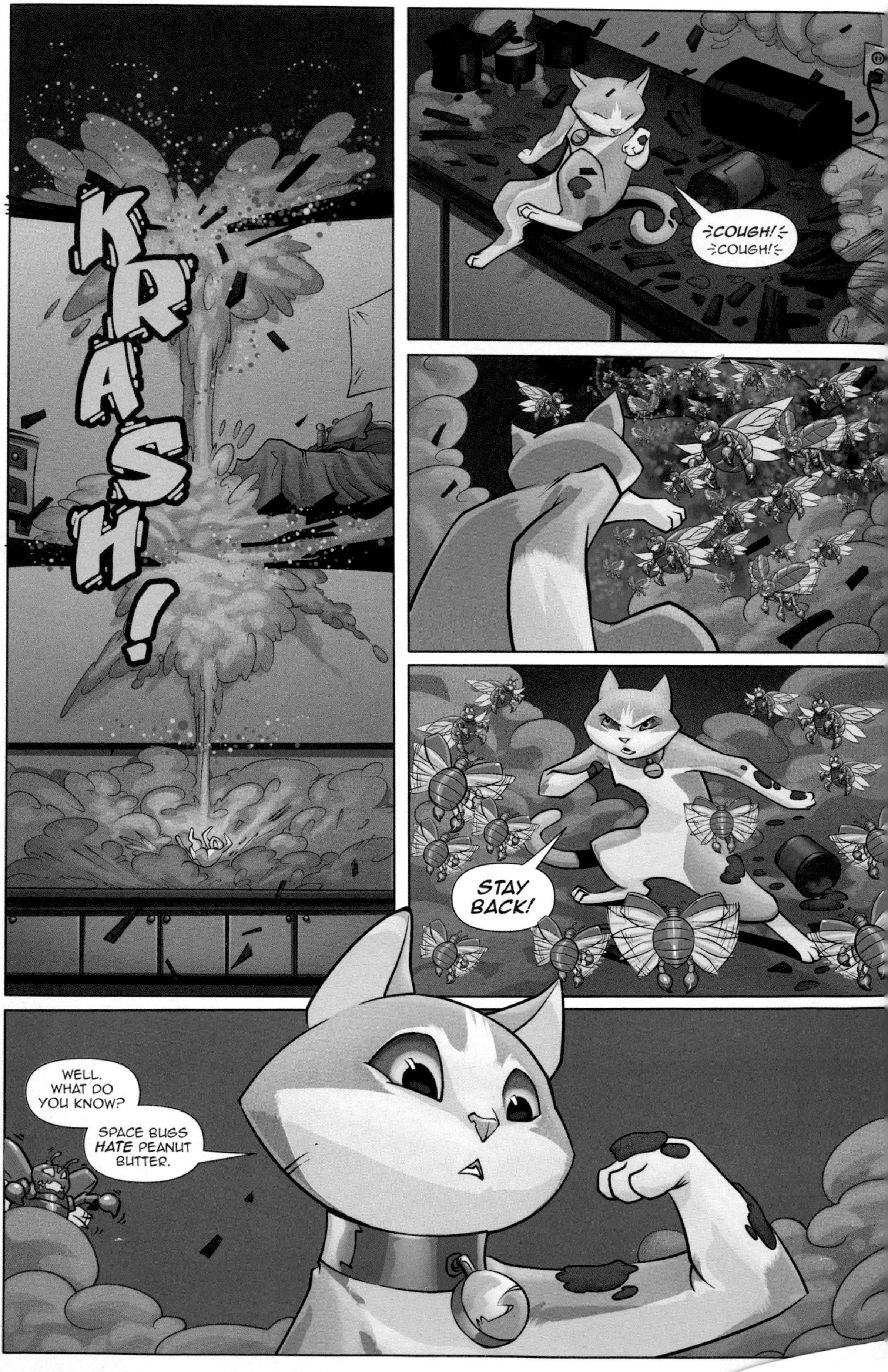
KRASH!
COUGH!
COUGH!
STAY BACK!
WELL. WHAT DO YOU KNOW?
SPACE BUGS HATE PEANUT BUTTER.

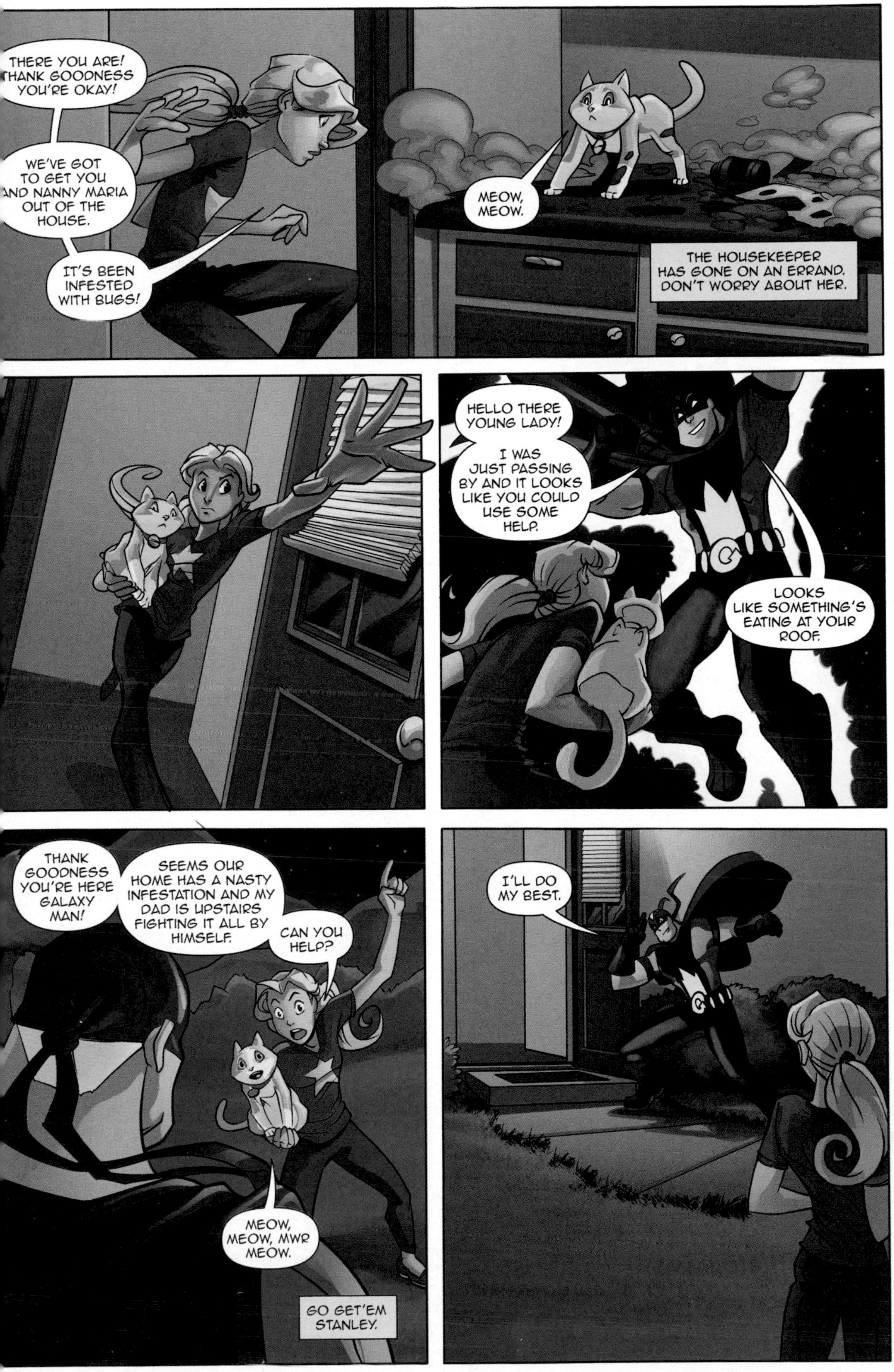
THERE YOU ARE! THANK GOODNESS YOU'RE OKAY!
WE'VE GOT TO GET YOU AND NANNY MARIA OUT OF THE HOUSE.
IT'S BEEN INFESTED WITH BUGS!
MEOW, MEOW.
THE HOUSEKEEPER HAS GONE ON AN ERRAND. DON'T WORRY ABOUT HER.
HELLO THERE YOUNG LADY!
I WAS JUST PASSING BY AND IT LOOKS LIKE YOU COULD USE SOME HELP.
LOOKS LIKE SOMETHING'S EATING AT YOUR ROOF.
THANK GOODNESS YOU'RE HERE GALAXY MAN!
SEEMS OUR HOME HAS A NASTY INFESTATION AND MY DAD IS UPSTAIRS FIGHTING IT ALL BY HIMSELF.
CAN YOU HELP?
MEOW, MEOW, MWR MEOW.
GO GET'EM STANLEY.
I'LL DO MY BEST.

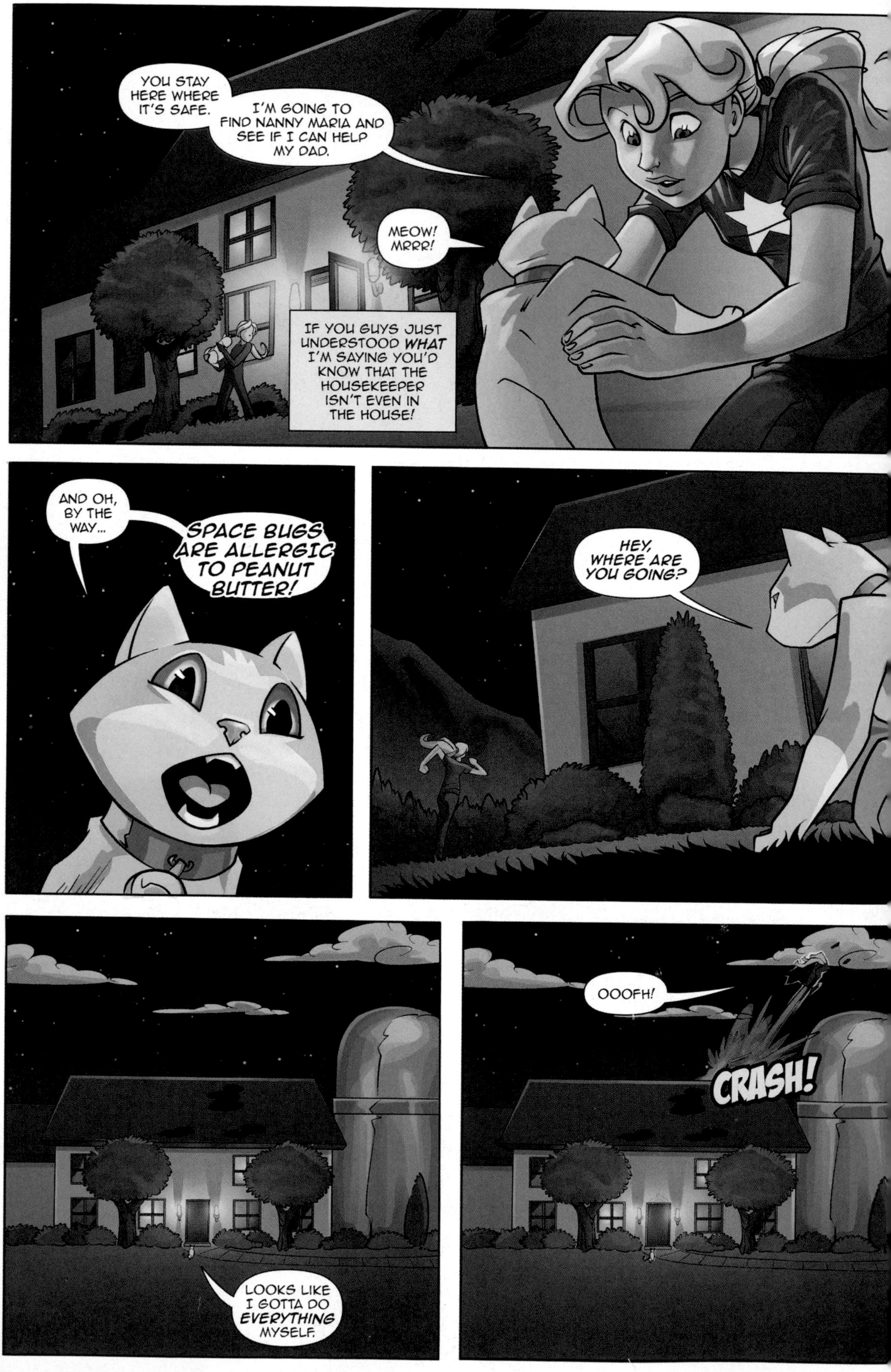
YOU STAY HERE WHERE IT'S SAFE.
I'M GOING TO FIND NANNY MARIA AND SEE IF I CAN HELP MY DAD.
MEOW! MRRR!
IF YOU GUYS JUST UNDERSTOOD WHAT I'M SAYING YOU'D KNOW THAT THE HOUSEKEEPER ISN'T EVEN IN THE HOUSE!
AND OH, BY THE WAY...
SPACE BUGS ARE ALLERGIC TO PEANUT BUTTER!
HEY, WHERE ARE YOU GOING?
LOOKS LIKE I GOTTA DO EVERYTHING MYSELF.
OOOFH!
CRASH!

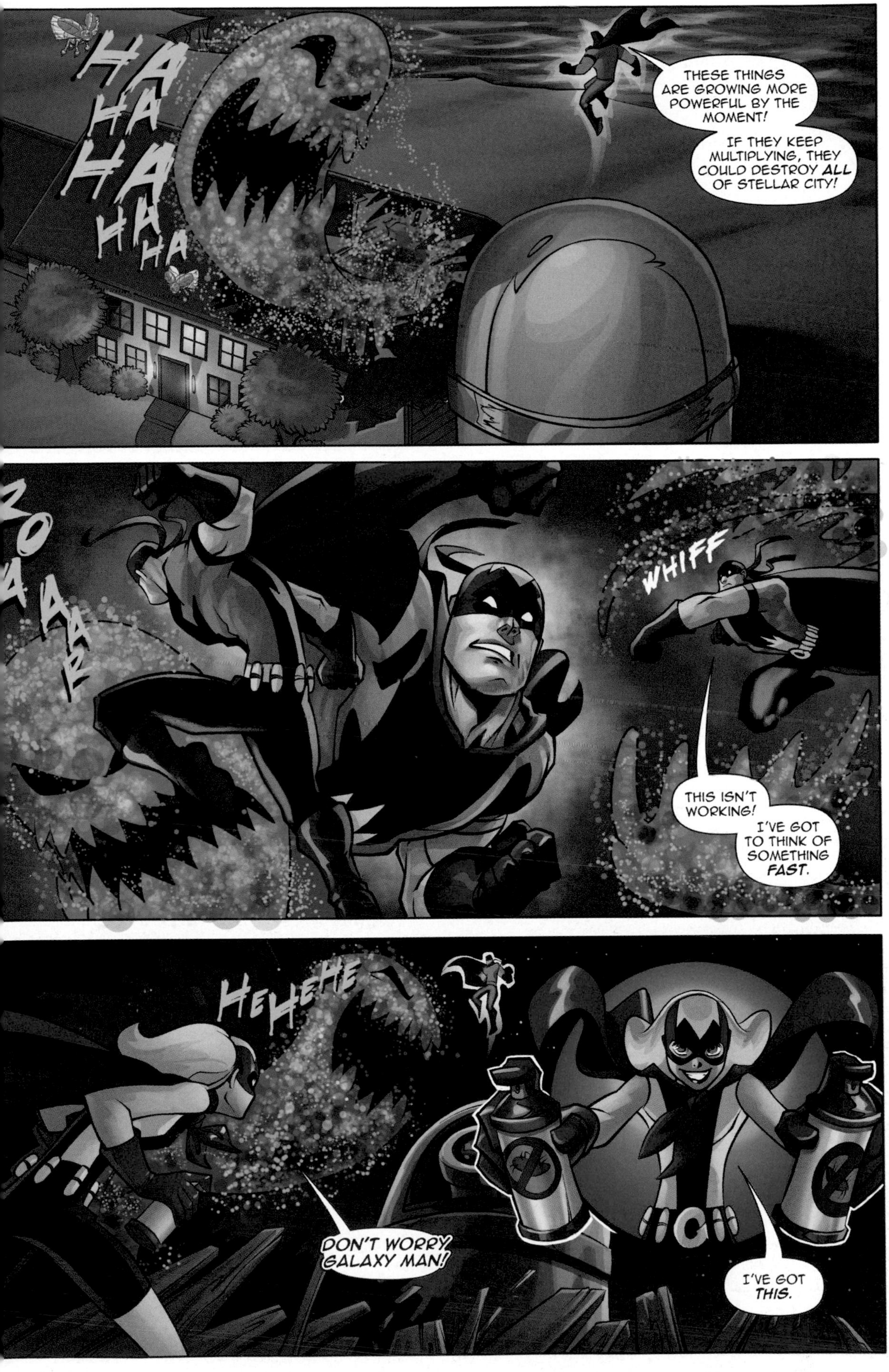
HA HA HA HA HA HA
THESE THINGS ARE GROWING MORE POWERFUL BY THE MOMENT!
IF THEY KEEP MULTIPLYING, THEY COULD DESTROY ALL OF STELLAR CITY!
WHIFF
THIS ISN'T WORKING!
I'VE GOT TO THINK OF SOMETHING FAST.
HEHEHE
DON'T WORRY GALAXY MAN!
I'VE GOT THIS.

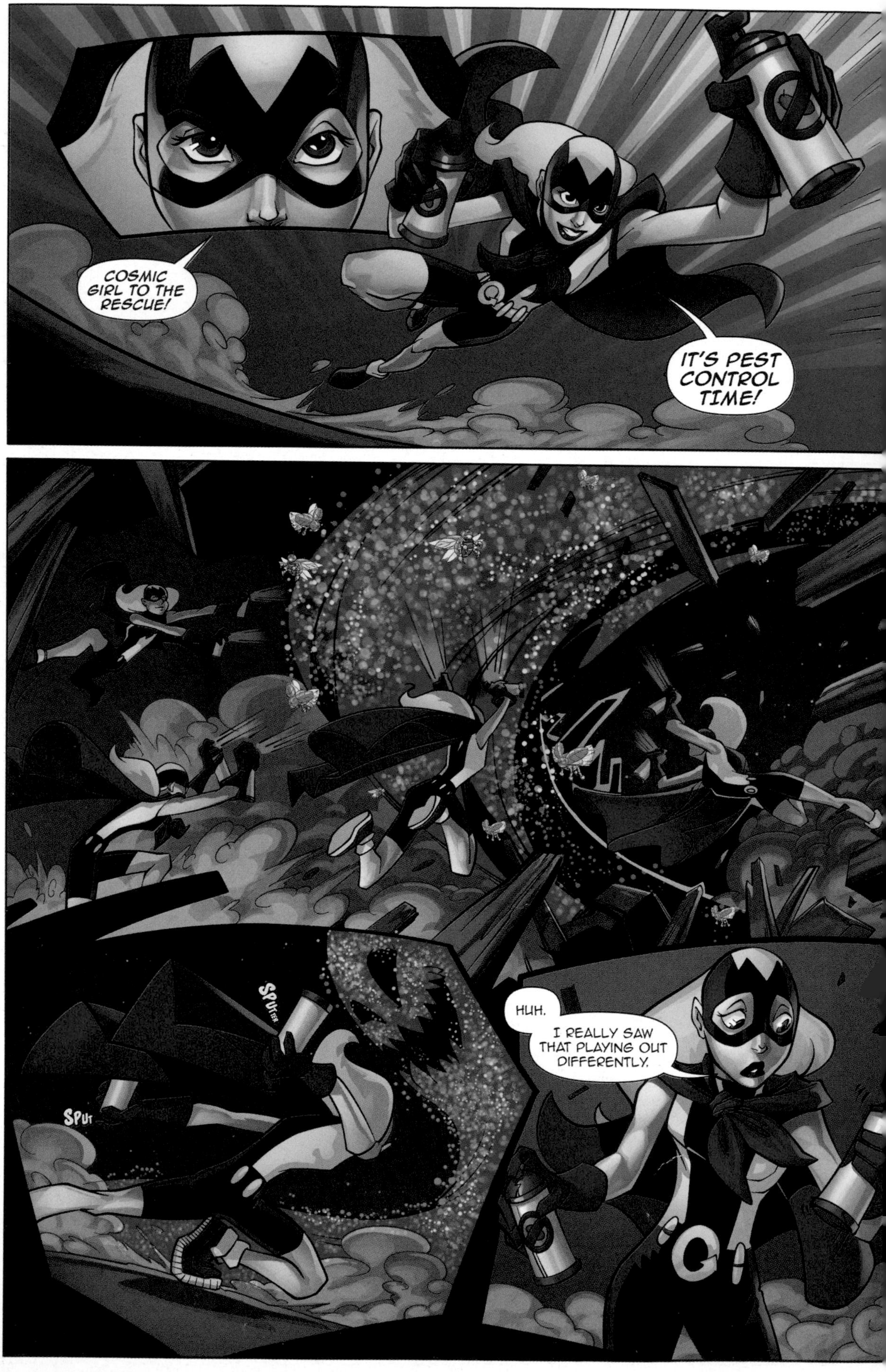
COSMIC GIRL TO THE RESCUE!
IT'S PEST CONTROL TIME!
SPUTTER
SPUT
HUH.
I REALLY SAW THAT PLAYING OUT DIFFERENTLY.

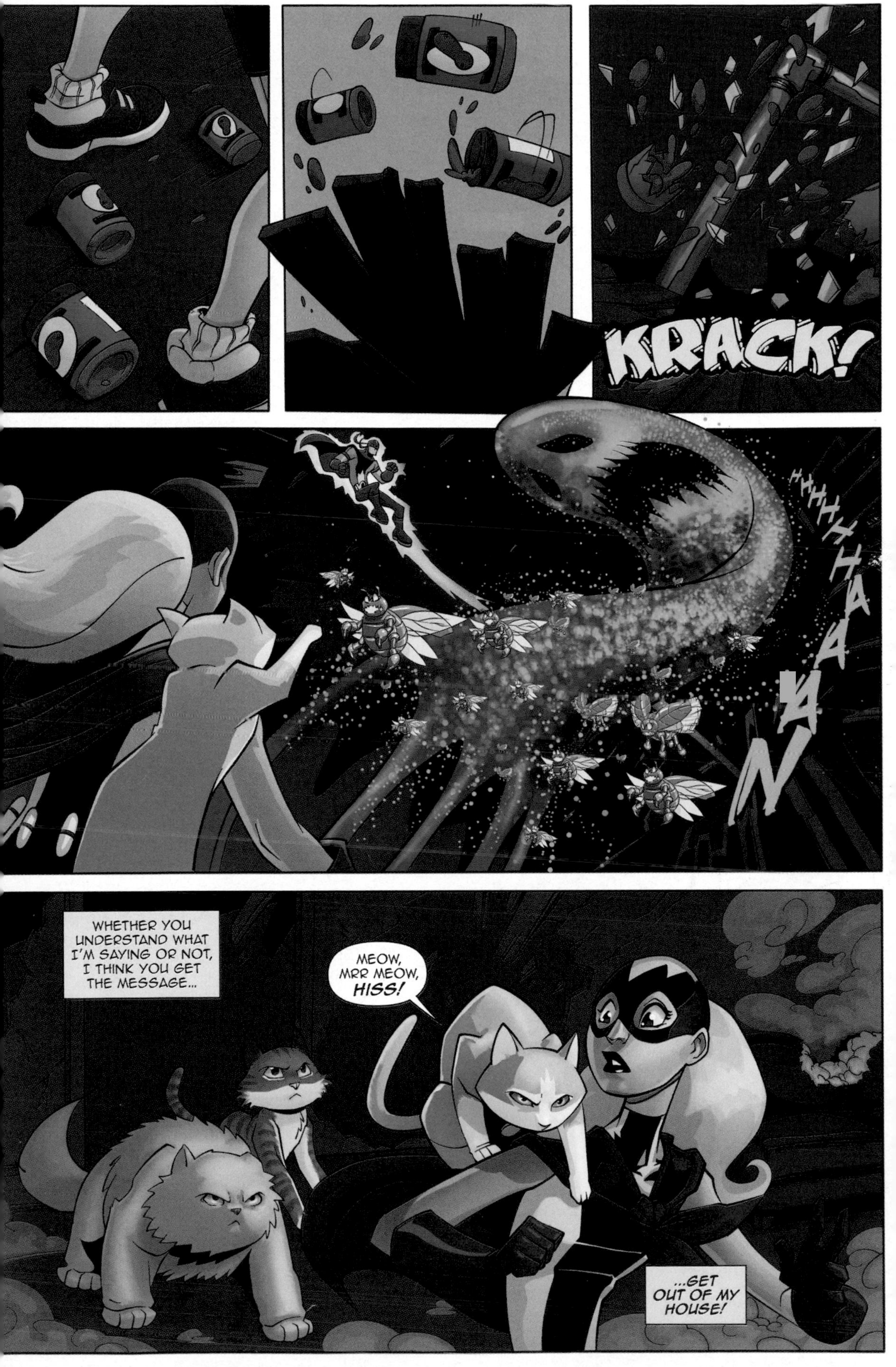
KRACK!
HHHHHHHAAAN
WHETHER YOU UNDERSTAND WHAT I'M SAYING OR NOT, I THINK YOU GET THE MESSAGE...
MEOW, MRR MEOW, HISS!
...GET OUT OF MY HOUSE!

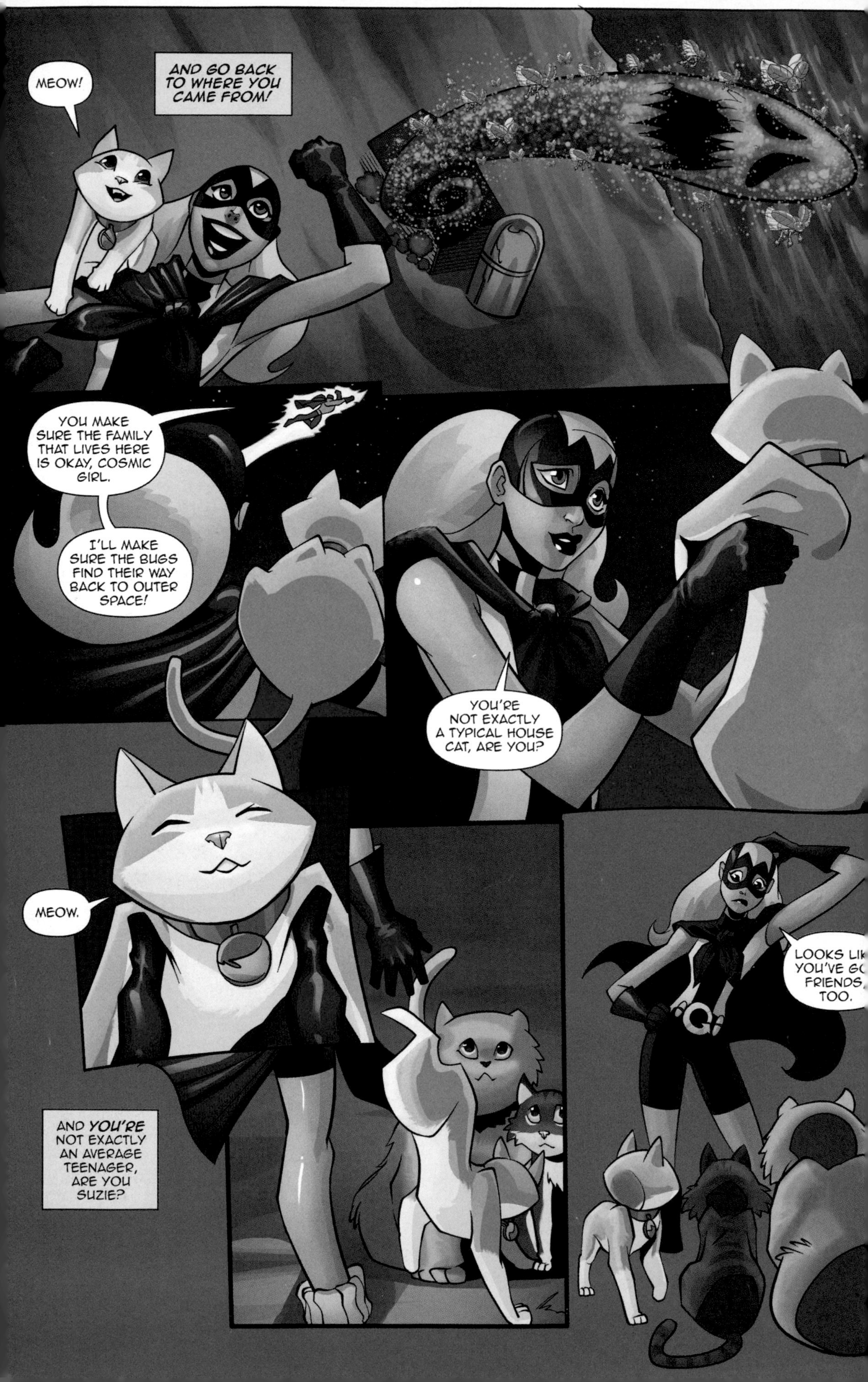
MEOW!
AND GO BACK TO WHERE YOU CAME FROM!
YOU MAKE SURE THE FAMILY THAT LIVES HERE IS OKAY, COSMIC GIRL.
I'LL MAKE SURE THE BUGS FIND THEIR WAY BACK TO OUTER SPACE!
YOU'RE NOT EXACTLY A TYPICAL HOUSE CAT, ARE YOU?
MEOW.
AND YOU'RE NOT EXACTLY AN AVERAGE TEENAGER, ARE YOU SUZIE?
LOOKS LI YOU'VE G FRIENDS TOO.

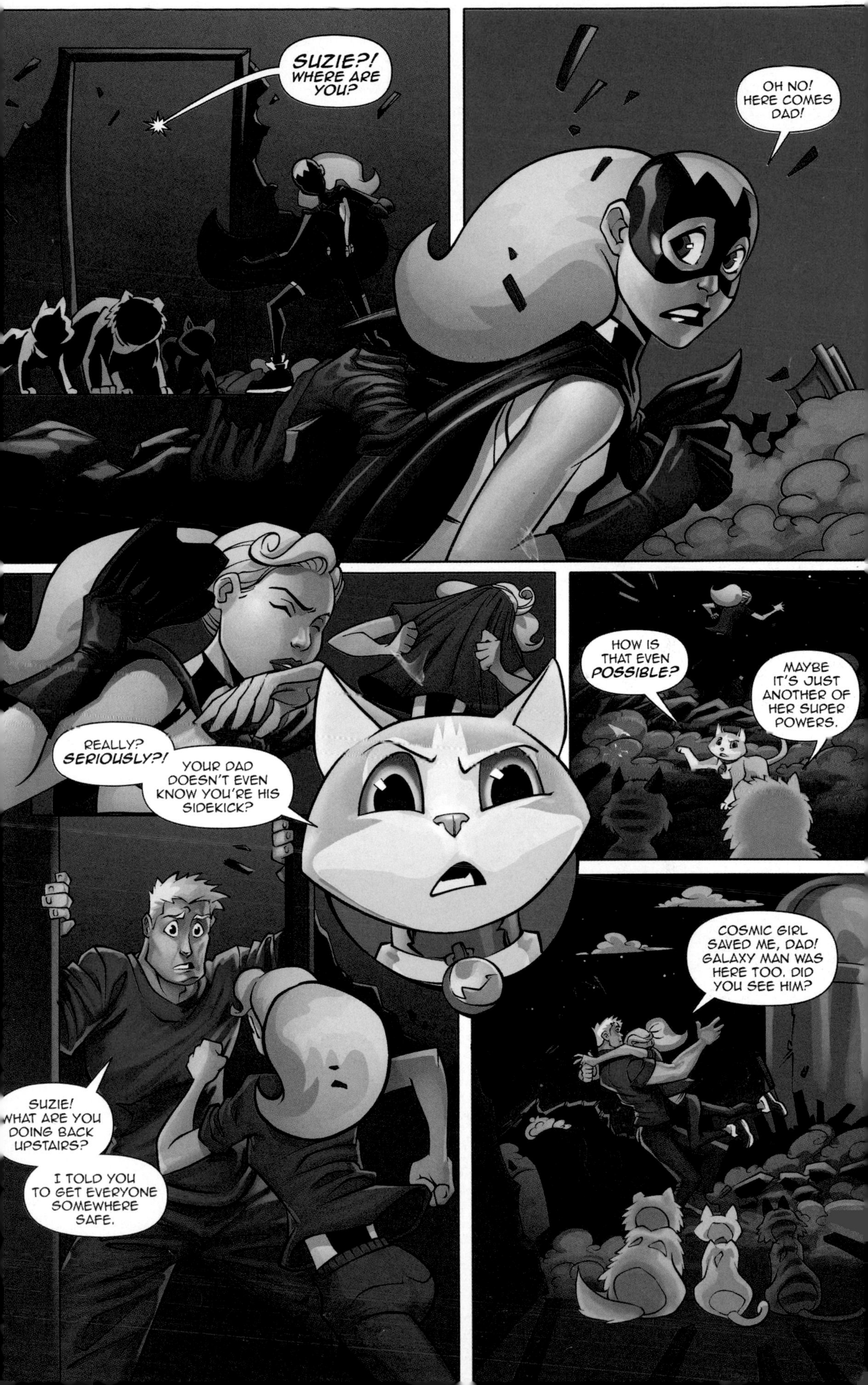
SUZIE?! WHERE ARE YOU?
OH NO! HERE COMES DAD!
REALLY? SERIOUSLY?!
YOUR DAD DOESN'T EVEN KNOW YOU'RE HIS SIDEKICK?
HOW IS THAT EVEN POSSIBLE?
MAYBE IT'S JUST ANOTHER OF HER SUPER POWERS.
SUZIE! WHAT ARE YOU DOING BACK UPSTAIRS?
I TOLD YOU TO GET EVERYONE SOMEWHERE SAFE.
COSMIC GIRL SAVED ME, DAD! GALAXY MAN WAS HERE TOO. DID YOU SEE HIM?

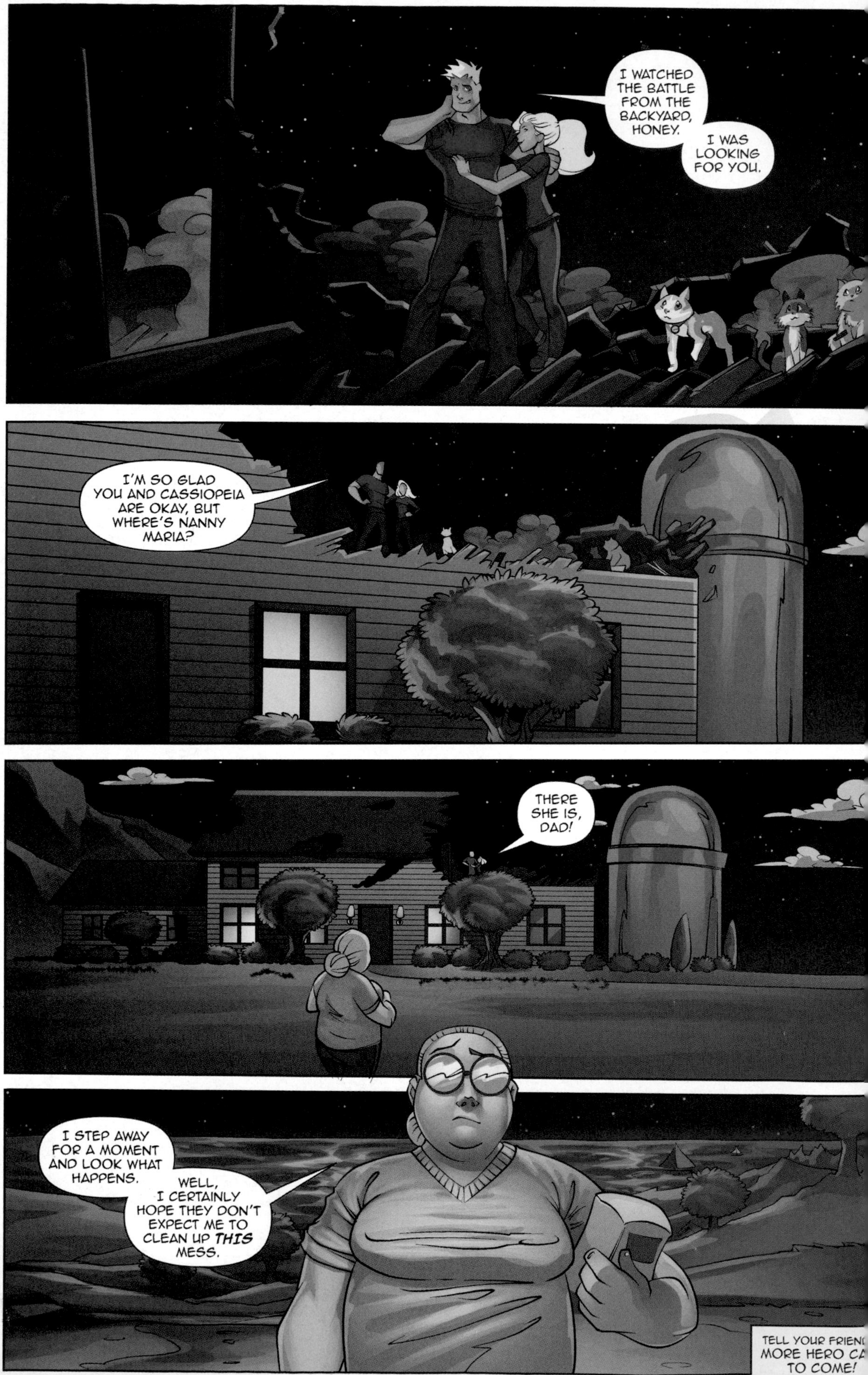
I WATCHED THE BATTLE FROM THE BACKYARD, HONEY.
I WAS LOOKING FOR YOU.
I'M SO GLAD YOU AND CASSIOPEIA ARE OKAY, BUT WHERE'S NANNY MARIA?
THERE SHE IS, DAD!
I STEP AWAY FOR A MOMENT AND LOOK WHAT HAPPENS.
WELL, I CERTAINLY HOPE THEY DON'T EXPECT ME TO CLEAN UP *THIS* MESS.
TELL YOUR FRIEN
MORE HERO CA
TO COME!

HEROCHAT

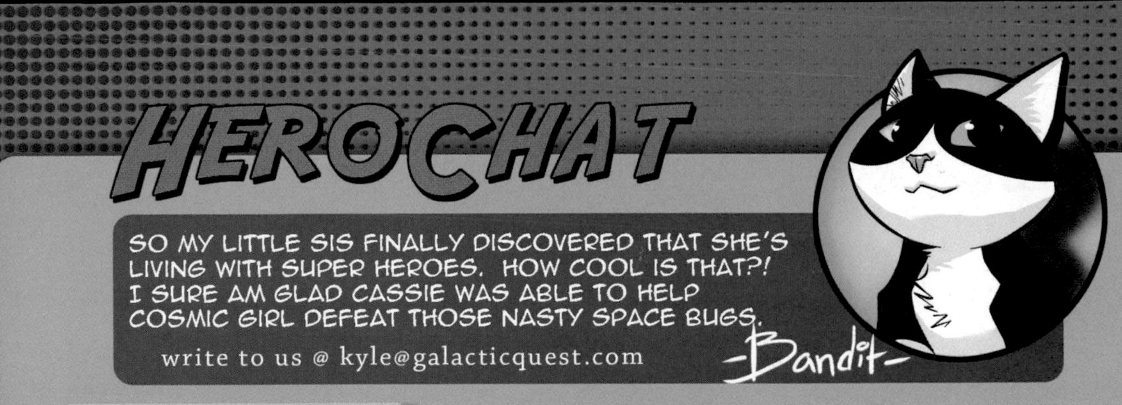

SO MY LITTLE SIS FINALLY DISCOVERED THAT SHE'S LIVING WITH SUPER HEROES. HOW COOL IS THAT?! I SURE AM GLAD CASSIE WAS ABLE TO HELP COSMIC GIRL DEFEAT THOSE NASTY SPACE BUGS.

-Bandit-

write to us @ kyle@galacticquest.com

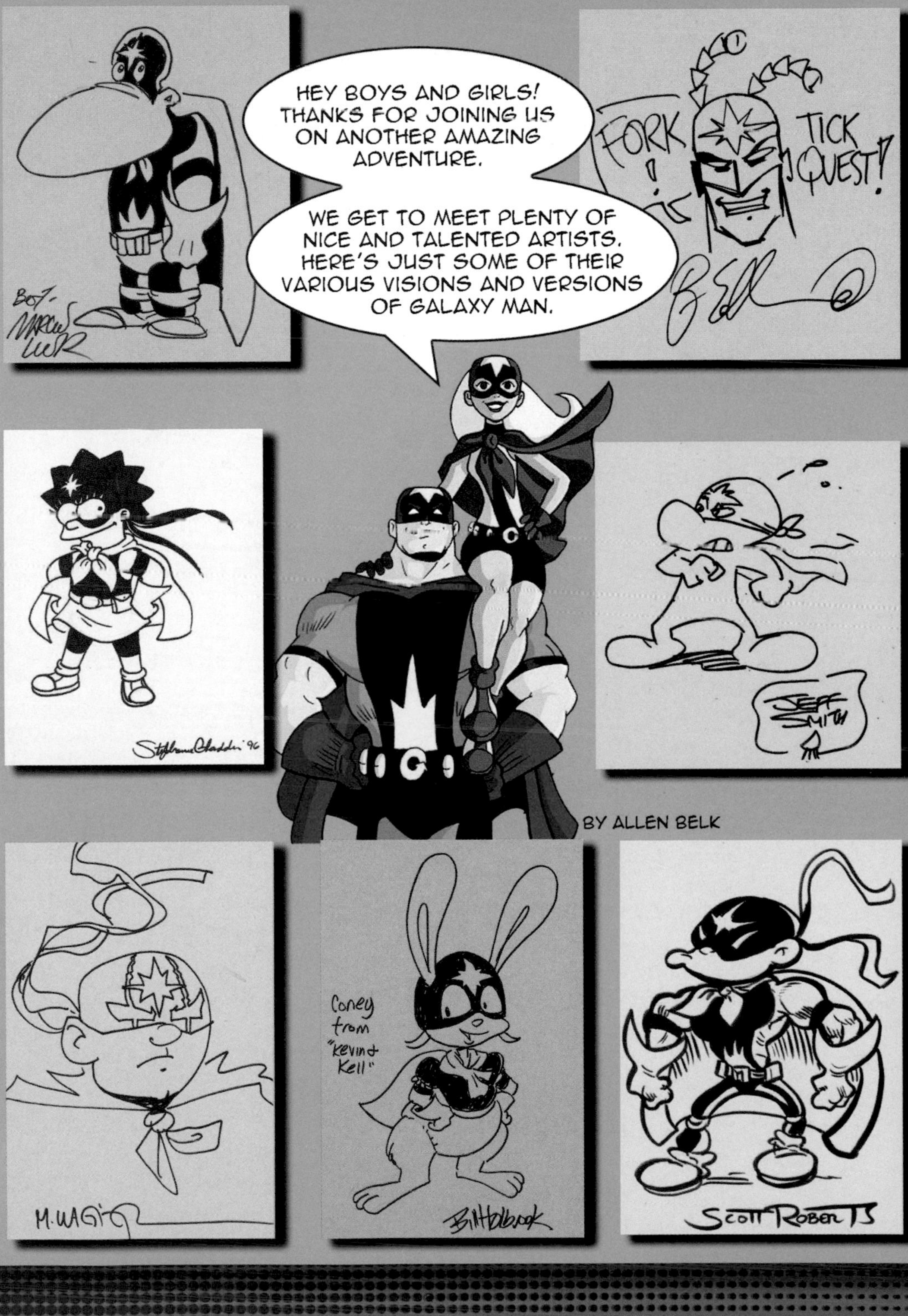
HEY BOYS AND GIRLS! THANKS FOR JOINING US ON ANOTHER AMAZING ADVENTURE.
WE GET TO MEET PLENTY OF NICE AND TALENTED ARTISTS. HERE'S JUST SOME OF THEIR VARIOUS VISIONS AND VERSIONS OF GALAXY MAN.
FORK!
TICK QUEST!
JEFF SMITH
BY ALLEN BELK
Coney from "Kevin & Kell"
Bill Holbrook
SCOTT ROBERTS

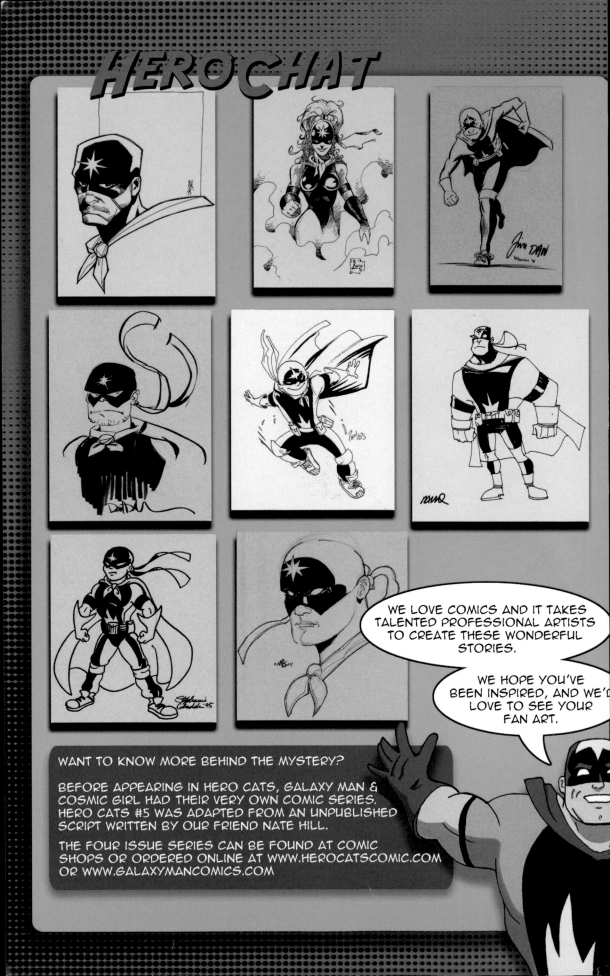

HEROCHAT

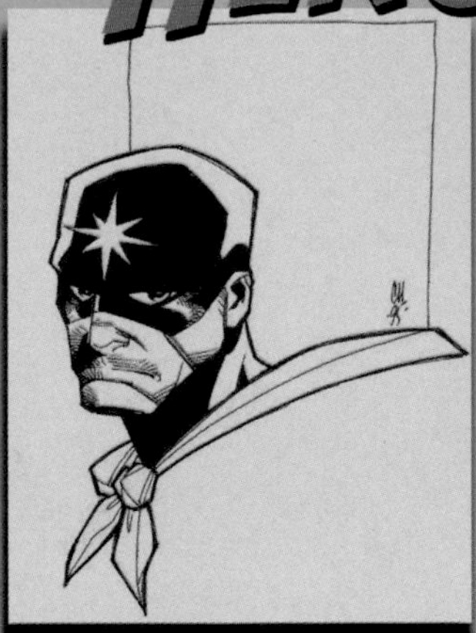
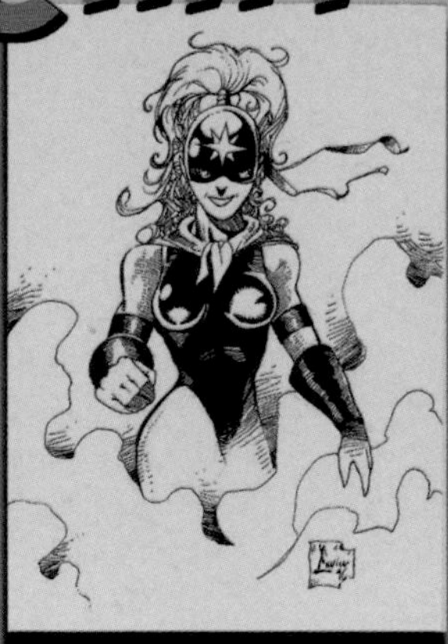
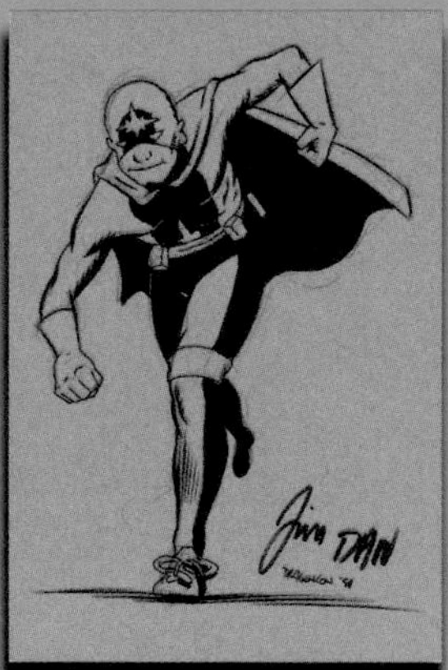
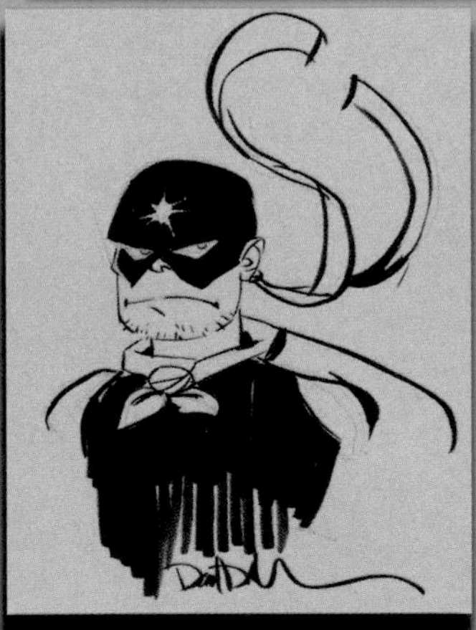
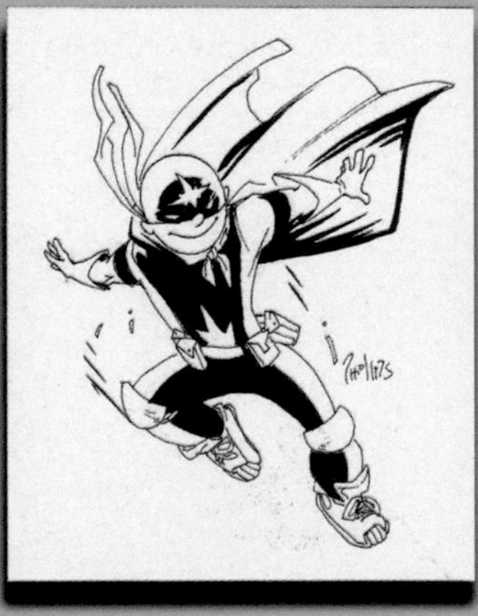
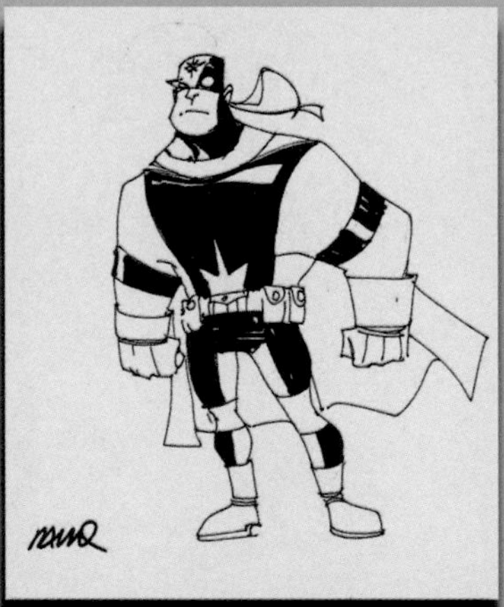
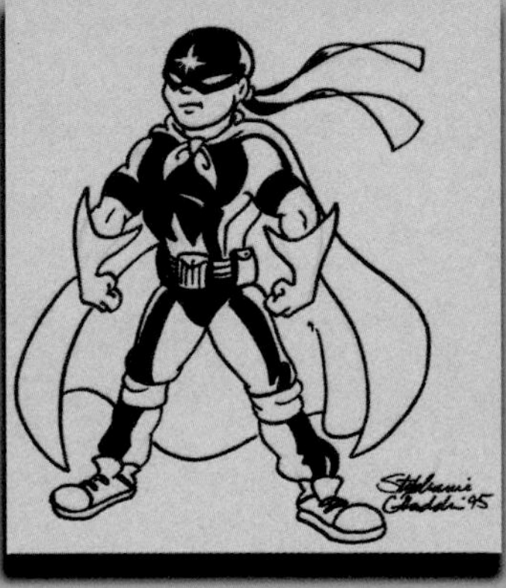
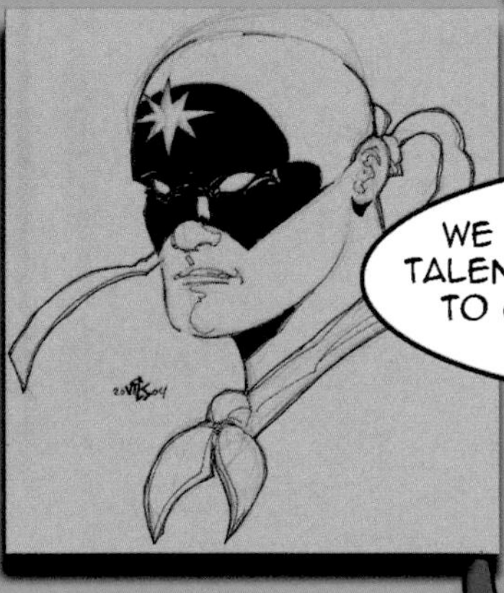
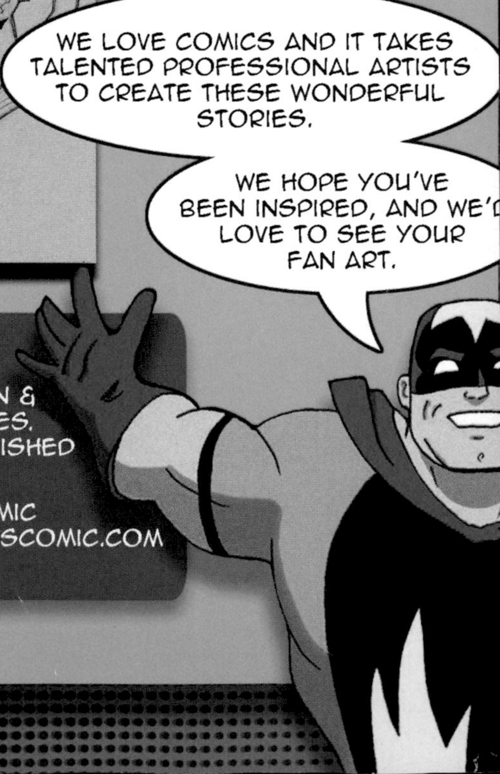
WE LOVE COMICS AND IT TAKES TALENTED PROFESSIONAL ARTISTS TO CREATE THESE WONDERFUL STORIES.
WE HOPE YOU'VE BEEN INSPIRED, AND WE'D LOVE TO SEE YOUR FAN ART.

WANT TO KNOW MORE BEHIND THE MYSTERY?

BEFORE APPEARING IN HERO CATS, GALAXY MAN & COSMIC GIRL HAD THEIR VERY OWN COMIC SERIES. HERO CATS #5 WAS ADAPTED FROM AN UNPUBLISHED SCRIPT WRITTEN BY OUR FRIEND NATE HILL.

THE FOUR ISSUE SERIES CAN BE FOUND AT COMIC SHOPS OR ORDERED ONLINE AT WWW.HEROCATSCOMIC.COM OR WWW.GALAXYMANCOMICS.COM

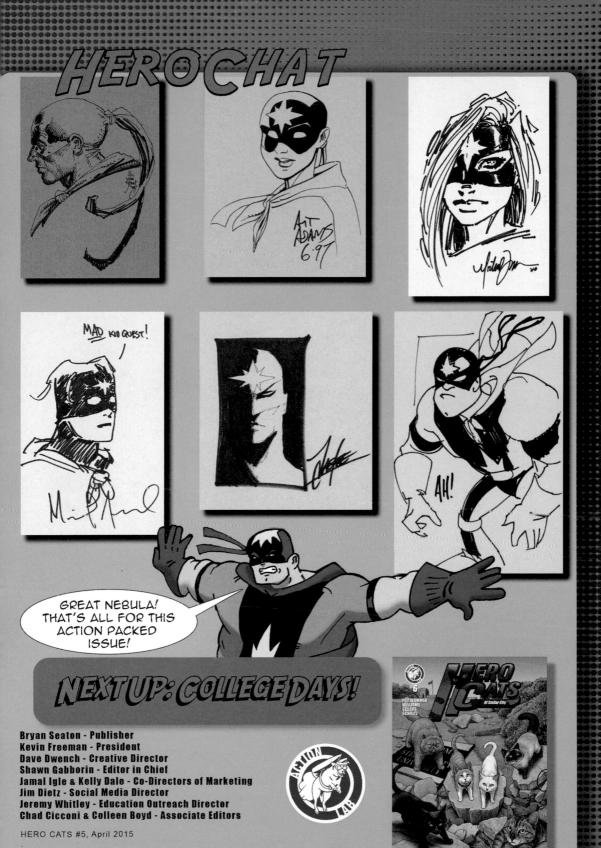

HEROCHAT

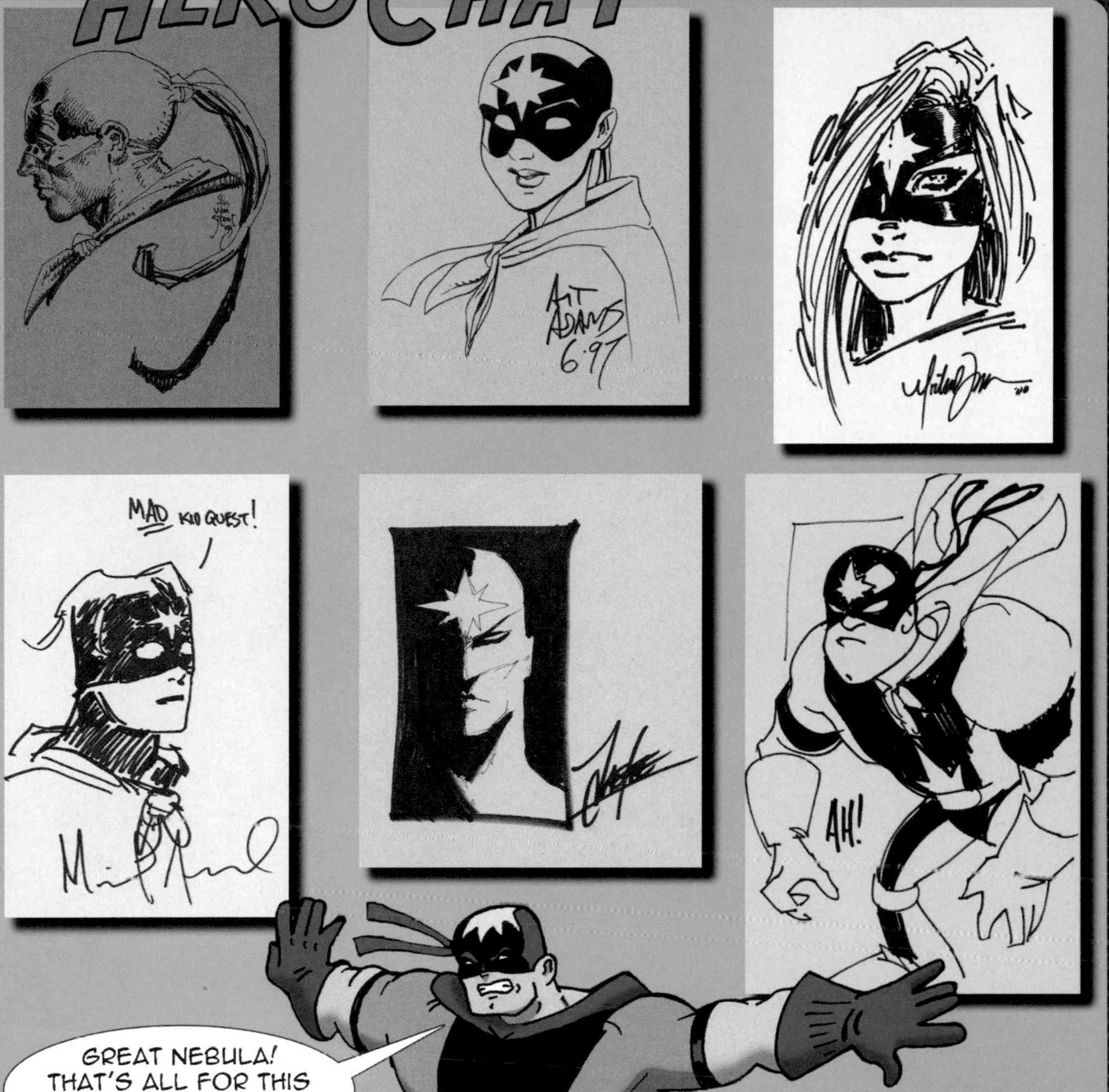
ART ADAMS 6·97
MAD KID QUEST!
AH!
GREAT NEBULA! THAT'S ALL FOR THIS ACTION PACKED ISSUE!

NEXT UP: COLLEGE DAYS!

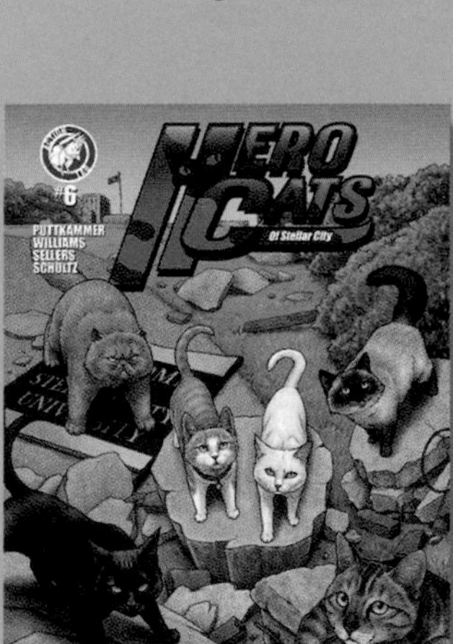
HERO CATS
of Stellar City
#6
PUTTKAMMER
WILLIAMS
SELLERS
SCHULTZ

Bryan Seaton - Publisher
Kevin Freeman - President
Dave Dwench - Creative Director
Shawn Gabborin - Editor in Chief
Jamal Igle & Kelly Dale - Co-Directors of Marketing
Jim Dietz - Social Media Director
Jeremy Whitley - Education Outreach Director
Chad Cicconi & Colleen Boyd - Associate Editors

HERO CATS #5, April 2015

Printed in Canada.

First Printing.

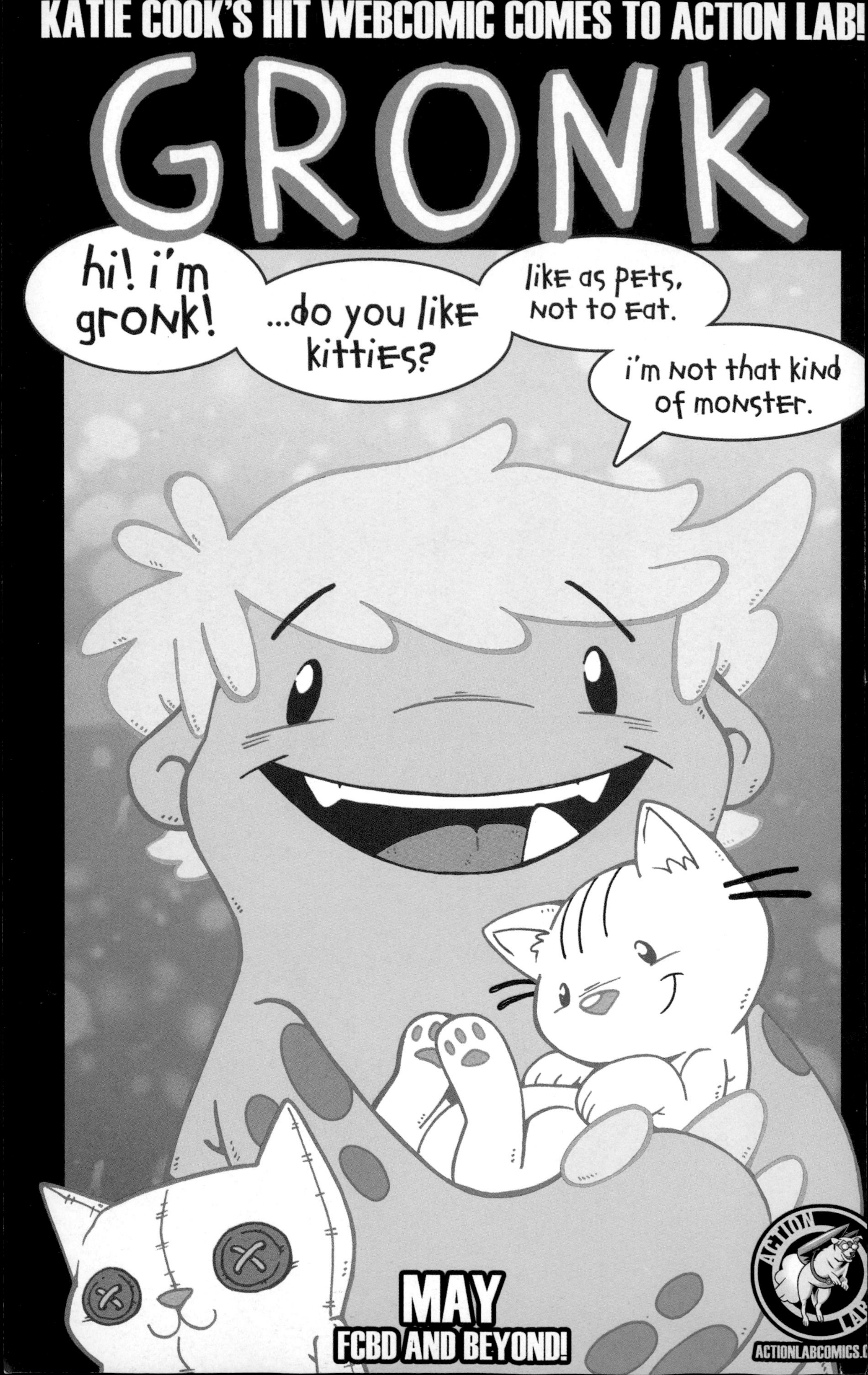
KATIE COOK'S HIT WEBCOMIC COMES TO ACTION LAB!
GRONK
hi! i'm gronk!
...do you like kitties?
like as pets, not to eat.
i'm not that kind of monster.
MAY
FCBD AND BEYOND!
ACTION LAB
ACTIONLABCOMICS.C

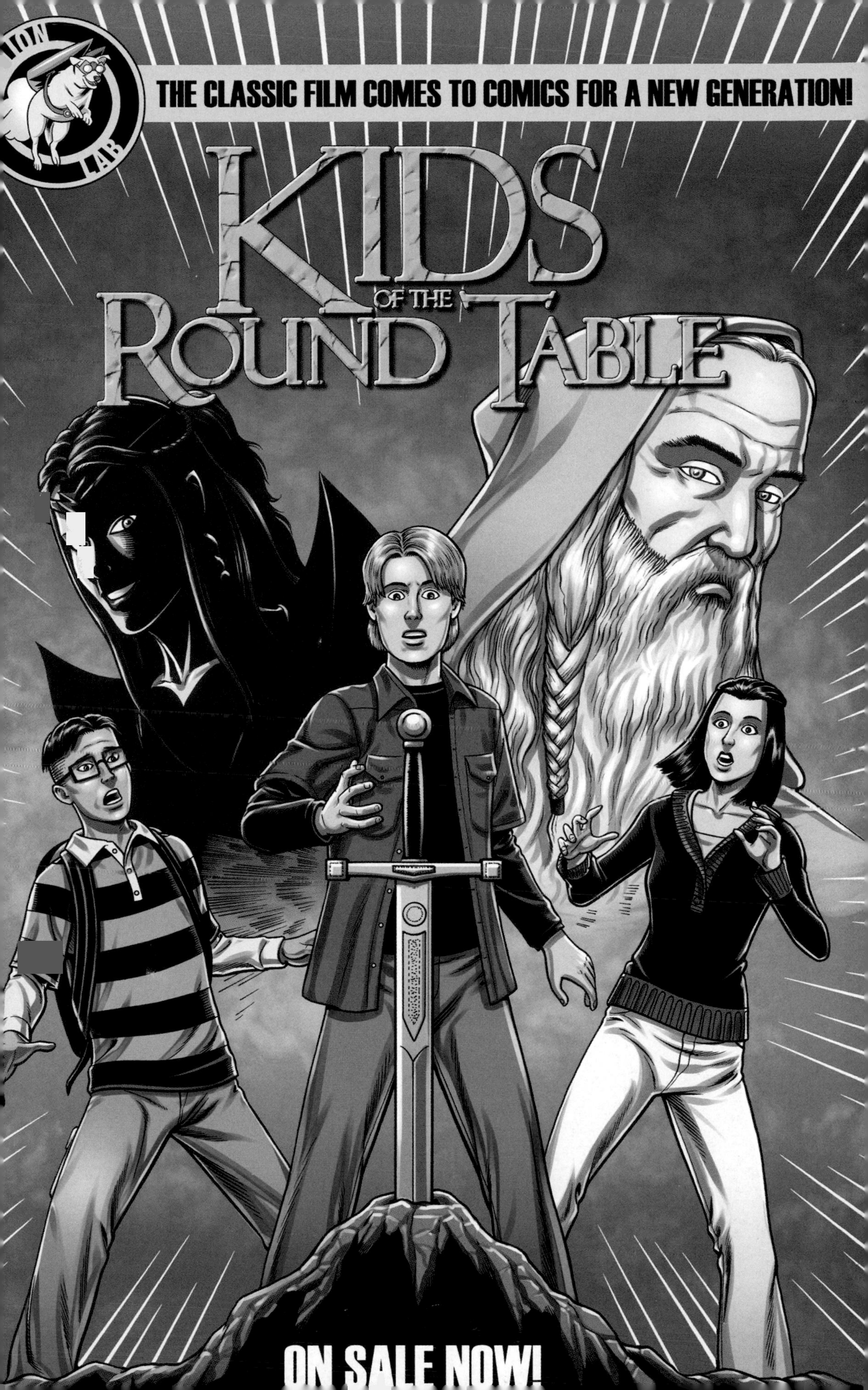
THE CLASSIC FILM COMES TO COMICS FOR A NEW GENERATION!
KIDS OF THE ROUND TABLE
ON SALE NOW!

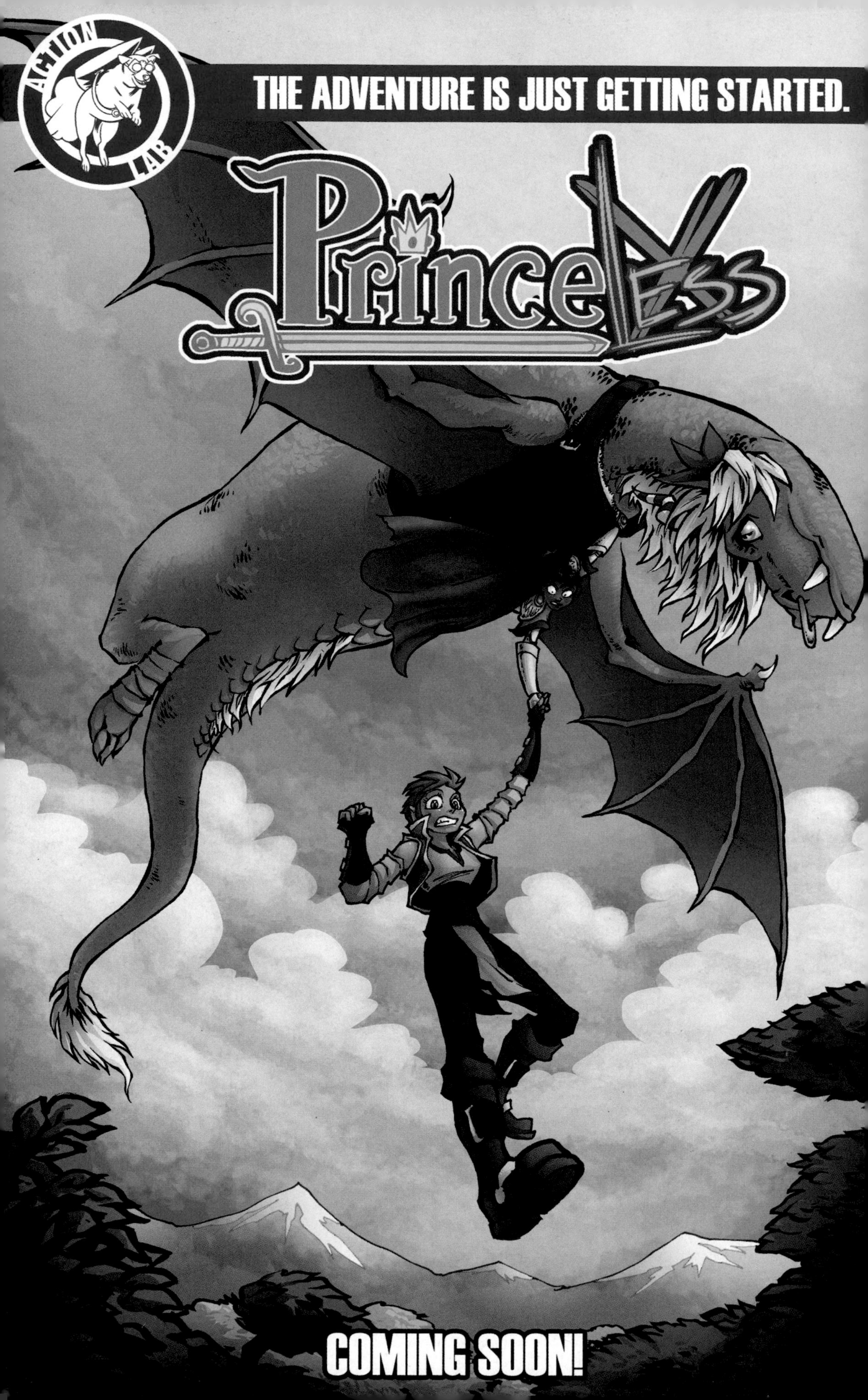
ACTION LAB
THE ADVENTURE IS JUST GETTING STARTED.
Princeless
COMING SOON!

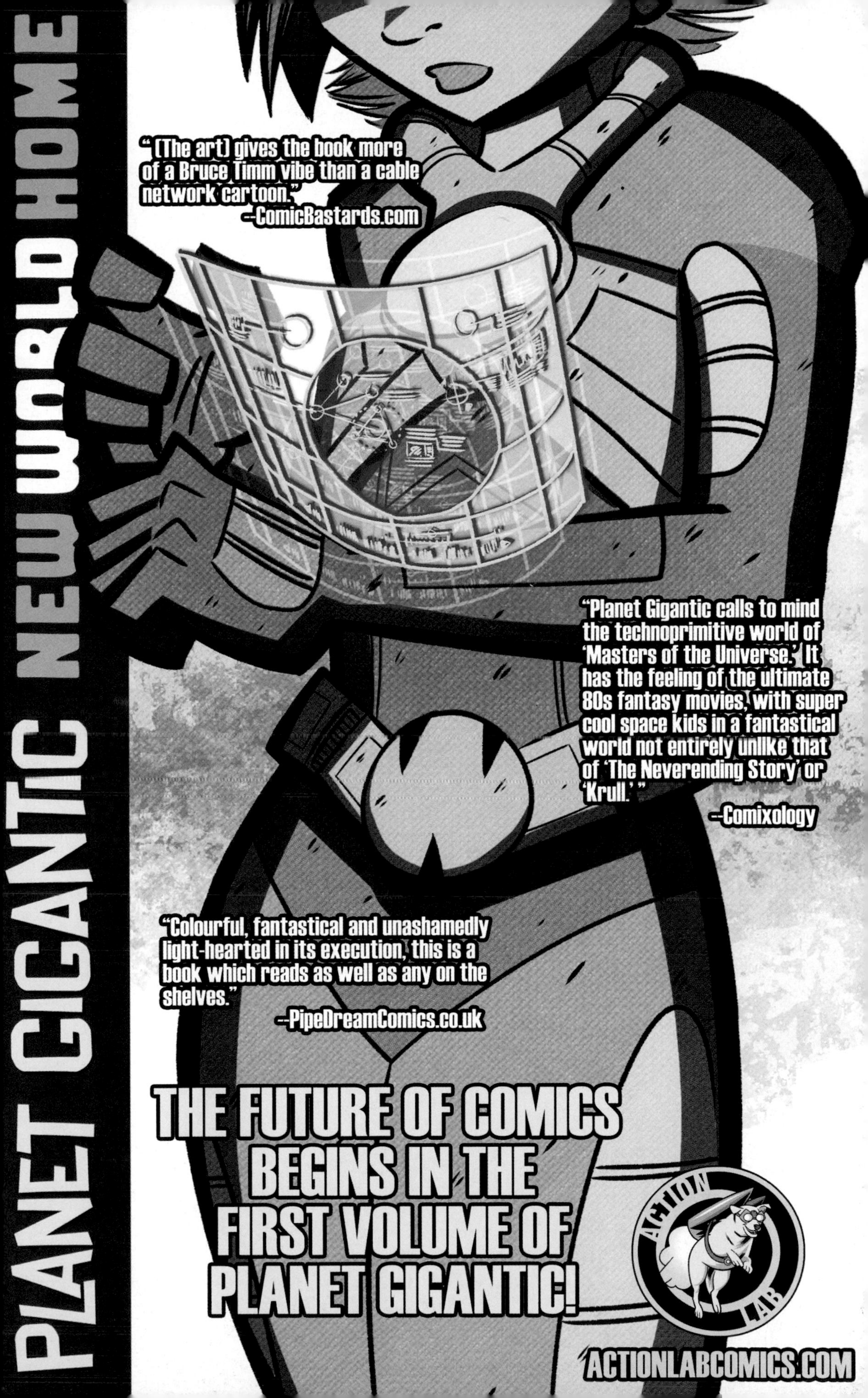
PLANET GIGANTIC NEW WORLD HOME
“(The art) gives the book more of a Bruce Timm vibe than a cable network cartoon.” --ComicBastards.com
“Planet Gigantic calls to mind the technoprimitive world of ‘Masters of the Universe.’ It has the feeling of the ultimate 80s fantasy movies, with super cool space kids in a fantastical world not entirely unlike that of ‘The Neverending Story’ or ‘Krull.’ ” --Comixology
“Colourful, fantastical and unashamedly light-hearted in its execution, this is a book which reads as well as any on the shelves.” --PipeDreamComics.co.uk
THE FUTURE OF COMICS BEGINS IN THE FIRST VOLUME OF PLANET GIGANTIC!
ACTION LAB
ACTIONLABCOMICS.COM

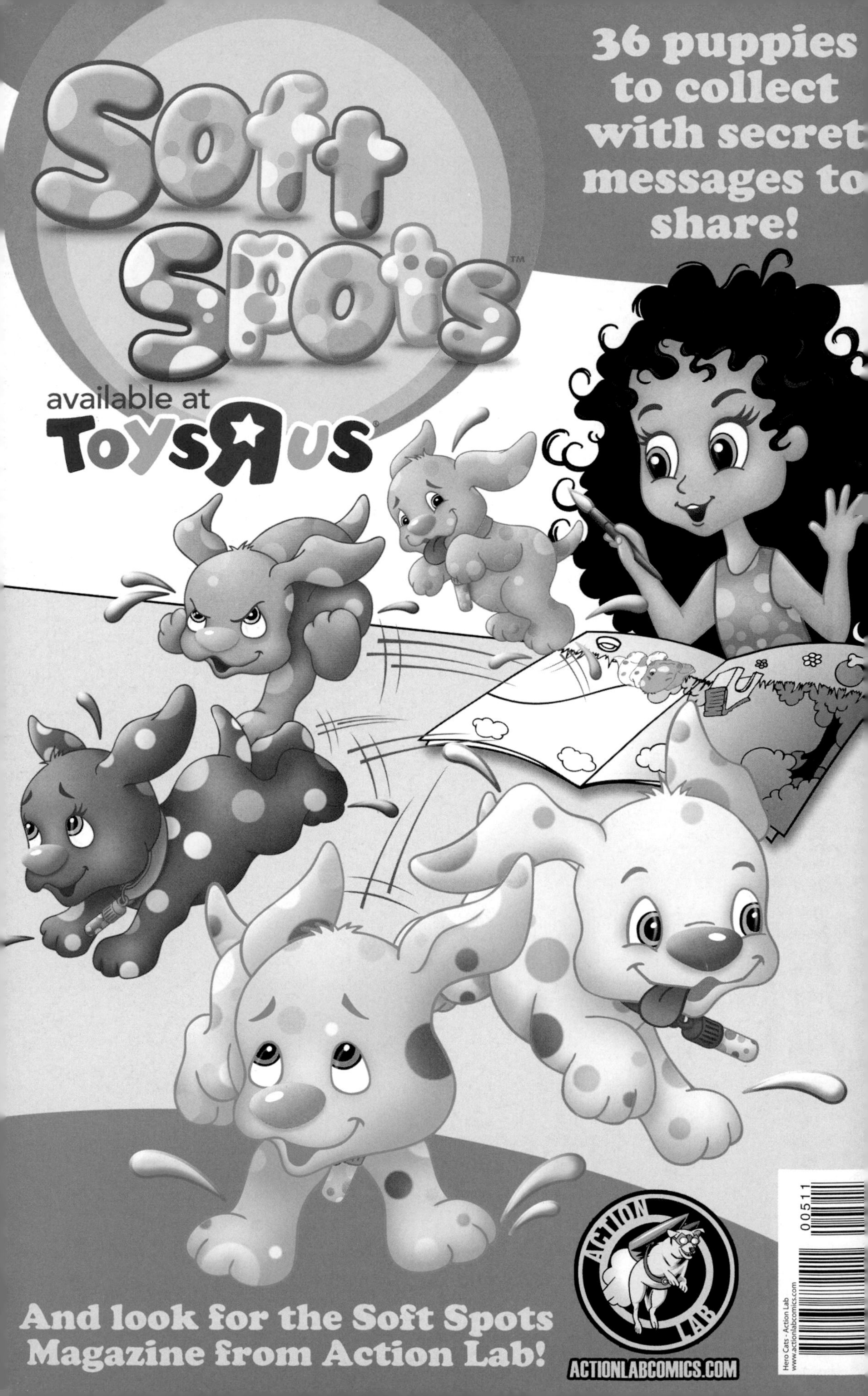

Soft Spots™
available at
Toys R Us
36 puppies to collect with secret messages to share!
And look for the Soft Spots Magazine from Action Lab!
ACTION LAB
ACTIONLABCOMICS.COM
Hero Cats - Action Lab
www.actionlabcomics.com
00511

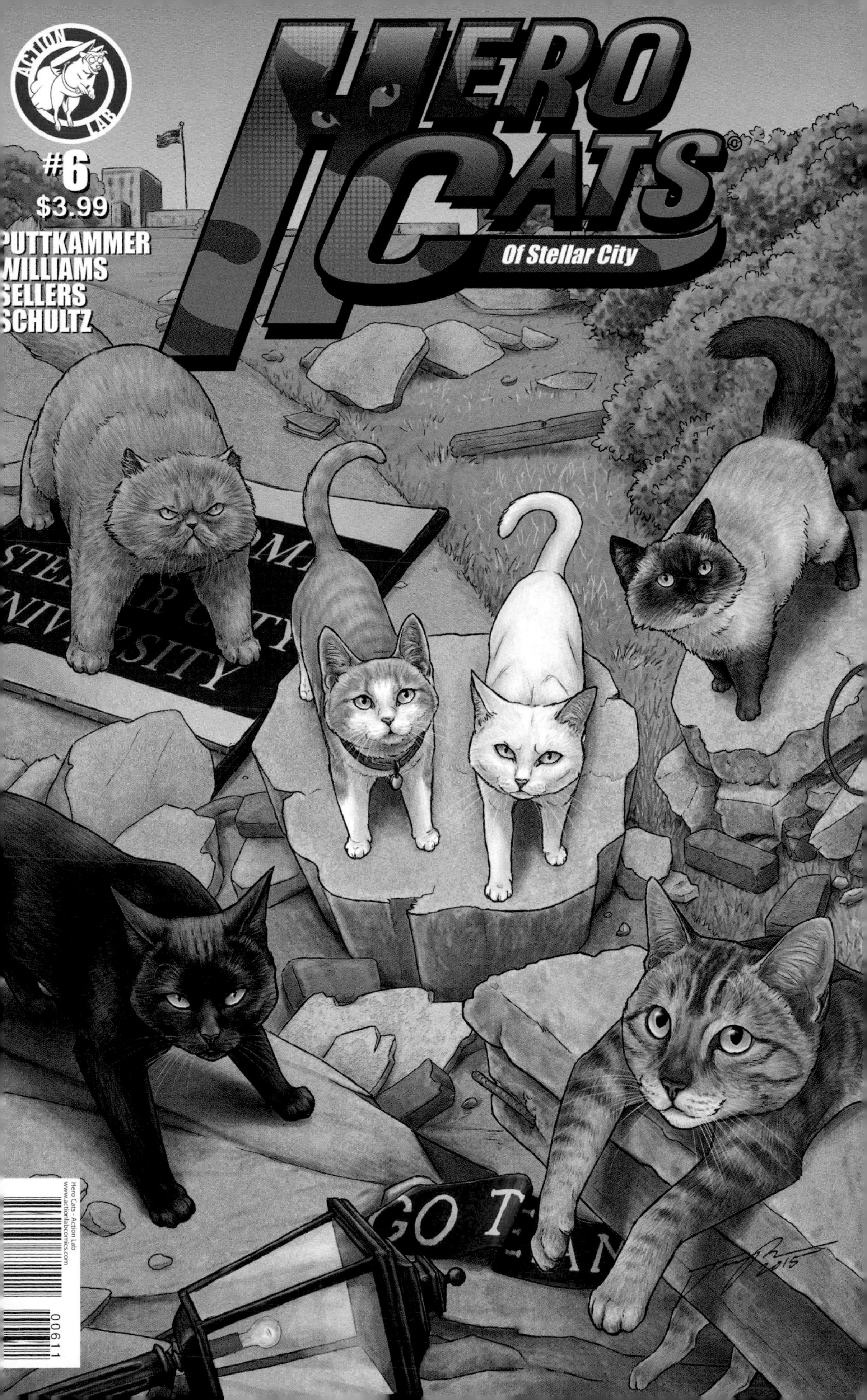
ACTION LAB
HERO CATS
Of Stellar City
#6
$3.99
PUTTKAMMER
WILLIAMS
SELLERS
SCHULTZ
Hero Cats - Action Lab
www.actionlabcomics.com

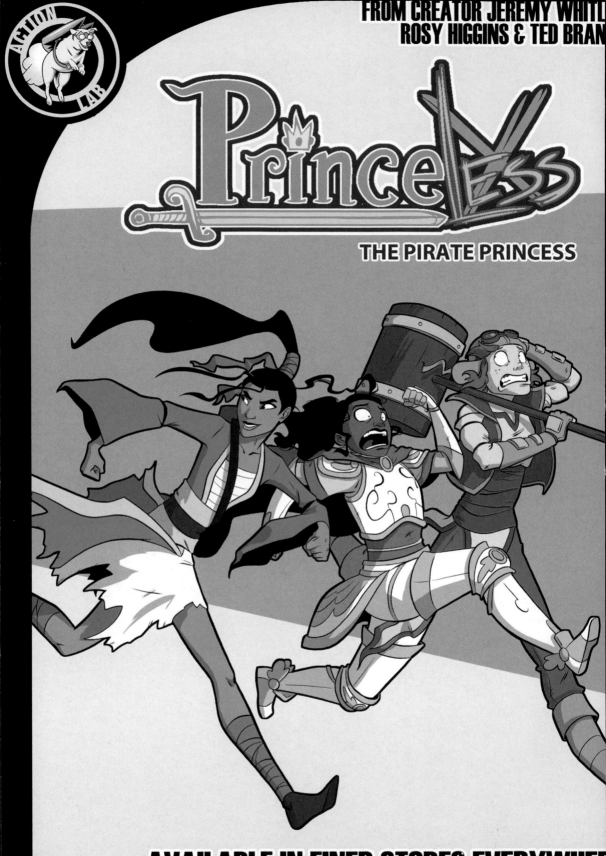

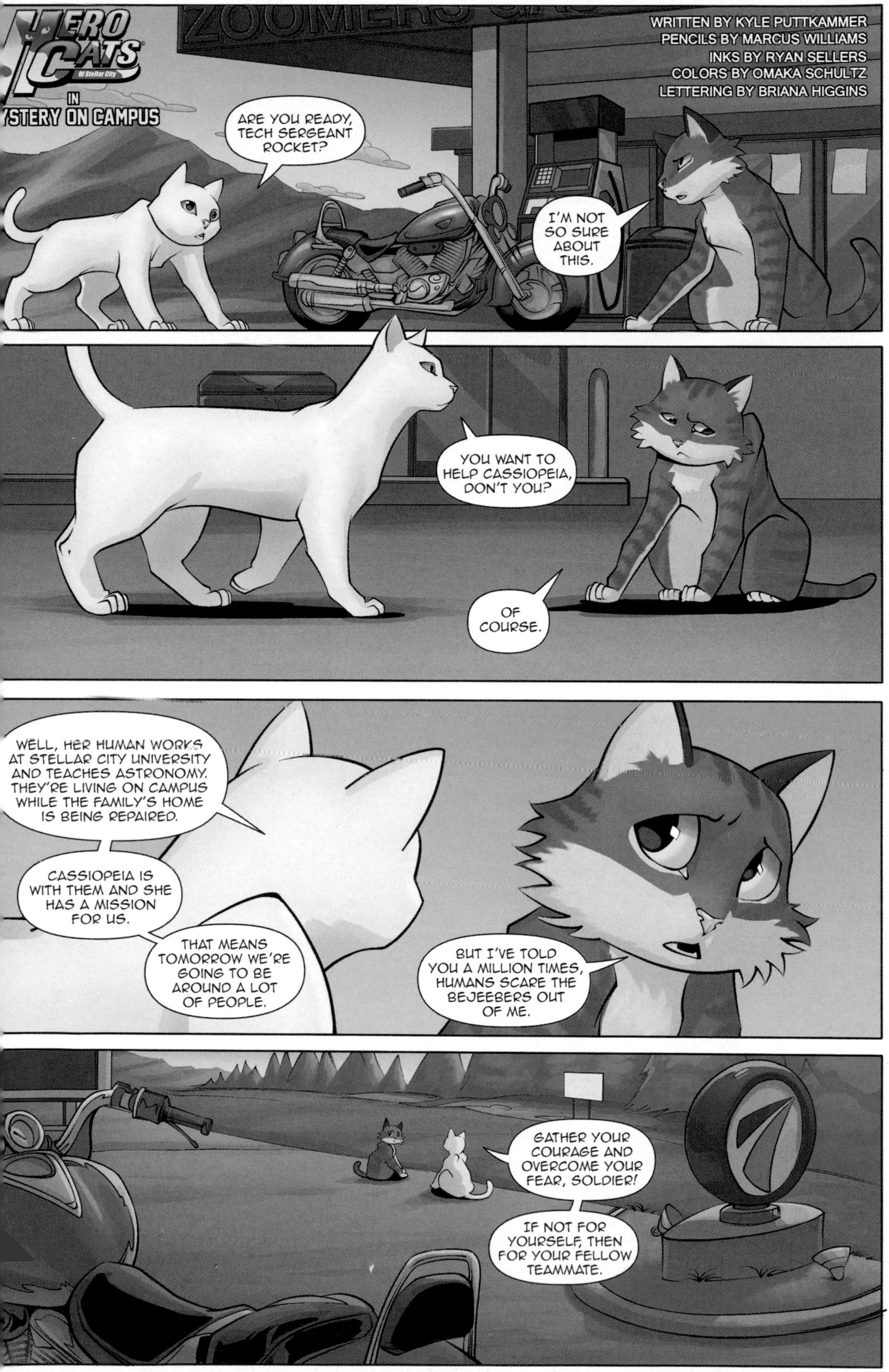
HERO CATS Of Stellar City
IN
YSTERY ON CAMPUS
ZOOMERS
WRITTEN BY KYLE PUTTKAMMER
PENCILS BY MARCUS WILLIAMS
INKS BY RYAN SELLERS
COLORS BY OMAKA SCHULTZ
LETTERING BY BRIANA HIGGINS
ARE YOU READY, TECH SERGEANT ROCKET?
I'M NOT SO SURE ABOUT THIS.
YOU WANT TO HELP CASSIOPEIA, DON'T YOU?
OF COURSE.
WELL, HER HUMAN WORKS AT STELLAR CITY UNIVERSITY AND TEACHES ASTRONOMY. THEY'RE LIVING ON CAMPUS WHILE THE FAMILY'S HOME IS BEING REPAIRED.
CASSIOPEIA IS WITH THEM AND SHE HAS A MISSION FOR US.
THAT MEANS TOMORROW WE'RE GOING TO BE AROUND A LOT OF PEOPLE.
BUT I'VE TOLD YOU A MILLION TIMES, HUMANS SCARE THE BEJEEBERS OUT OF ME.
GATHER YOUR COURAGE AND OVERCOME YOUR FEAR, SOLDIER!
IF NOT FOR YOURSELF, THEN FOR YOUR FELLOW TEAMMATE.

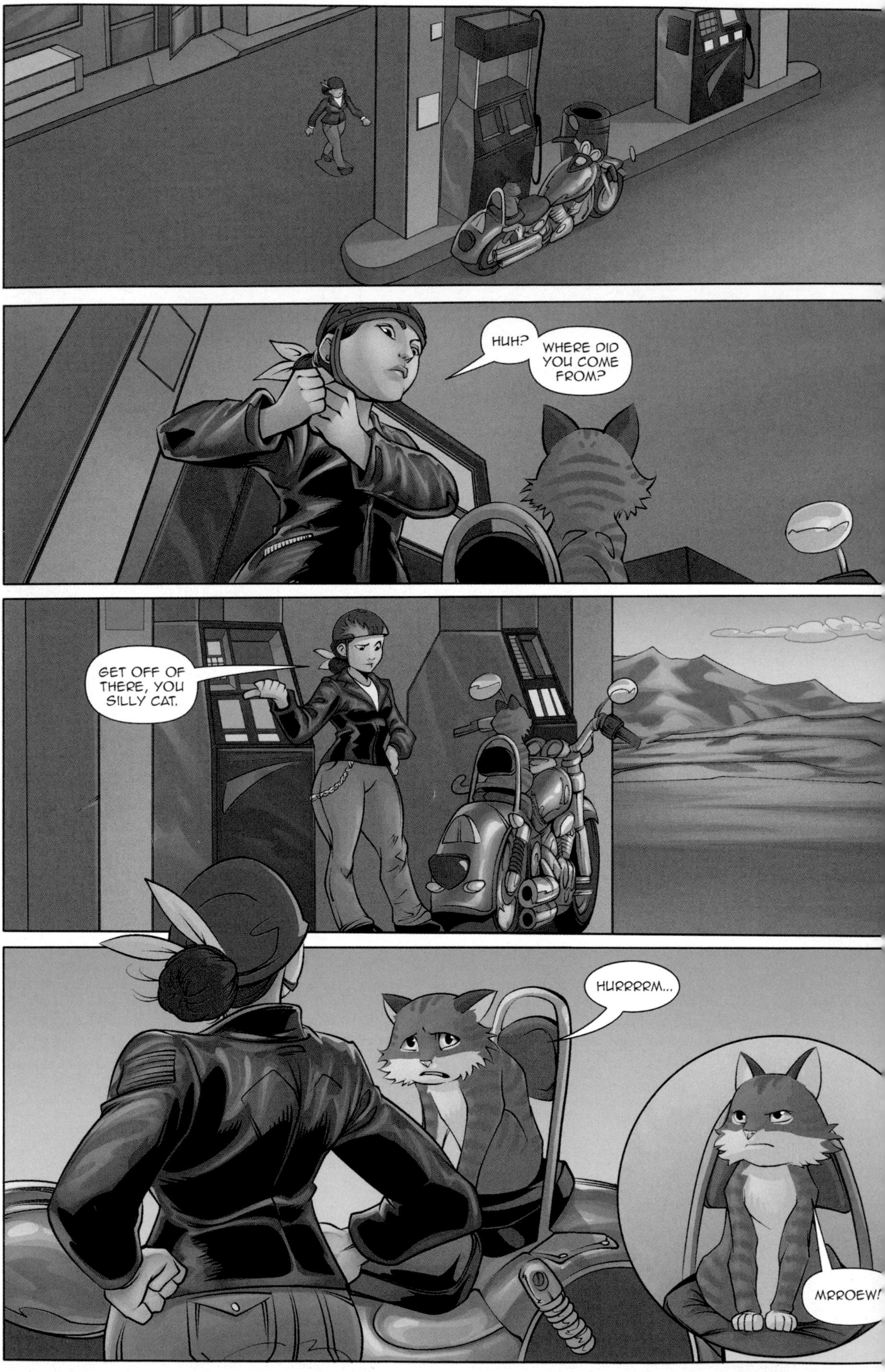
HUH?
WHERE DID YOU COME FROM?
GET OFF OF THERE, YOU SILLY CAT.
HURRRRM...
MRROEW!

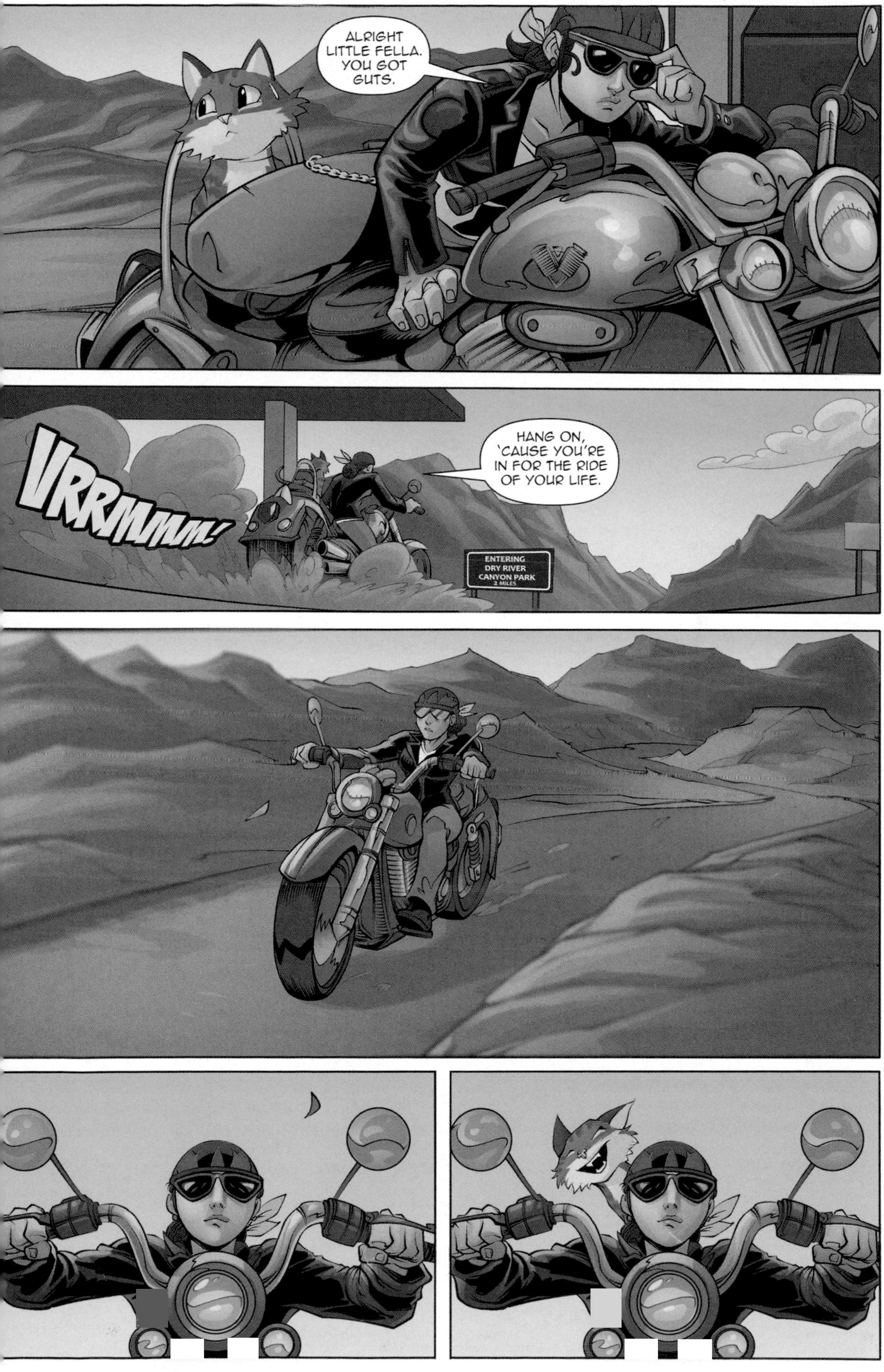
ALRIGHT LITTLE FELLA. YOU GOT GUTS.
VRRMMMM!
HANG ON, 'CAUSE YOU'RE IN FOR THE RIDE OF YOUR LIFE.
ENTERING DRY RIVER CANYON PARK 2 MILES

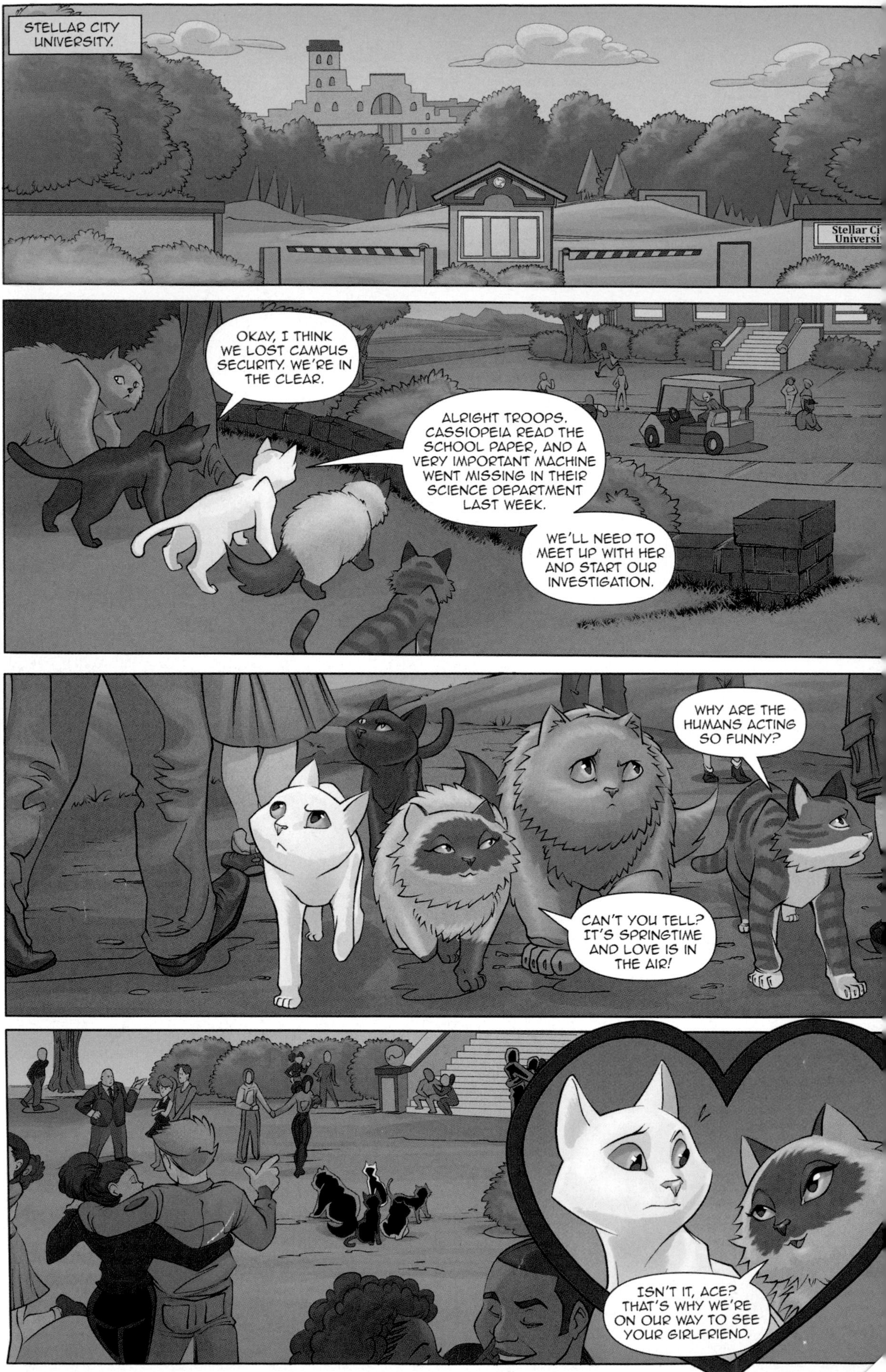
STELLAR CITY UNIVERSITY.
Stellar City University
OKAY, I THINK WE LOST CAMPUS SECURITY. WE'RE IN THE CLEAR.
ALRIGHT TROOPS. CASSIOPEIA READ THE SCHOOL PAPER, AND A VERY IMPORTANT MACHINE WENT MISSING IN THEIR SCIENCE DEPARTMENT LAST WEEK.
WE'LL NEED TO MEET UP WITH HER AND START OUR INVESTIGATION.
WHY ARE THE HUMANS ACTING SO FUNNY?
CAN'T YOU TELL? IT'S SPRINGTIME AND LOVE IS IN THE AIR!
ISN'T IT, ACE? THAT'S WHY WE'RE ON OUR WAY TO SEE YOUR GIRLFRIEND.

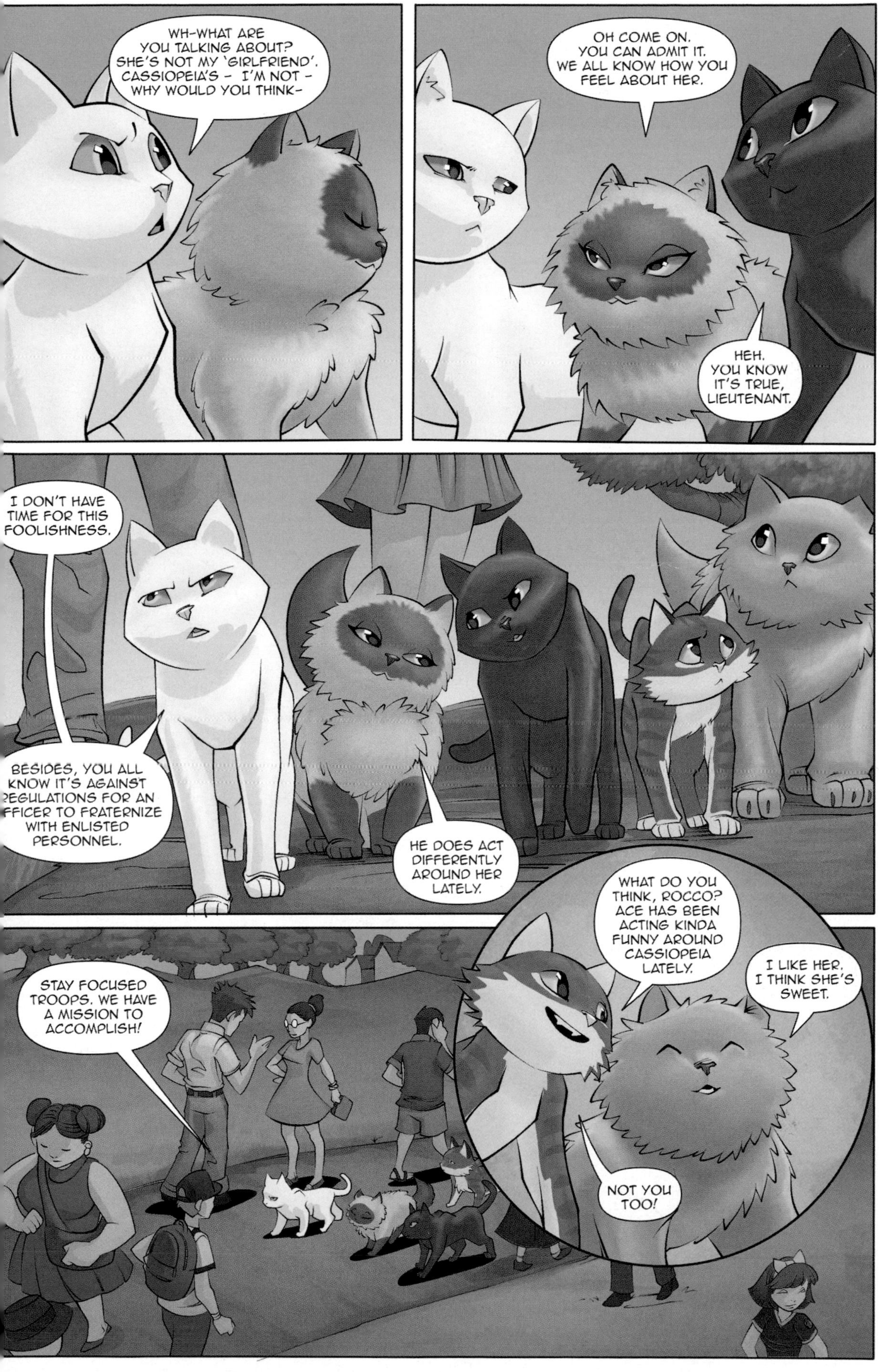
WH-WHAT ARE YOU TALKING ABOUT? SHE'S NOT MY 'GIRLFRIEND'. CASSIOPEIA'S – I'M NOT – WHY WOULD YOU THINK–
OH COME ON. YOU CAN ADMIT IT. WE ALL KNOW HOW YOU FEEL ABOUT HER.
HEH. YOU KNOW IT'S TRUE, LIEUTENANT.
I DON'T HAVE TIME FOR THIS FOOLISHNESS.
BESIDES, YOU ALL KNOW IT'S AGAINST REGULATIONS FOR AN OFFICER TO FRATERNIZE WITH ENLISTED PERSONNEL.
HE DOES ACT DIFFERENTLY AROUND HER LATELY.
STAY FOCUSED TROOPS. WE HAVE A MISSION TO ACCOMPLISH!
WHAT DO YOU THINK, ROCCO? ACE HAS BEEN ACTING KINDA FUNNY AROUND CASSIOPEIA LATELY.
I LIKE HER. I THINK SHE'S SWEET.
NOT YOU TOO!

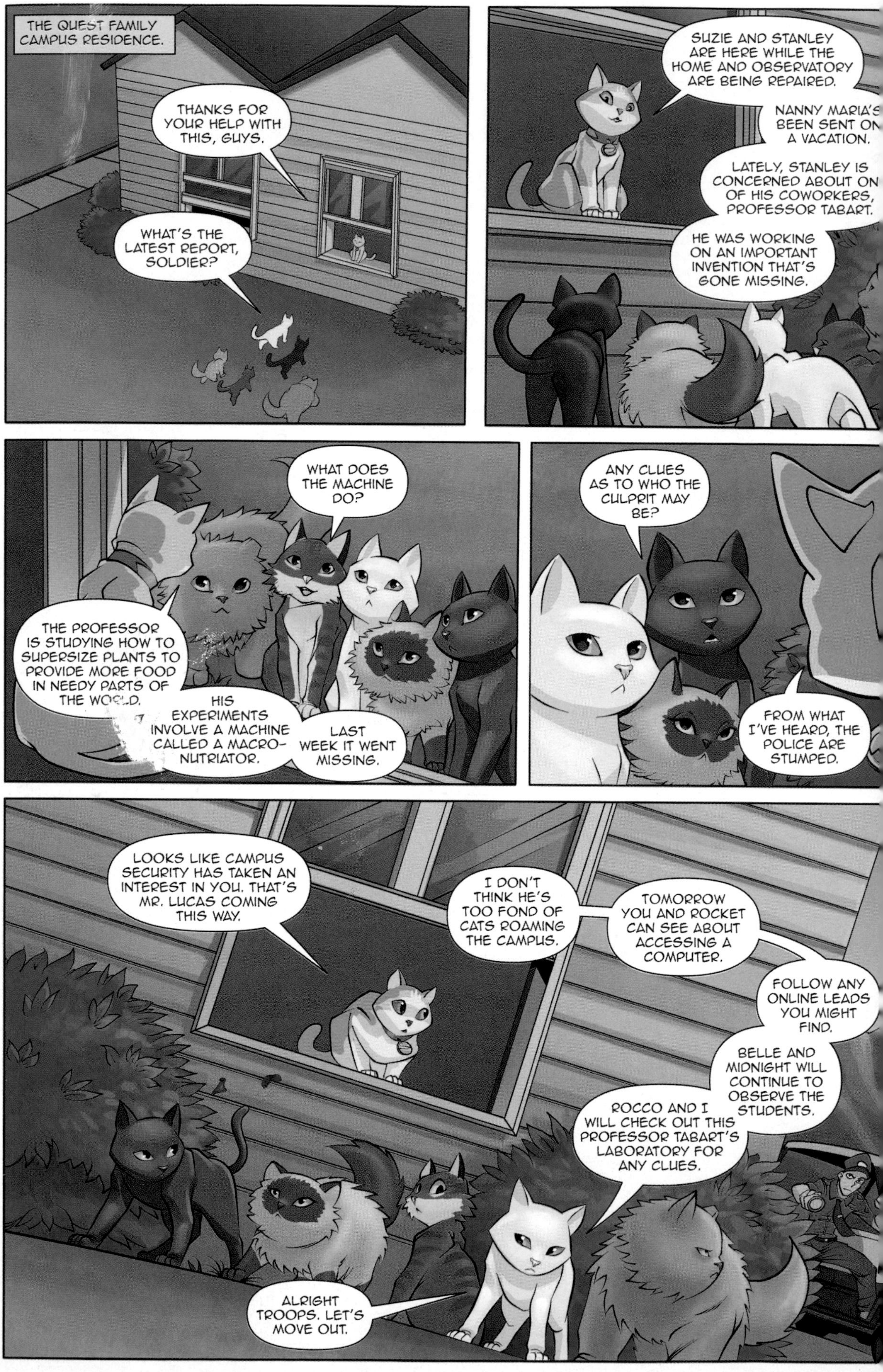
THE QUEST FAMILY CAMPUS RESIDENCE.
THANKS FOR YOUR HELP WITH THIS, GUYS.
WHAT'S THE LATEST REPORT, SOLDIER?
SUZIE AND STANLEY ARE HERE WHILE THE HOME AND OBSERVATORY ARE BEING REPAIRED.
NANNY MARIA'S BEEN SENT ON A VACATION.
LATELY, STANLEY IS CONCERNED ABOUT ONE OF HIS COWORKERS, PROFESSOR TABART.
HE WAS WORKING ON AN IMPORTANT INVENTION THAT'S GONE MISSING.
WHAT DOES THE MACHINE DO?
THE PROFESSOR IS STUDYING HOW TO SUPERSIZE PLANTS TO PROVIDE MORE FOOD IN NEEDY PARTS OF THE WORLD.
HIS EXPERIMENTS INVOLVE A MACHINE CALLED A MACRO-NUTRIATOR.
LAST WEEK IT WENT MISSING.
ANY CLUES AS TO WHO THE CULPRIT MAY BE?
FROM WHAT I'VE HEARD, THE POLICE ARE STUMPED.
LOOKS LIKE CAMPUS SECURITY HAS TAKEN AN INTEREST IN YOU. THAT'S MR. LUCAS COMING THIS WAY.
I DON'T THINK HE'S TOO FOND OF CATS ROAMING THE CAMPUS.
TOMORROW YOU AND ROCKET CAN SEE ABOUT ACCESSING A COMPUTER.
FOLLOW ANY ONLINE LEADS YOU MIGHT FIND.
BELLE AND MIDNIGHT WILL CONTINUE TO OBSERVE THE STUDENTS.
ROCCO AND I WILL CHECK OUT THIS PROFESSOR TABART'S LABORATORY FOR ANY CLUES.
ALRIGHT TROOPS. LET'S MOVE OUT.

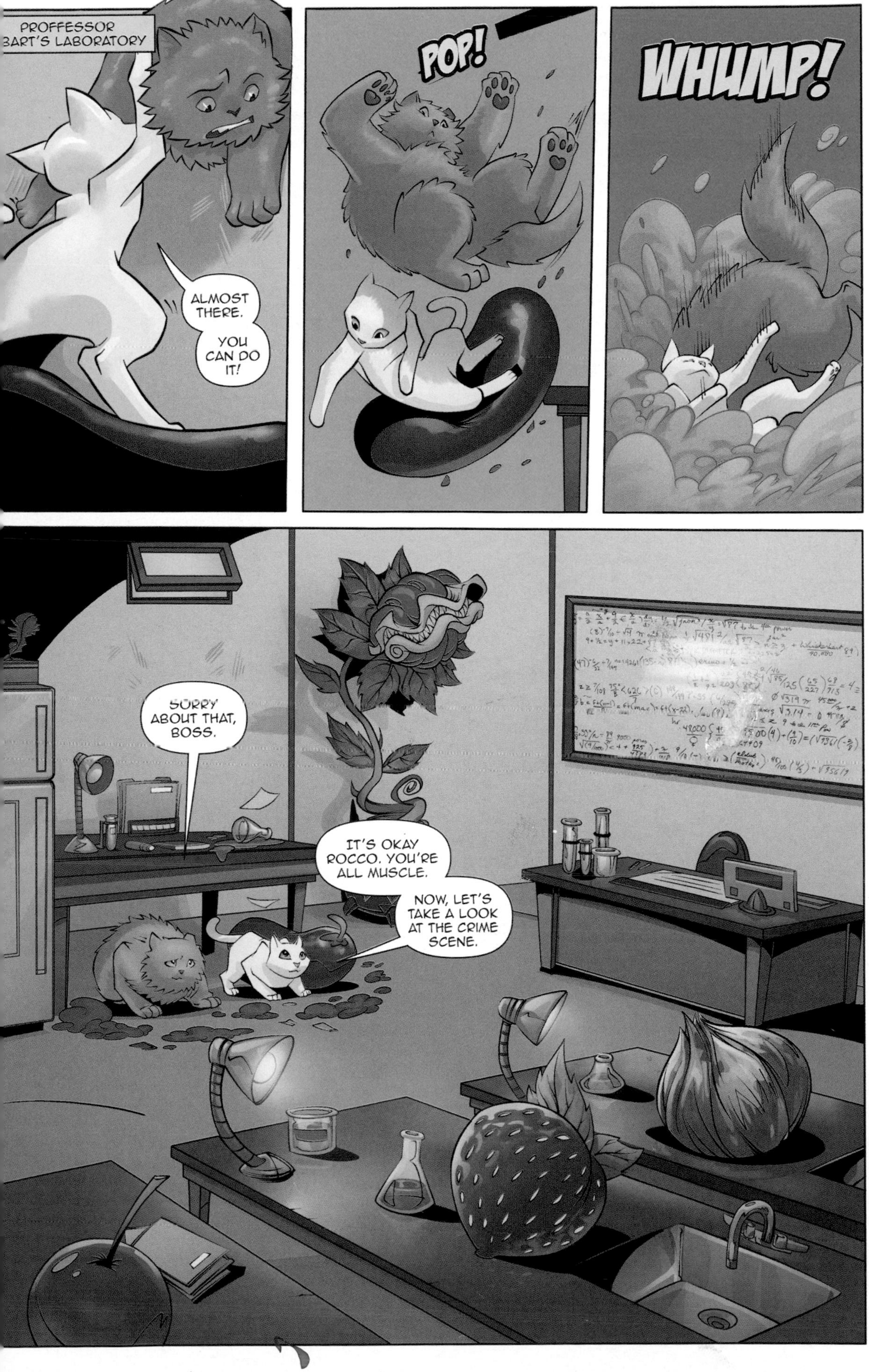
PROFFESSOR BART'S LABORATORY
ALMOST THERE.
YOU CAN DO IT!
POP!
WHUMP!
SORRY ABOUT THAT, BOSS.
IT'S OKAY ROCCO. YOU'RE ALL MUSCLE.
NOW, LET'S TAKE A LOOK AT THE CRIME SCENE.

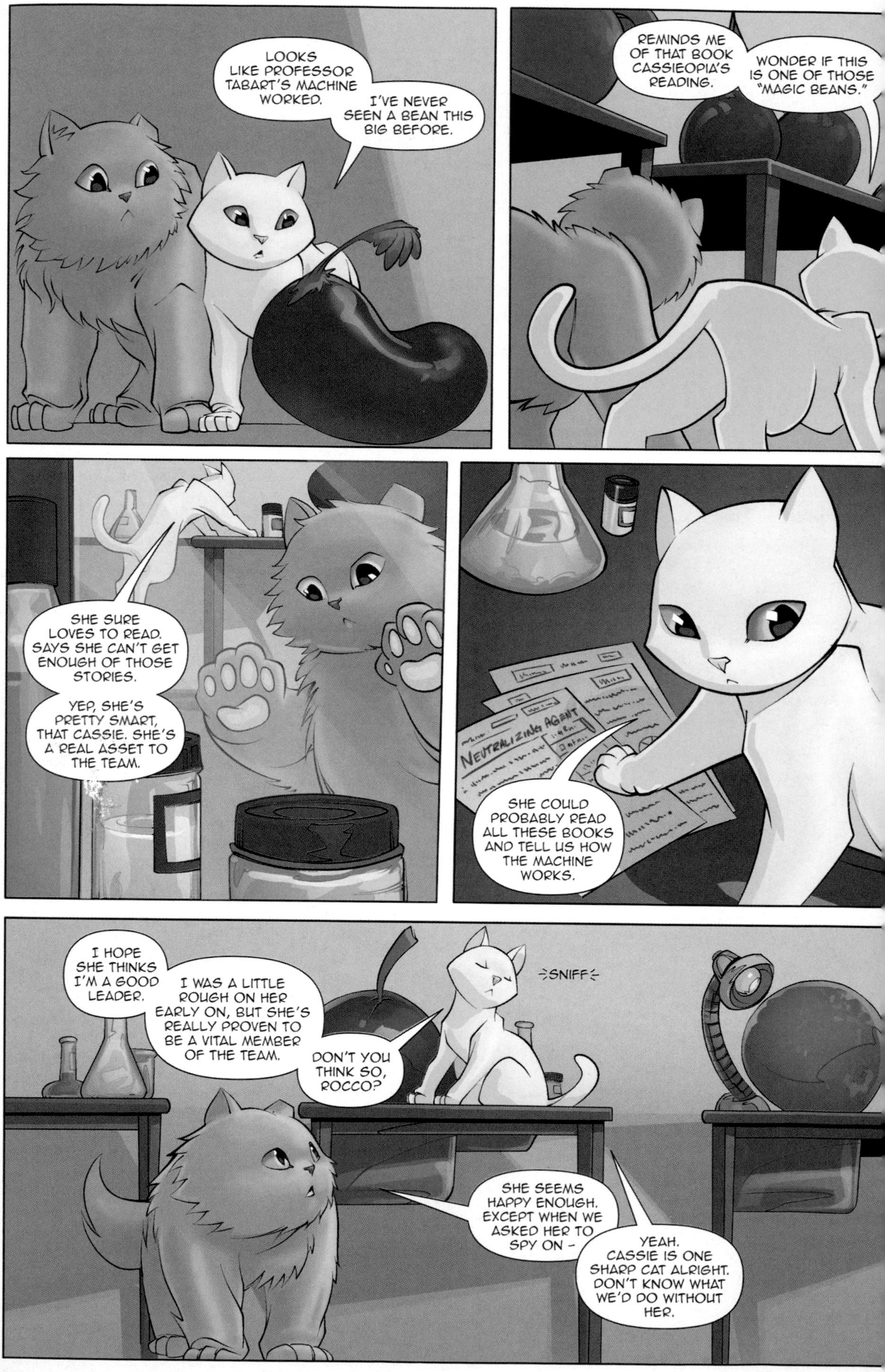

LOOKS LIKE PROFESSOR TABART'S MACHINE WORKED.
I'VE NEVER SEEN A BEAN THIS BIG BEFORE.
REMINDS ME OF THAT BOOK CASSIEOPIA'S READING.
WONDER IF THIS IS ONE OF THOSE "MAGIC BEANS."
SHE SURE LOVES TO READ. SAYS SHE CAN'T GET ENOUGH OF THOSE STORIES.
YEP, SHE'S PRETTY SMART, THAT CASSIE. SHE'S A REAL ASSET TO THE TEAM.
NEUTRALIZING AGENT
SHE COULD PROBABLY READ ALL THESE BOOKS AND TELL US HOW THE MACHINE WORKS.
I HOPE SHE THINKS I'M A GOOD LEADER.
I WAS A LITTLE ROUGH ON HER EARLY ON, BUT SHE'S REALLY PROVEN TO BE A VITAL MEMBER OF THE TEAM.
DON'T YOU THINK SO, ROCCO?
SNIFF
SHE SEEMS HAPPY ENOUGH. EXCEPT WHEN WE ASKED HER TO SPY ON –
YEAH. CASSIE IS ONE SHARP CAT ALRIGHT. DON'T KNOW WHAT WE'D DO WITHOUT HER.

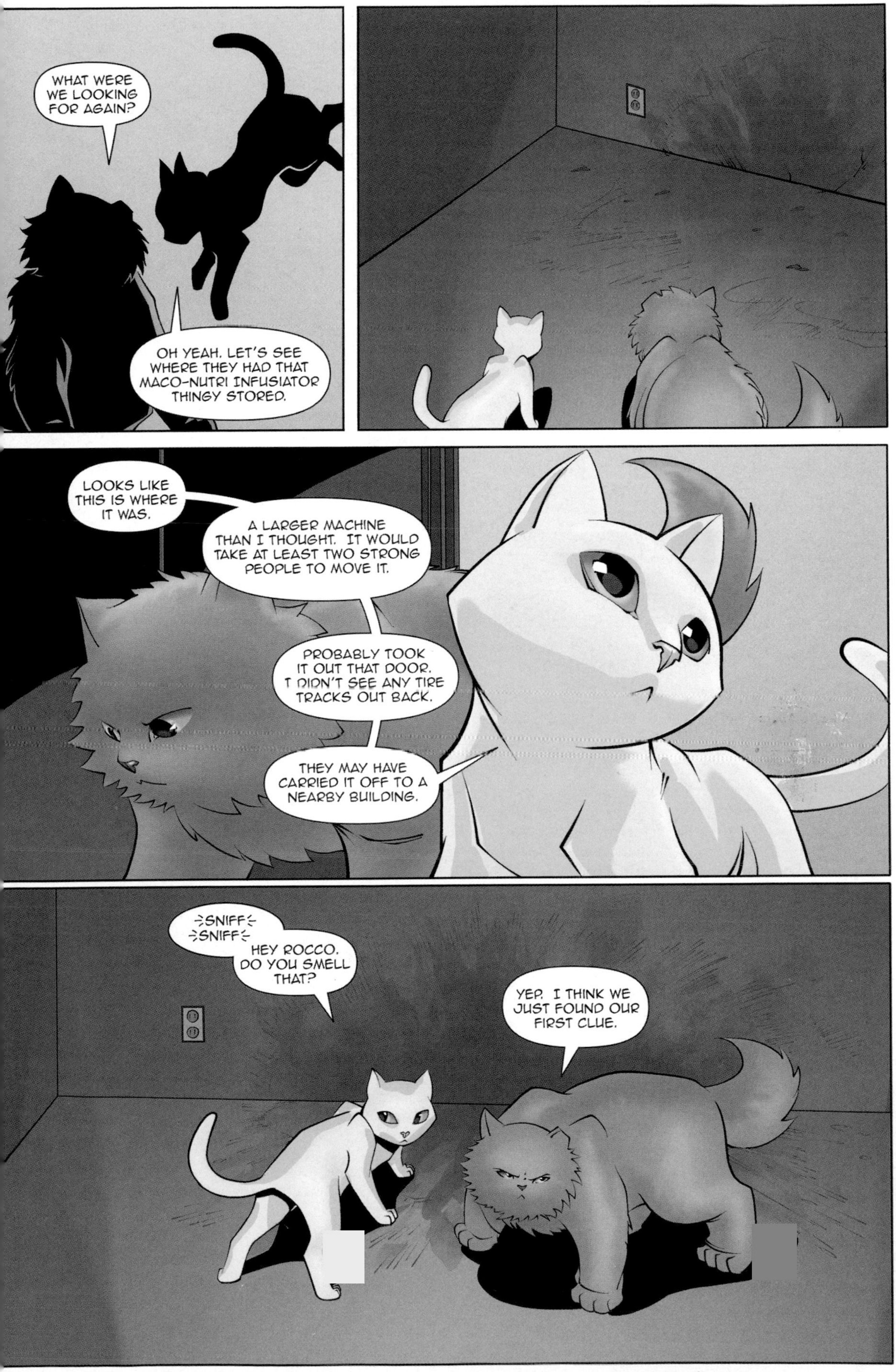
WHAT WERE WE LOOKING FOR AGAIN?
OH YEAH. LET'S SEE WHERE THEY HAD THAT MACO-NUTRI INFUSIATOR THINGY STORED.
LOOKS LIKE THIS IS WHERE IT WAS.
A LARGER MACHINE THAN I THOUGHT. IT WOULD TAKE AT LEAST TWO STRONG PEOPLE TO MOVE IT.
PROBABLY TOOK IT OUT THAT DOOR. I DIDN'T SEE ANY TIRE TRACKS OUT BACK.
THEY MAY HAVE CARRIED IT OFF TO A NEARBY BUILDING.
SNIFF SNIFF HEY ROCCO. DO YOU SMELL THAT?
YEP. I THINK WE JUST FOUND OUR FIRST CLUE.

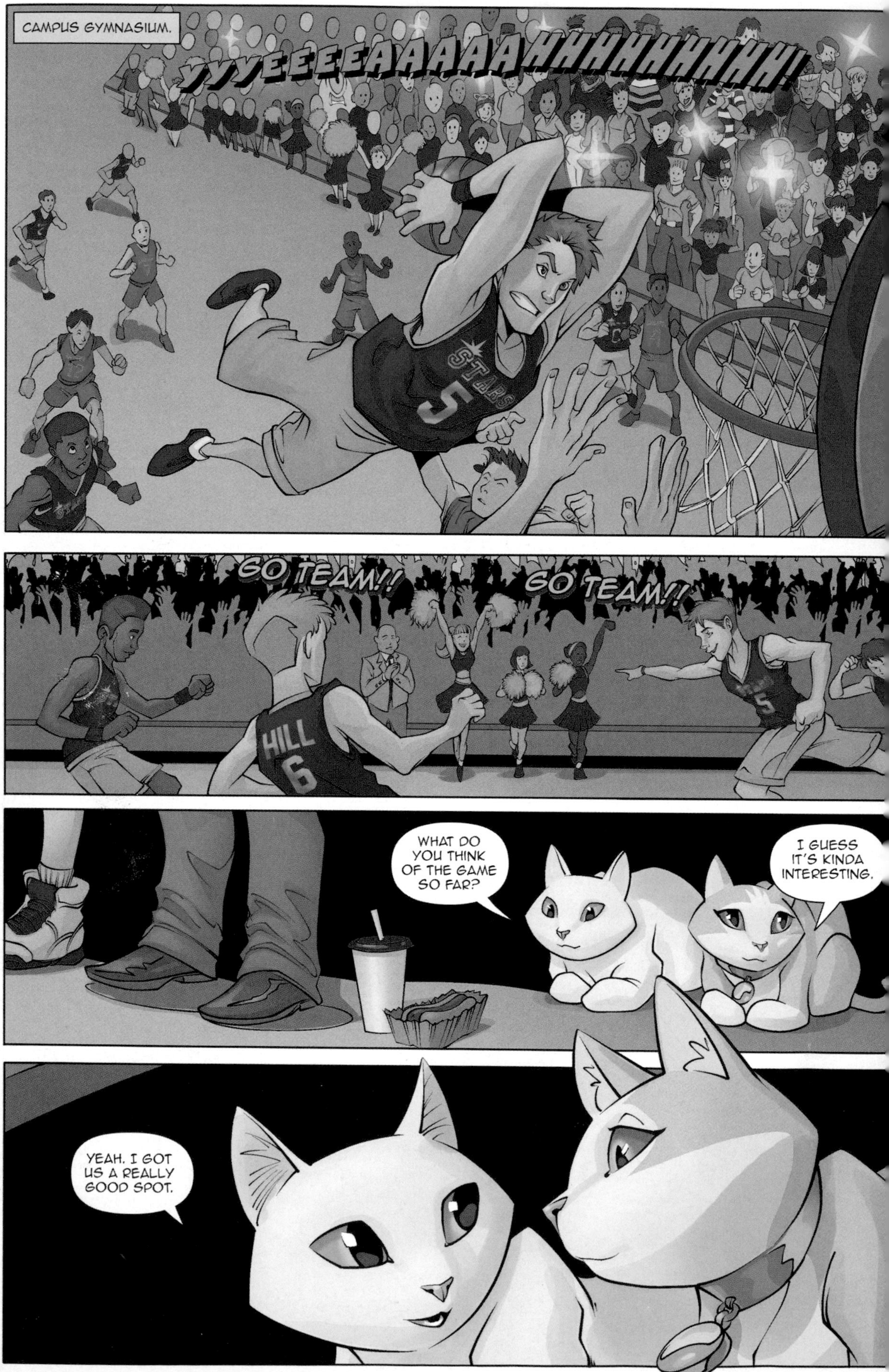
CAMPUS GYMNASIUM.
YYYEEEEAAAAAHHHHHHHHHH!
STARS
5
GO TEAM!!
GO TEAM!!
HILL
6
5
WHAT DO YOU THINK OF THE GAME SO FAR?
I GUESS IT'S KINDA INTERESTING.
YEAH. I GOT US A REALLY GOOD SPOT.

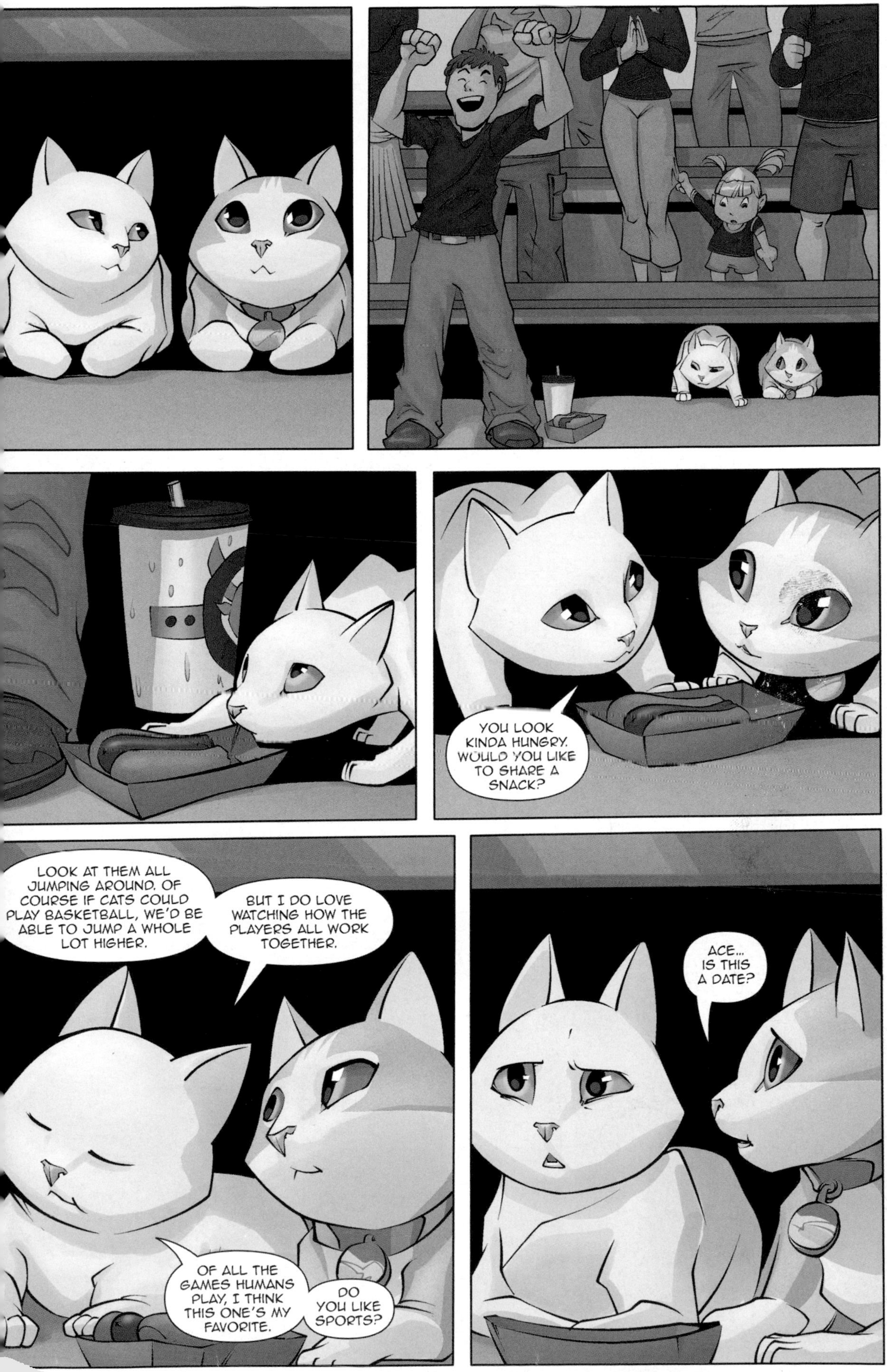
YOU LOOK KINDA HUNGRY. WOULD YOU LIKE TO SHARE A SNACK?
LOOK AT THEM ALL JUMPING AROUND. OF COURSE IF CATS COULD PLAY BASKETBALL, WE'D BE ABLE TO JUMP A WHOLE LOT HIGHER.
BUT I DO LOVE WATCHING HOW THE PLAYERS ALL WORK TOGETHER.
OF ALL THE GAMES HUMANS PLAY, I THINK THIS ONE'S MY FAVORITE.
DO YOU LIKE SPORTS?
ACE... IS THIS A DATE?

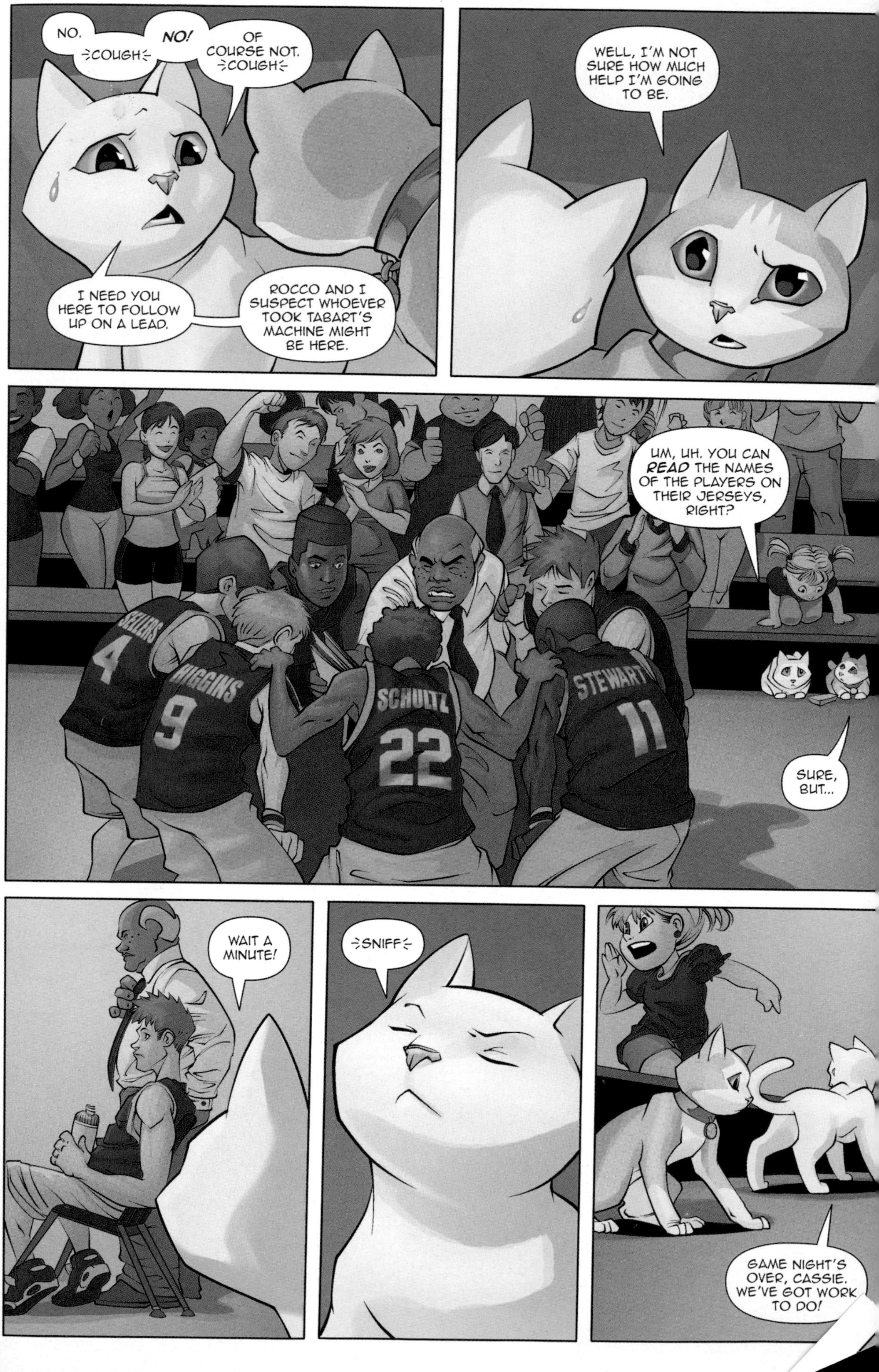

NO.
≈COUGH≈
NO!
OF COURSE NOT.
≈COUGH≈
I NEED YOU HERE TO FOLLOW UP ON A LEAD.
ROCCO AND I SUSPECT WHOEVER TOOK TABART'S MACHINE MIGHT BE HERE.
WELL, I'M NOT SURE HOW MUCH HELP I'M GOING TO BE.
UM, UH. YOU CAN *READ* THE NAMES OF THE PLAYERS ON THEIR JERSEYS, RIGHT?
SELLERS 4
HIGGINS 9
SCHULTZ 22
STEWART 11
SURE, BUT...
WAIT A MINUTE!
≈SNIFF≈
GAME NIGHT'S OVER, CASSIE. WE'VE GOT WORK TO DO!

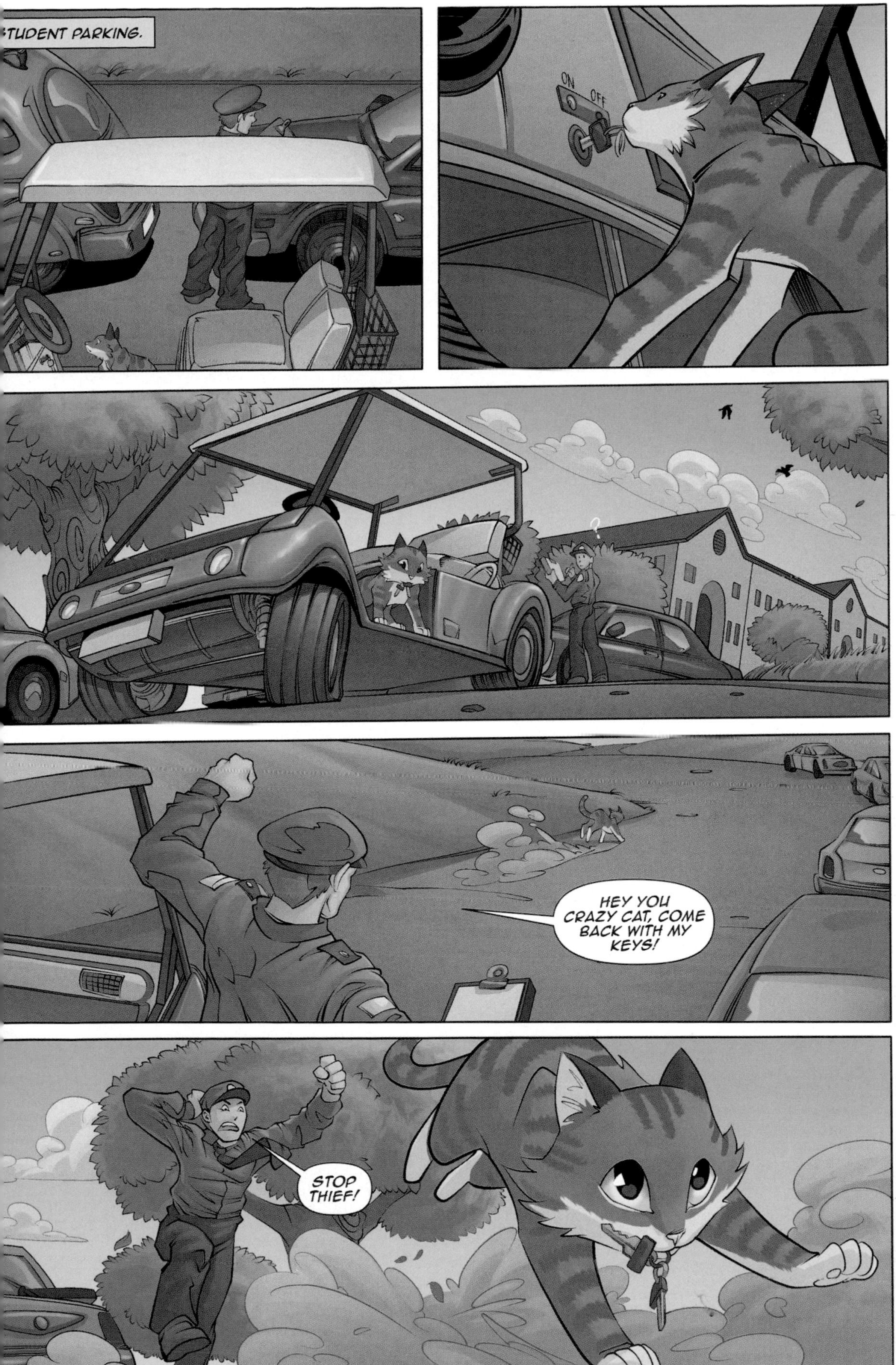
STUDENT PARKING.
ON
OFF
?
HEY YOU CRAZY CAT, COME BACK WITH MY KEYS!
STOP THIEF!

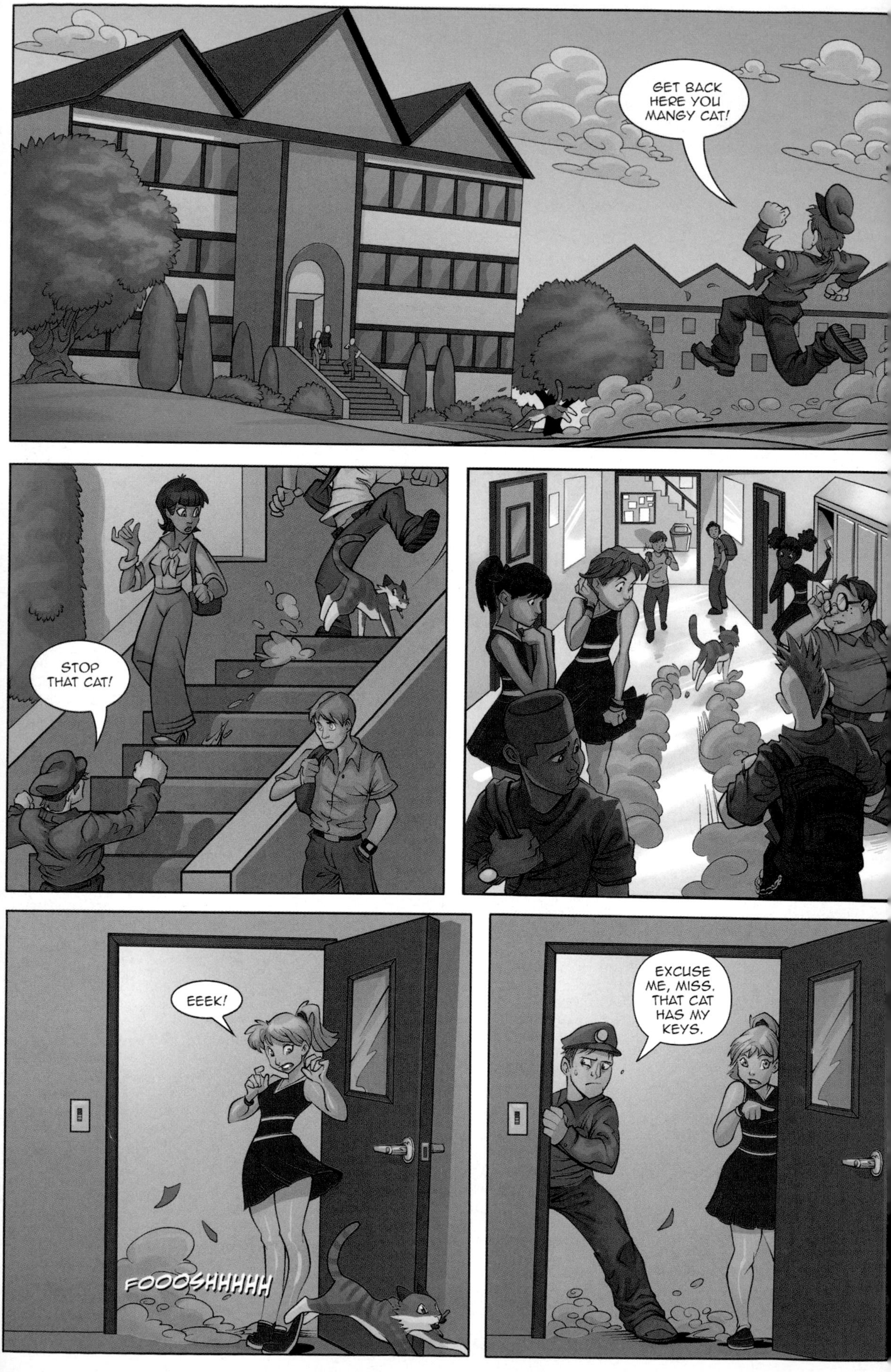
GET BACK HERE YOU MANGY CAT!
STOP THAT CAT!
EEEK!
FOOOSHHHHH
EXCUSE ME, MISS. THAT CAT HAS MY KEYS.

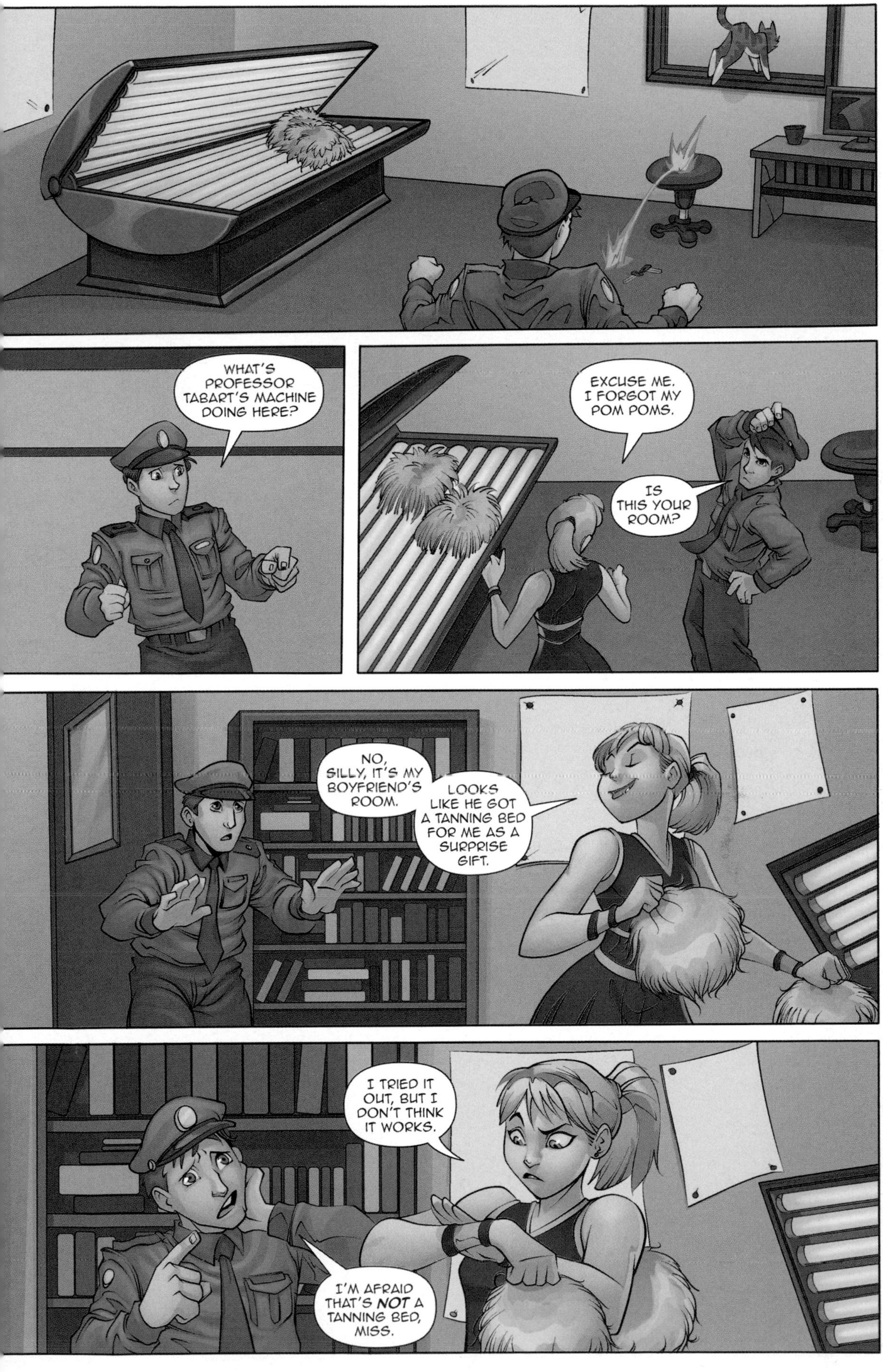
WHAT'S PROFESSOR TABART'S MACHINE DOING HERE?
EXCUSE ME. I FORGOT MY POM POMS.
IS THIS YOUR ROOM?
NO, SILLY, IT'S MY BOYFRIEND'S ROOM.
LOOKS LIKE HE GOT A TANNING BED FOR ME AS A SURPRISE GIFT.
I TRIED IT OUT, BUT I DON'T THINK IT WORKS.
I'M AFRAID THAT'S **NOT** A TANNING BED, MISS.

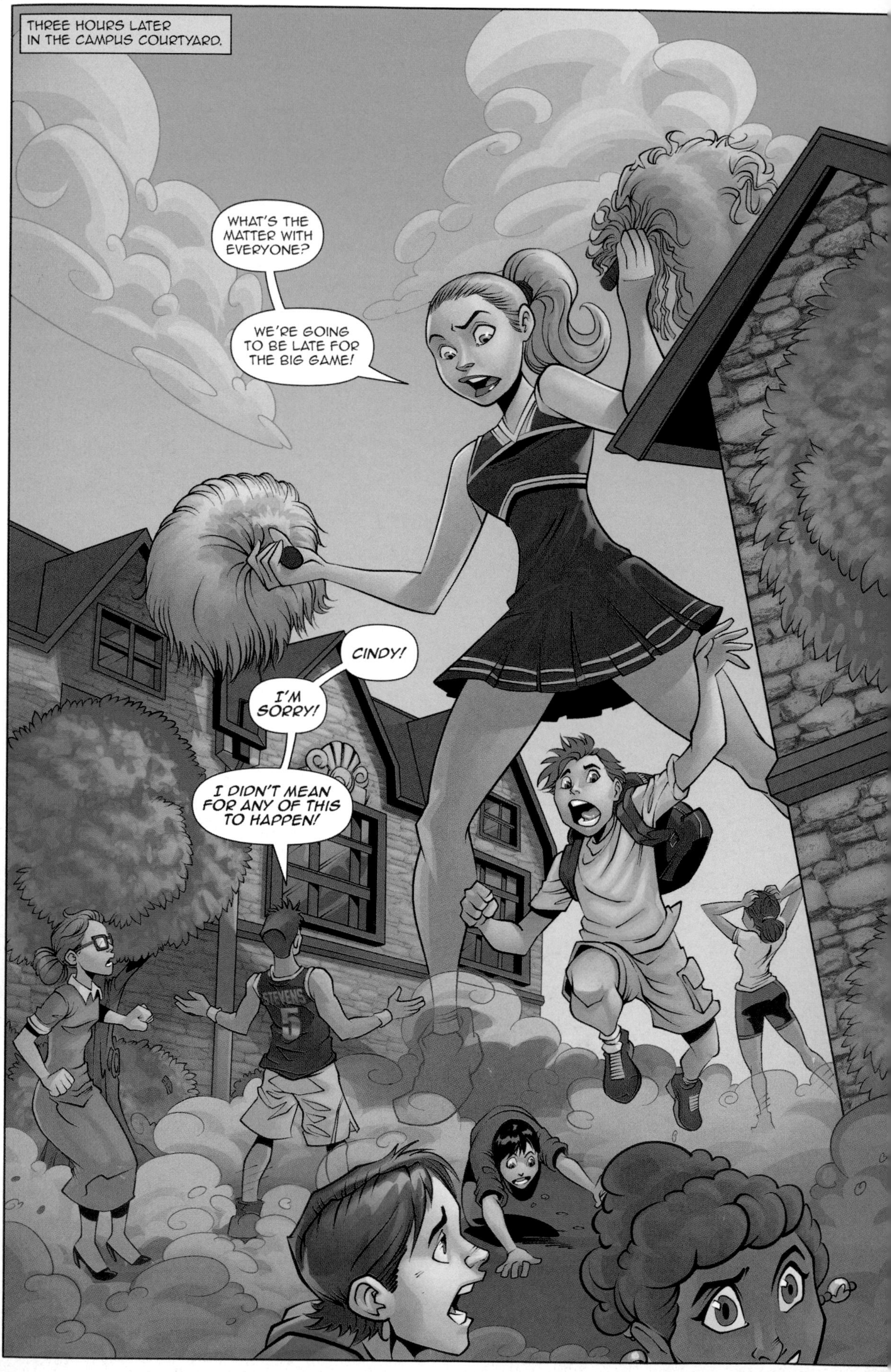
THREE HOURS LATER IN THE CAMPUS COURTYARD.
WHAT'S THE MATTER WITH EVERYONE?
WE'RE GOING TO BE LATE FOR THE BIG GAME!
CINDY!
I'M SORRY!
I DIDN'T MEAN FOR ANY OF THIS TO HAPPEN!
STEVENS
5

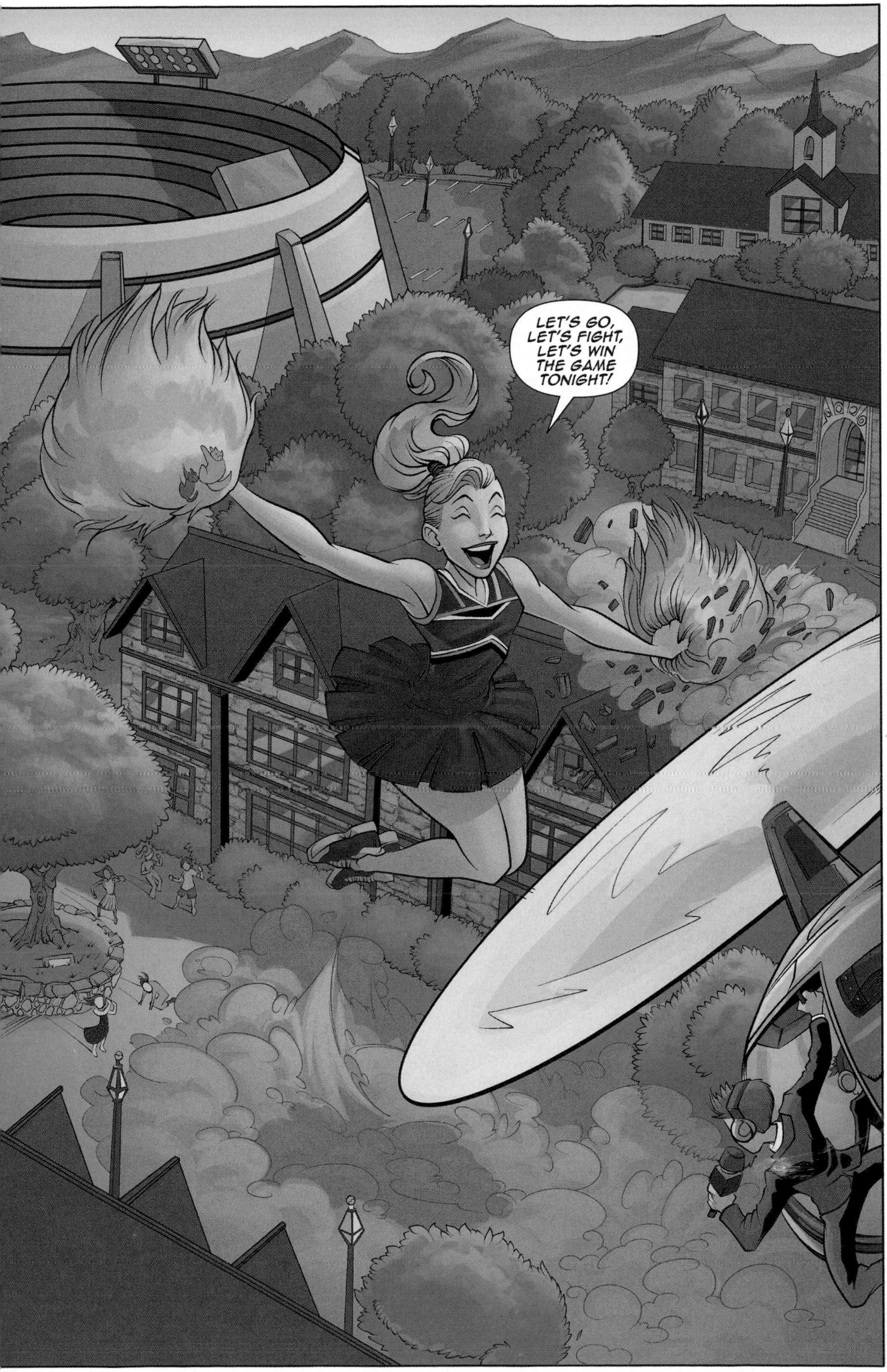
LET'S GO, LET'S FIGHT, LET'S WIN THE GAME TONIGHT!

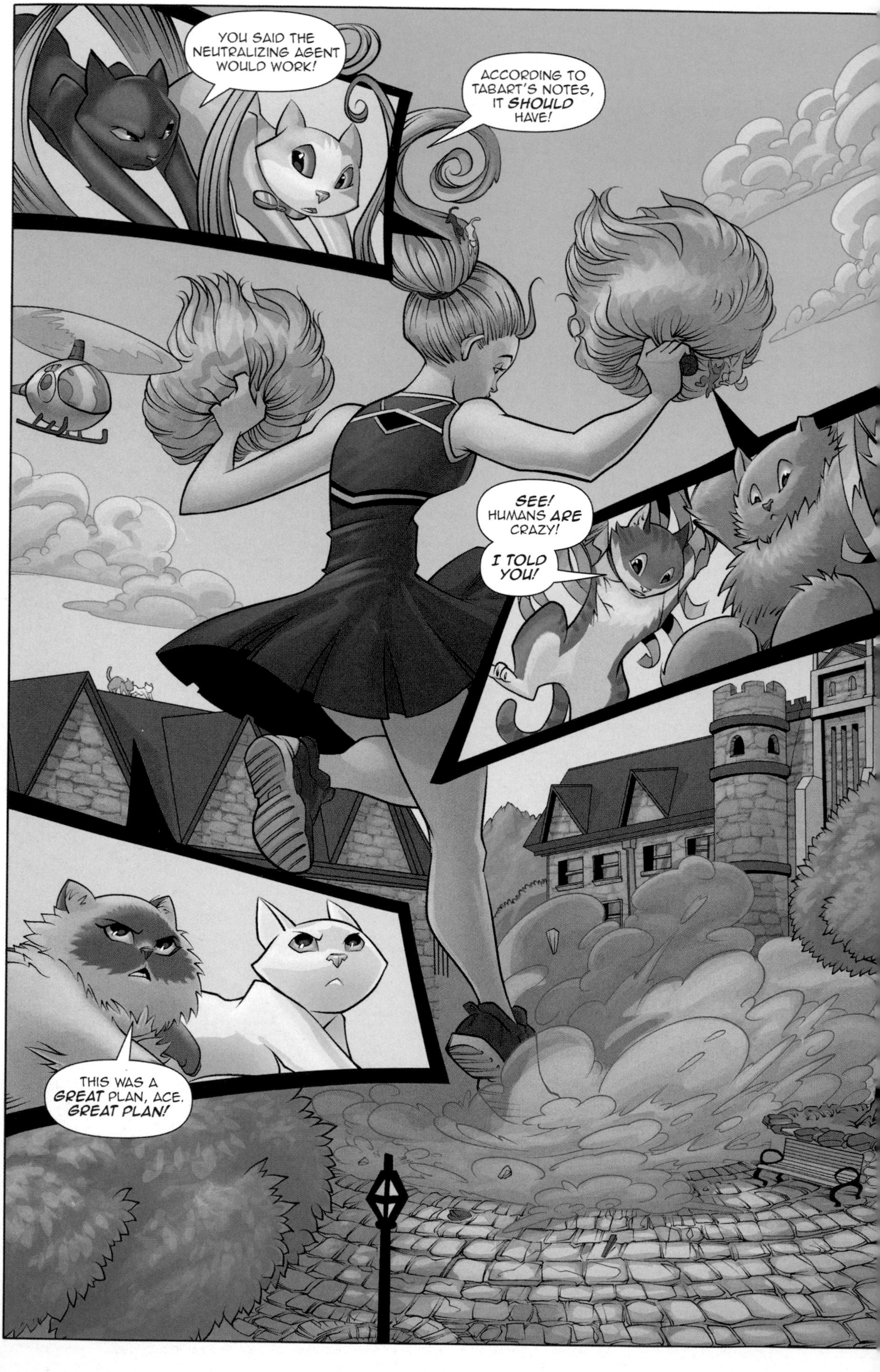
YOU SAID THE NEUTRALIZING AGENT WOULD WORK!
ACCORDING TO TABART'S NOTES, IT *SHOULD* HAVE!
SEE! HUMANS *ARE* CRAZY!
I TOLD YOU!
THIS WAS A *GREAT* PLAN, ACE. *GREAT PLAN!*

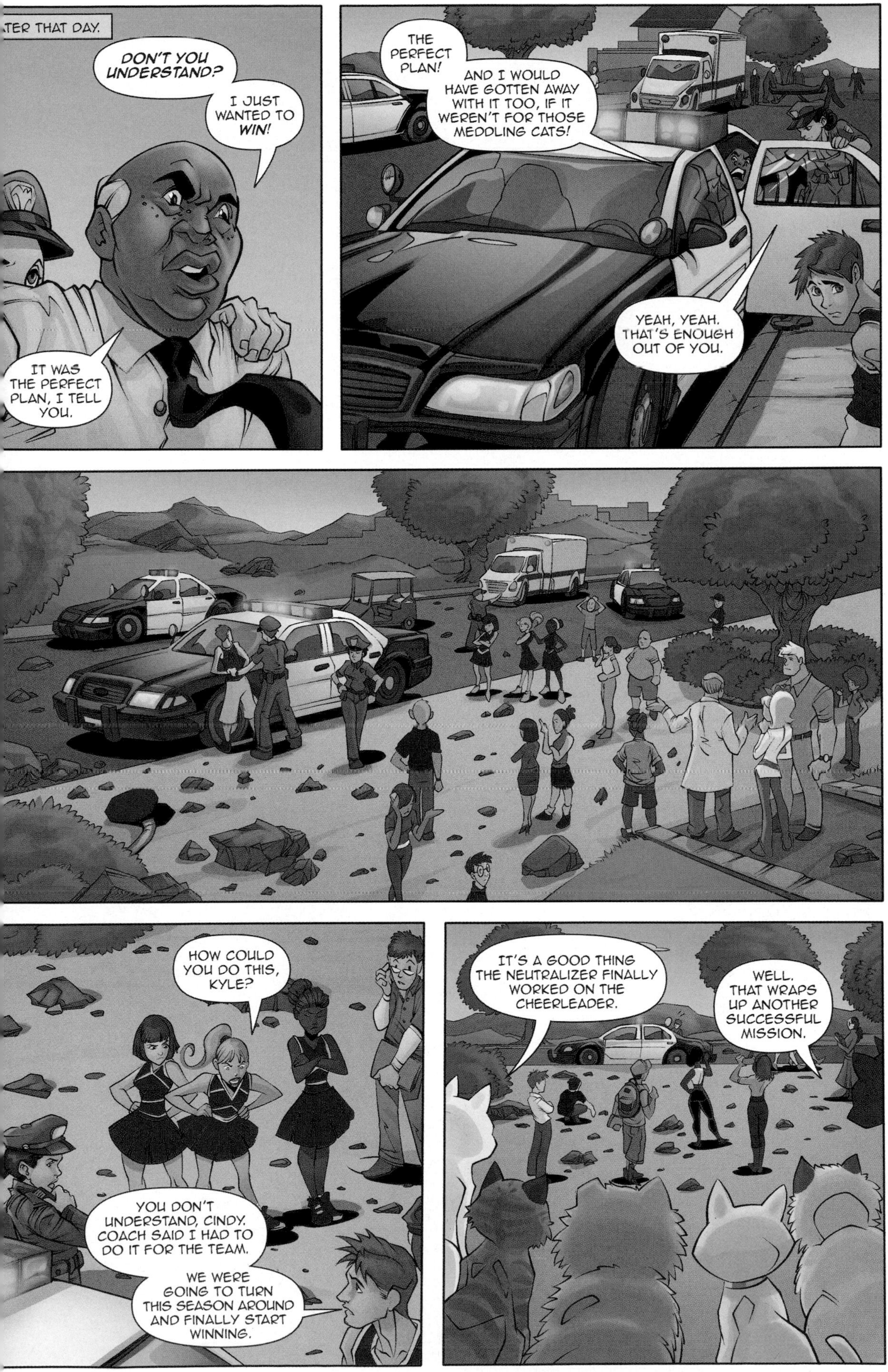

LATER THAT DAY.
DON'T YOU UNDERSTAND?
I JUST WANTED TO WIN!
IT WAS THE PERFECT PLAN, I TELL YOU.
THE PERFECT PLAN!
AND I WOULD HAVE GOTTEN AWAY WITH IT TOO, IF IT WEREN'T FOR THOSE MEDDLING CATS!
YEAH, YEAH. THAT'S ENOUGH OUT OF YOU.
HOW COULD YOU DO THIS, KYLE?
YOU DON'T UNDERSTAND, CINDY. COACH SAID I HAD TO DO IT FOR THE TEAM.
WE WERE GOING TO TURN THIS SEASON AROUND AND FINALLY START WINNING.
IT'S A GOOD THING THE NEUTRALIZER FINALLY WORKED ON THE CHEERLEADER.
WELL. THAT WRAPS UP ANOTHER SUCCESSFUL MISSION.

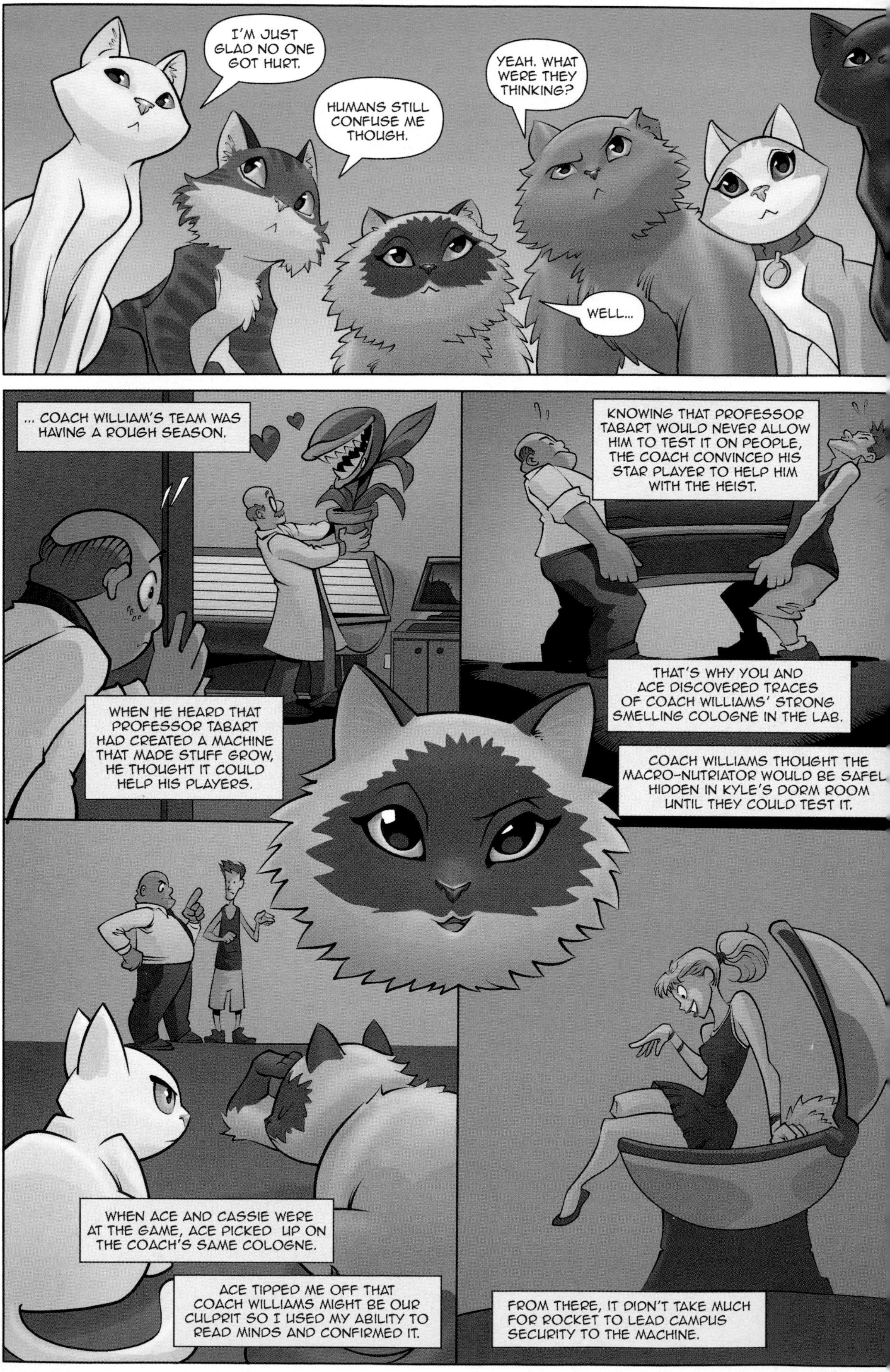
I'M JUST GLAD NO ONE GOT HURT.
HUMANS STILL CONFUSE ME THOUGH.
YEAH. WHAT WERE THEY THINKING?
WELL...
... COACH WILLIAM'S TEAM WAS HAVING A ROUGH SEASON.
WHEN HE HEARD THAT PROFESSOR TABART HAD CREATED A MACHINE THAT MADE STUFF GROW, HE THOUGHT IT COULD HELP HIS PLAYERS.
KNOWING THAT PROFESSOR TABART WOULD NEVER ALLOW HIM TO TEST IT ON PEOPLE, THE COACH CONVINCED HIS STAR PLAYER TO HELP HIM WITH THE HEIST.
THAT'S WHY YOU AND ACE DISCOVERED TRACES OF COACH WILLIAMS' STRONG SMELLING COLOGNE IN THE LAB.
COACH WILLIAMS THOUGHT THE MACRO-NUTRIATOR WOULD BE SAFEL HIDDEN IN KYLE'S DORM ROOM UNTIL THEY COULD TEST IT.
WHEN ACE AND CASSIE WERE AT THE GAME, ACE PICKED UP ON THE COACH'S SAME COLOGNE.
ACE TIPPED ME OFF THAT COACH WILLIAMS MIGHT BE OUR CULPRIT SO I USED MY ABILITY TO READ MINDS AND CONFIRMED IT.
FROM THERE, IT DIDN'T TAKE MUCH FOR ROCKET TO LEAD CAMPUS SECURITY TO THE MACHINE.

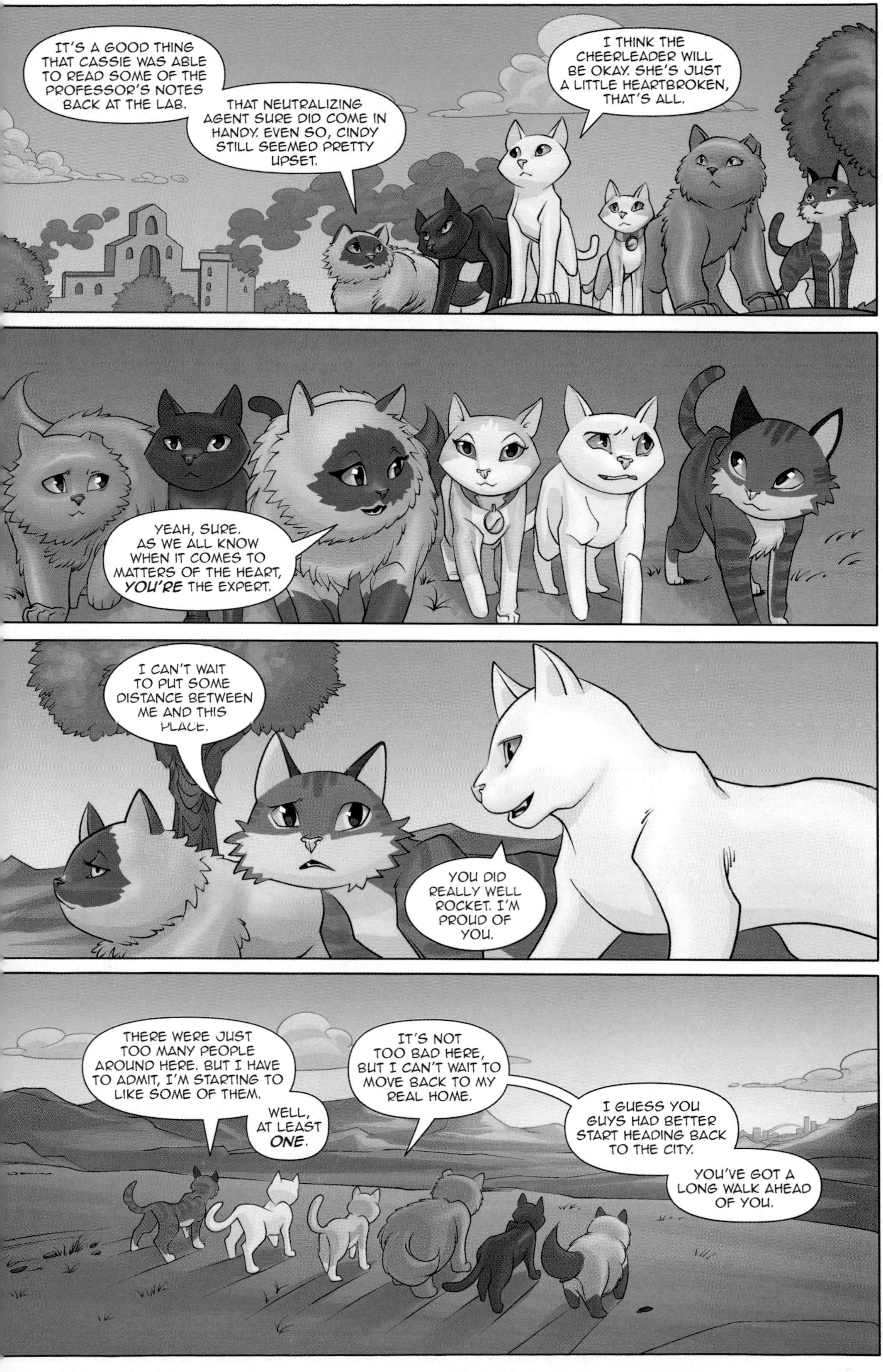
IT'S A GOOD THING THAT CASSIE WAS ABLE TO READ SOME OF THE PROFESSOR'S NOTES BACK AT THE LAB.
THAT NEUTRALIZING AGENT SURE DID COME IN HANDY. EVEN SO, CINDY STILL SEEMED PRETTY UPSET.
I THINK THE CHEERLEADER WILL BE OKAY. SHE'S JUST A LITTLE HEARTBROKEN, THAT'S ALL.
YEAH, SURE. AS WE ALL KNOW WHEN IT COMES TO MATTERS OF THE HEART, *YOU'RE* THE EXPERT.
I CAN'T WAIT TO PUT SOME DISTANCE BETWEEN ME AND THIS PLACE.
YOU DID REALLY WELL ROCKET. I'M PROUD OF YOU.
THERE WERE JUST TOO MANY PEOPLE AROUND HERE. BUT I HAVE TO ADMIT, I'M STARTING TO LIKE SOME OF THEM.
WELL, AT LEAST ***ONE***.
IT'S NOT TOO BAD HERE, BUT I CAN'T WAIT TO MOVE BACK TO MY REAL HOME.
I GUESS YOU GUYS HAD BETTER START HEADING BACK TO THE CITY.
YOU'VE GOT A LONG WALK AHEAD OF YOU.

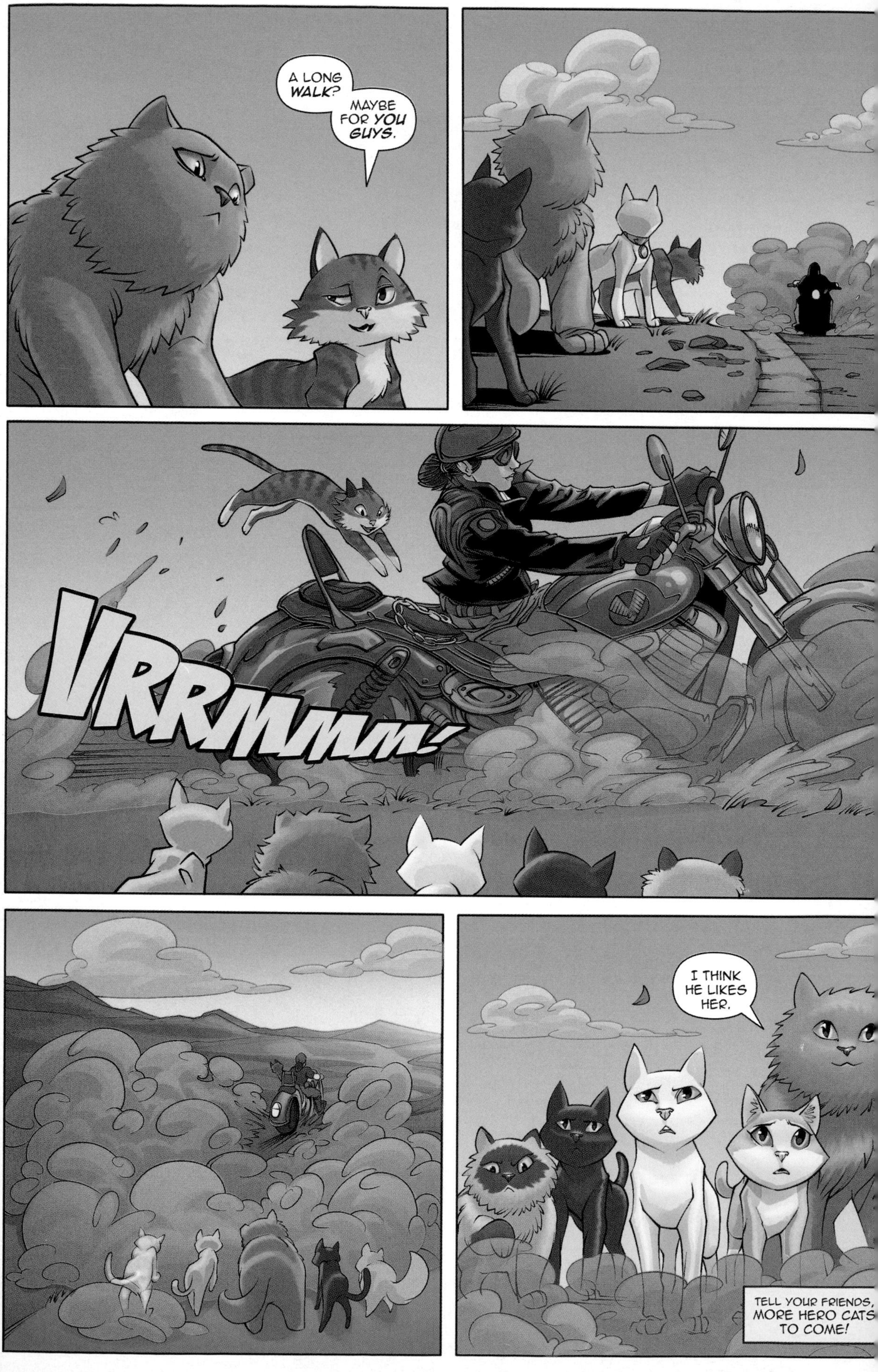
A LONG WALK?
MAYBE FOR YOU GUYS.
VRRMMMM!
I THINK HE LIKES HER.
TELL YOUR FRIENDS, MORE HERO CATS TO COME!

HEROCHAT

HEY KIDS & CATS. YOU MAY REMEMBER BACK IN HERO CATS #1 THAT I PROMISED TO TELL YOU MY STORY. WELL HOLD TIGHT, IT'S UP NEXT! UNTIL THEN, HERE'S SOME LETTERS AND UPDATES FROM OUR NEW FRIENDS.

write to us @ kyle@galacticquest.com

Hi kyle

Thank you for the great comic!
– Matthew Lazorwitz

All The Rage! Co...
Festus MO...

...d Games in
... Cats.
Brandon

...Toronto
...ernier

Hi Kyle,
I just finished Hero Cats #5 on my break, another slam dunk!
Suzy Colombo

Dear Kyle,
I have loved the hero cats series and an idea to make my own hero! I will freak out if you ever considered having Anastasia in your comic.
Your fan,
Meghan Strickland

NEXT UP: BANDIT AND BEYOND!

Bryan Seaton - Publisher
Kevin Freeman - President
Dave Dwench - Creative Director
Shawn Gabborin - Editor in Chief
Jamal Igle & Vito Delsante - Co-Directors of Marketing
Jim Dietz - Social Media Director
Jeremy Whitley - Education Outreach Director
Chad Cicconi & Colleen Boyd - Associate Editors

#7
$3.99
PUTTKAMMER
WILLIAMS
SELLERS
SCHULTZ

INTRODUCING THE NEWEST HERO CAT
BANDIT

HERO CATS #6, June 2015

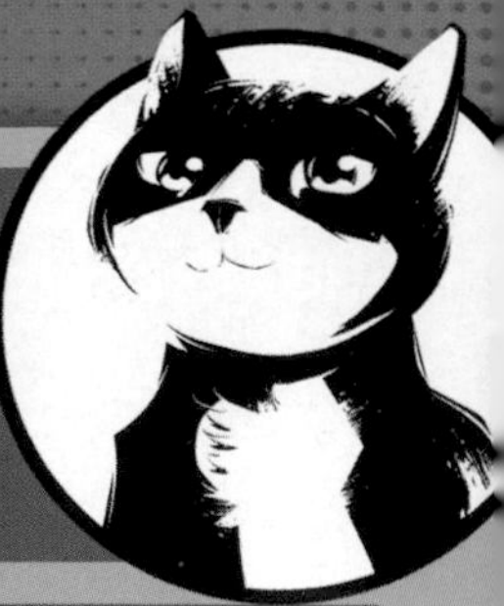

HAVE YOU SEEN THE VIDEO ON YOUTUBE ABOUT THE CAT THAT SAVED A YOUNG BOY? WE DID! LOOKS LIKE THERE ARE EVEN MORE HERO CATS OUT THERE THAN WE EVER KNEW. CHECK OUT MARCUS'S VERY SPECIAL ILLUSTRATION OF TARA!

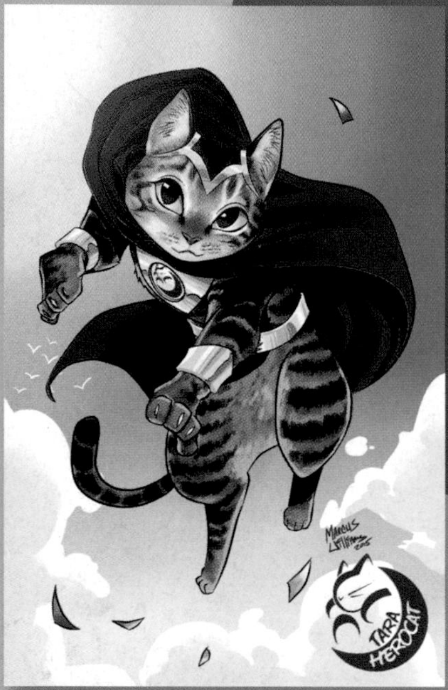
TARA HEROCAT

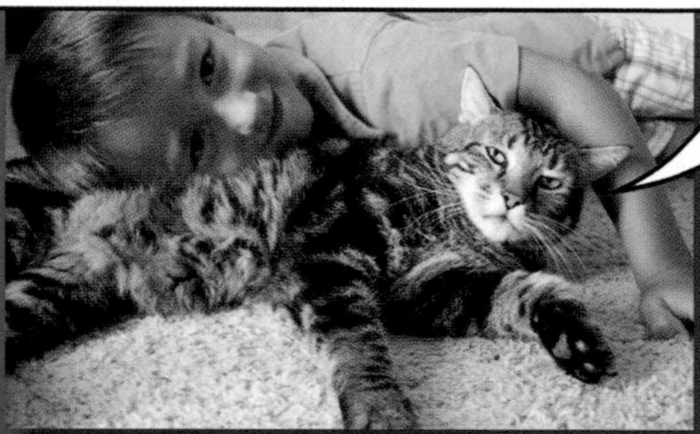
I SAVED MY BEST FRIEND FROM A MEAN DOG. WHY? BECAUSE I LOVE JEREMY AND WILL ALWAYS BE THERE FOR HIM.

TARATHEHEROCAT.COM

"HEY HERO CAT FANS! MY NAME IS ALEX OGLE AND I'M WORKING ON THE ART FOR A NEW MIDNIGHT SERIES. I LOOK FORWARD TO SHARING IT WITH YOU SOON!"

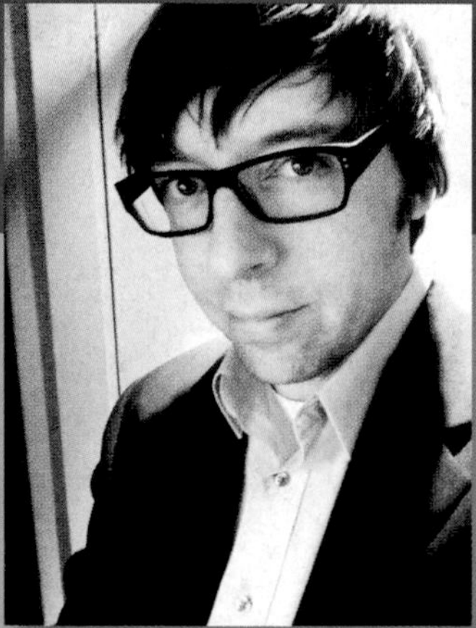

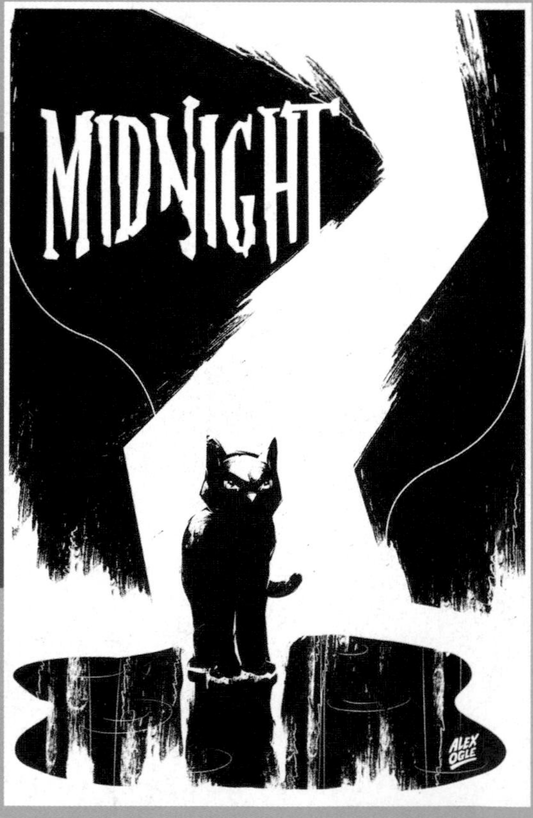
MIDNIGHT
ALEX OGLE

ALEXOGLE.COM

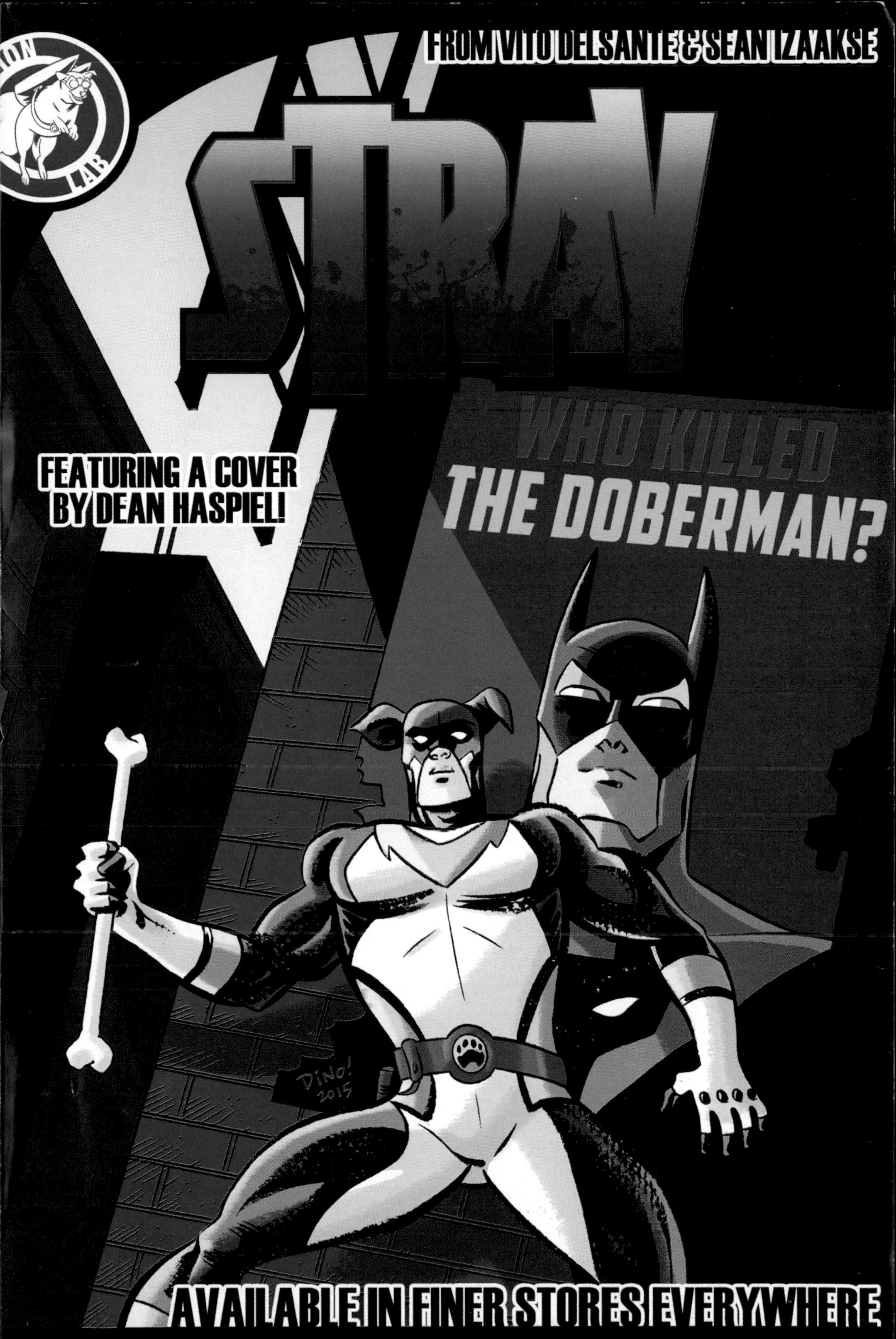

FROM VITO DELSANTE & SEAN IZAAKSE
LAB
STRAY
FEATURING A COVER BY DEAN HASPIEL!
WHO KILLED THE DOBERMAN?
DINO! 2015
AVAILABLE IN FINER STORES EVERYWHERE

Collecting the hit mini-series, STRAY tells the story of Rodney Weller, the former sidekick known as "the Rottweiler." When his mentor, the Doberman, is murdered, Rodney has to decide if he wants to come back to the world of capes and masks and, if he does, who he wants to be. Cover by Emmy Award winner, Dean Haspiel (The Fox)! Collects Stray #1-4.